Praise for *New York Times* and *USA TODAY* bestselling author RaeAnne Thayne

"Hope's Crossing is a charming series that lives up to its name. Reading these stories of small-town life engages the reader's heart and emotions, inspiring hope and the belief miracles are possible."
—Debbie Macomber, #1 *New York Times* bestselling author

"RaeAnne Thayne is quickly becoming one of my favorite authors.... Once you start reading, you aren't going to be able to stop."
—*Fresh Fiction* on *Snow Angel Cove*

"A sometimes heartbreaking tale of love and relationships in a small Colorado town.... Poignant and sweet, this tale of second chances will appeal to fans of military-flavored sweet romance."
—*Publishers Weekly* on *Christmas in Snowflake Canyon*

"Thayne, once again, delivers a heartfelt story of a caring community and a caring romance between adults who have triumphed over tragedies."
—*Booklist* on *Woodrose Mountain*

"Thayne pens another winner by combining her huge, boisterous cast of familiar, lovable characters with a beautiful setting and a wonderful story. Her main characters are strong and three-dimensional, with enough heat between them to burn the pages."
—*RT Book Reviews* on *Currant Creek Valley*

"Thayne's beautiful, honest storytelling goes straight to the heart.... [A] moving yet powerful romance."
—*RT Book Reviews* on *Wild Iris Ridge*

Also available from RaeAnne Thayne
and HQN Books

The Haven Point series

Redemption Bay
Snow Angel Cove

The Hope's Crossing series

Wild Iris Ridge
Christmas in Snowflake Canyon
Willowleaf Lane
Currant Creek Valley
Sweet Laurel Falls
Woodrose Mountain
Blackberry Summer

RaeAnne Thayne

EVERGREEN SPRINGS

HQN™

ISBN-13: 978-0-373-78859-0

Evergreen Springs

Recycling programs
for this product may
not exist in your area.

www.HQNBooks.com

Printed in U.S.A.

In memory of my dear father-in-law, Donald Thayne,
who loved me like a daughter from the moment we met.
Aloha 'Oe.

As always, I offer my endless thanks
to my beloved family for their patience
and encouragement, to all the hardworking people at
HQN Books who had a hand in bringing this book to life
and especially to you, my wonderful readers.

CHAPTER ONE

DEVIN SHAW WAS BORED.

She supposed that particular state of affairs wasn't necessarily a bad thing in her current role as substitute attending physician at the Lake Haven Hospital emergency department. While a juicy trauma might be professionally stimulating and serve to break up the monotony, she adored all her neighbors in Haven Point and the greater Lake Haven area too much to wish that sort of stress and pain on anyone.

Better to be stuck at the nurses' station of the small emergency department trying without success—and not for the first time, alas—to learn how to knit.

"No. Your problem here has to do with the amount of tension on the working yarn," Greta Ward insisted. "If you don't have the right tension, you'll end up losing control and making a huge mess you will only have to undo."

The scarily efficient charge nurse of the emergency department at the Lake Haven Hospital leaned over her and tugged the yarn around her fingers in some kind of complicated way that Devin knew she would never be able to replicate.

"There. That's better. Try again."

Devin concentrated, nibbling on her bottom lip as she tried to work the needles that seemed unwieldy and awkward, no matter how she tried.

After her third time tangling the yarn into a total mess, Devin sighed and admitted defeat. Again. Every time they happened to be assigned to work together, Greta took a moment to try teaching her to knit. And every time, she came up short.

"People who find knitting at all relaxing have to be crazy. I think I must have some kind of mental block. It's just not coming."

"You're not trying hard enough," Greta insisted.

"I am! I swear I am."

"Even my eight-year-old granddaughter can do it," she said sternly. "Once you get past the initial learning curve, this is something you'll love the rest of your life."

"I think it's funny." Callie Bennett, one of the other nurses and also one of Devin's good friends, smirked as she observed her pitiful attempts over the top of her magazine.

"Oh, yes. Hilarious," Devin said drily.

"It is! You're a physician who can set a fractured radius, suture a screaming six-year-old's finger and deliver a baby, all with your eyes closed."

"Not quite," Devin assured her. "I open my eyes at the end of childbirth so I can see to cut the umbilical cord."

Callie chuckled. "Seriously, you're one of the best doctors at this hospital. I love working with you and wish you worked here permanently. You're cool under pressure and always seem to know just how to deal with every situation. But I hate to break it to you, hon, you're all thumbs when it comes to knitting, no matter how hard you try."

"I'm going to get the hang of this tonight," she insisted. "If Greta's eight-year-old granddaughter can do it, so can I."

She picked up the needles again and concentrated under the watchful eye of the charge nurse until she'd successfully finished the first row of what she hoped would eventually be a scarf.

"Not bad," Greta said. "Now just do that about four hundred more times and you might have enough for a decent-sized scarf."

Devin groaned. Already, she was wishing she had stuck to reading the latest medical journals to pass the time instead of trying to knit yet again.

"I've got to go back to my office and finish the schedule for next month," Greta said. "Keep going and remember—ten rows a day keeps the psychiatrist away."

Devin laughed but didn't look up from the stitches.

"How do you always pick the slowest nights to fill in?" Callie asked after Greta left the nurses' station.

"I have no idea. Just lucky, I guess."

It wasn't exactly true. Her nights weren't always quiet. The past few times she had substituted for the regular emergency department doctors at Lake Haven Hospital had been low-key like this one, but that definitely wasn't always the case. A month earlier, she worked the night of the first snowfall and had been on her feet all night, between car accidents, snow shovel injuries and a couple of teenagers who had taken a snowmobile through a barbed-wire fence.

Like so much of medicine, emergency medicine was all a roll of the dice.

Devin loved her regular practice as a family physician in partnership with Russell Warrick, who had been her own doctor when she was a kid. She loved having a day-to-day relationship with her patients and the idea that she could treat an entire family from cradle to grave.

Even so, she didn't mind filling in at the emergency department when the three rotating emergency medicine physicians in the small hospital needed an extra hand. The challenge and variety of it exercised her brain and sharpened her reflexes—except tonight, when the only thing sharp seemed to be these knitting needles that had become her nemesis.

She was on her twelfth row when she heard a commotion out in the reception area.

"We need a doctor here, right now."

"Can you tell me what's going on?" Devin heard the receptionist ask in a calm voice.

Devin didn't wait around to hear the answer. She and Callie both sprang into action. Though the emergency department usually followed triage protocol, with prospective patients screened by one of the certified nurse assistants first to determine level of urgency, that seemed superfluous when the newcomers were the only patients here. By default, they automatically moved to the front of the line, since there wasn't one.

She walked through the doorway to the reception desk and her initial impression was of a big, tough-looking man, a very pregnant woman in one of the hospital wheelchairs and a couple of scared-looking kids.

"What's the problem?"

"Are you a doctor?" the man demanded. "I know how emergency rooms work. You tell your story to a hundred different people before you finally see somebody who can actually help you. I don't want to go through that."

She gave a well-practiced smile. "I'm Dr. Shaw, the attending physician here tonight. What seems to be the problem?"

"Devin? Is that you?"

The pregnant woman looked up and met her gaze and Devin immediately recognized her. "Tricia! Hello."

Tricia Barrett had been a friend in high school, though she hadn't seen her in years. Barrett had been her maiden name, anyway. Devin couldn't remember the last name of the man she married.

"Hi," Tricia said, her features pale and her arms tight on the armrests of the wheelchair. "I would say it's great to see you again, but, well, not really, under these circumstances. No offense."

Devin stepped closer to her and gave her a calming smile. "None taken. Believe me, I get it. Why don't you tell me what's going on."

Tricia shifted in the wheelchair. "Nothing. Someone is overreacting."

"She slipped on a patch of ice about an hour ago and hurt her ankle." The man with her overrode her objections. "I'm not sure it's broken but she needs an X-ray."

At first she thought he might be Tricia's husband but on closer inspection, she recognized him, only because she'd seen him around town here and there over the past few years.

Cole Barrett, Tricia's older brother, was a rather hard man to overlook—six feet two inches of gorgeousness, with vivid blue eyes, sinfully long eyelashes and sun-streaked brown hair usually hidden by a cowboy hat.

He had been wild back in the day, if she remembered correctly, and still hadn't lost that edgy, bad-boy outlaw vibe.

In a small community like Haven Point, most people knew each other—or at least knew *of* each other. She hadn't met the man but she knew he lived in the mountains above town and that he had inherited a sprawling, successful ranch from his grandparents.

If memory served, he had once been some kind of hotshot rodeo cowboy.

With that afternoon shadow and his wavy brown hair a little disordered, he looked as if he had just climbed either off a horse or out of some lucky woman's bed. Not that it was any of her business. Disreputable cowboys were definitely *not* her type.

Devin dismissed the man from her mind and focused instead on her patient, where her attention should have been in the first place.

"Have you been able to put weight on your ankle?"

"No, but I haven't really tried. This is all so silly," Tricia insisted. "I'm sure it's not broken."

She winced suddenly, her face losing another shade or two of color, and pressed a hand to her abdomen.

Devin didn't miss the gesture and her attention sharpened. "How long have you been having contractions?"

"I'm sure they're only Braxton Hicks."

"How far along are you?"

"Thirty-four weeks. With twins, if you couldn't tell by the basketball here."

Her brother frowned. "You're having contractions? Why didn't you say anything?"

"Because you're already freaking out over a stupid sprained ankle. I didn't want to send you into total panic mode."

"What's happening?" the girl said. "What are contractions?"

"It's something a woman's body does when she's almost ready to have a baby," Tricia explained.

"Are you having the babies *tonight*?" she asked, big blue eyes wide. "I thought they weren't supposed to be here until after Christmas."

"I hope not," Tricia answered. "Sometimes I guess you have practice contractions. I'm sure that's what these are."

For the first time, she started to look uneasy and Devin knew she needed to take control of the situation.

"I don't want to send you up to Obstetrics until we take a look at the ankle. We can hook up all the fetal monitoring equipment down here in the emergency department to see what's going on and put your minds at ease."

"Thanks. I'm sure everything's fine. I'm going to be embarrassed for worrying everyone."

"Never worry about that," Devin assured her.

"I'm sorry to bother you, but I need to get some information so we can enter it into the computer and make an ID band." Brittney Calloway, the receptionist, stepped forward, clipboard in hand.

"My insurance information is in my purse," Tricia said. "Cole, can you find it and give her what she needs?"

He looked as if he didn't want to leave his sister's side but the little boy was already looking bored.

Whose were they? The girl looked to be about eight, blonde and ethereal like Tricia but with Cole's blue eyes, and the boy was a few years younger with darker coloring and big brown eyes.

She hadn't heard the man had kids—in fact, as far as she knew, he had lived alone at Evergreen Springs the past two years since his grandmother died.

"You can come back to the examination room after you're done out here, or you can stay out in the waiting room."

He looked at the children and then back at his sister, obviously torn. "We'll wait out here, if you think you'll be okay."

"I'll be fine," she assured him. "I'm sorry to be such a pain."

He gave his sister a soft, affectionate smile that would have made Devin's knees go weak, if she weren't made of sterner stuff. "You're not a pain. You're just stubborn," he said gruffly. "You should have called me the minute you fell instead of waiting until I came back to the house and you definitely should have said something about the contractions."

"We'll take care of her and try to keep you posted."

"Thanks." He nodded and shepherded the two children to the small waiting room, with his sister's purse in hand.

Devin forced herself to put him out of her mind and focus on her patient.

Normally, the nurses and aides would take a patient into a room and start a chart but since she knew Tricia and the night was slow, Devin didn't mind coming into her care from the beginning.

"You're thirty-three weeks?" she asked as she pushed her into the largest exam room in the department.

"Almost thirty-four. Tuesday."

"With twins. Congratulations. Are they fraternal or identical?"

"Fraternal. A boy and a girl. The girl is measuring bigger, according to my ob-gyn back in California."

"Did your OB clear you for travel this close to your due date?"

"Yes. Everything has been uncomplicated. A textbook pregnancy, Dr. Adams said."

"When was your last appointment?"

"I saw my regular doctor the morning before Thanksgiving. She knew I was flying out to spend the holiday with Cole and the kids. I was supposed to be back the next Sunday, but, well, I decided to stay."

She paused and her chin started to quiver. "Everything is such a mess and I can't go home and now I've sprained my ankle. How am I going to get around on crutches when I'm as big as a barn?"

Something else was going on here, something that had nothing to do with sprained ankles. Why couldn't she go home? Devin squeezed her hand. "Let's not get ahead of ourselves."

"No. You're right." Tricia drew a breath. When she spoke her voice only wobbled a little. "I have an appointment Monday for a checkup with a local doctor. Randall or Crandall or something like that. I can't remember. I just know my records have been transferred there."

"Randall. Jim Randall."

He was one of her favorite colleagues in the area, compassionate and kind and more than competent. Whenever she had a complicated obstetrics patient in her family medicine practice, she sent her to Jim.

As Devin guided Tricia from the wheelchair to the narrow bed in the room, the pregnant woman paused on the edge, her hand curved around her abdomen and her face contorted with pain. She drew in a sharp breath and let it out slowly. "Ow. That was a big one."

And not far apart from the first contraction she'd had a few minutes earlier, Devin thought in concern, her priorities shifting as Callie came in. "Here we are. This is Callie. She's an amazing nurse and right now she's going to gather some basic information and help you into a gown. I'll be back when she's done to take a look at things."

Tricia grabbed her hand. "You'll be back?"

"In just a moment, I promise. I'm going to write orders for the X-ray and the fetal heartbeat monitoring and put a call in to Dr. Randall. I'll also order some basic urine and blood tests, too, then I'll be right back."

"Okay. Okay." Tricia gave a wobbly smile. "Thanks. I can't tell you how glad I am that you're here."

"I'm not going anywhere. I promise."

HE TRULY DETESTED HOSPITALS.

Cole shifted in the uncomfortable chair, his gaze on the little Christmas tree in the corner with its colorful lights and garland made out of rolled bandages.

Given the setting and the time of year, it was hard not to flash back to that miserable Christmas he was eleven, when his mother lay dying. That last week of her life, Stan had taken him and Tricia to the hospital just about every evening. They would sit in the waiting room near a pitiful little Christmas tree like this one and do homework or read or just gaze out the window at the falling snow in the moonlight, scared and sad and a little numb after months of their mother's chemotherapy and radiation.

He pushed away the memory, especially of all that came after, choosing instead to focus on the two good things that had come from hospitals: his kids, though he had only been there for Jazmyn's birth.

He could still remember walking through the halls and wanting to stop everybody there and share a drink with them and tell them about his beautiful new baby girl.

Emphasis on the part about sharing a drink. He sighed. By the time Sharla went into labor with Ty, things had been so terrible between them that she hadn't even told him the kid was on the way.

"I'm bored," the kid in question announced. "There's nothing to do."

Cole pointed to the small flat-screen TV hanging on the wall, showing some kind of talking heads on a muted news program. "Want to watch something? I'm sure we could find the remote somewhere. I can ask at the desk."

"I bet there's nothing on." Jazmyn slumped in her seat.

"Let's take a look. Maybe we could find a Christmas special or something."

Neither kid looked particularly enthusiastic but he headed over to the reception desk in search of a remote.

The woman behind the desk was a cute, curvy blonde with a friendly smile. Her name badge read Brittney and she had been watching him from under her fake eyelashes since he had filled out his sister's paperwork.

"Hi. Can I help you?" she asked.

"Hi, Brittney. I wonder if we can use the TV remote. My kids are getting a little restless."

"Oh. Sure. No prob." Her smile widened with a flirtatious look in her eyes. He'd like to think he was imagining it but he'd seen that look too many times from buckle bunnies on the rodeo circuit to mistake it for anything else.

He shifted, feeling self-conscious. A handful of years ago, he would have taken her up on the unspoken invitation in those big blue eyes. He would have done his best to tease out her phone number or would have made arrangements with her to meet up for a drink when her shift was over.

He might even have found a way to slip away with her on her next break to make out in a stairwell somewhere.

Though he had been a long, long time without a woman, he did his best to ignore the look. He hated the man he used to be and anything that reminded him of it.

"Thanks," he said stiffly when she handed over the remote. He took it from her and headed back to the kids.

"Here we go. Let's see what we can find."

He didn't have high hopes of finding a kids' show on at 7:00 p.m. on a Friday night but he was pleasantly surprised when the next click of the remote landed them on what looked like a stop-action animated holiday show featuring an elf, a snowman and a reindeer wearing a cowboy hat.

"How's this?" he asked.

"Okay," Ty said, agreeable as always.

"Looks like a little kids' show," Jazmyn said with a sniff but he noticed that after about two seconds, she was as interested in the action as her younger brother.

Jaz was quite a character, bossy and opinionated and domineering to her little brother and everyone else. How could he blame her for those sometimes annoying traits, which she had likely developed from being forced into little-mother mode for her brother most of the time and even for their mother if Sharla was going through a rough patch?

He leaned back in the chair and wished he had a cowboy hat like the reindeer so he could yank it down over his face, stretch out his boots and take a rest for five freaking minutes.

Between the ranch and the kids and now Tricia, he felt stretched to the breaking point.

Tricia. What was he supposed to do with her? A few weeks ago, he thought she was only coming for Thanksgiving. The kids, still lost and grieving and trying to settle into their new routine with him, showed unusual excitement at the idea of seeing their aunt from California, the one who showered them with presents and cards.

She had assured him her doctor said she was fine to travel. Over their Skype conversation, she had given him a bright smile and told him she wanted to come out while she still could. Her husband was on a business trip, she told him, and she didn't want to spend Thanksgiving on her own.

How the hell was he supposed to have figured out she was running away?

He sighed. His life had seemed so much less complicated two months ago.

He couldn't say it had ever been *uncomplicated*, but he had found a groove the past few years. His world consisted of the ranch, his child support payments, regular check-ins with his parole officer and the biweekly phone calls and occasional visits to wherever Sharla in her wanderlust called home that week so he could stay in touch with his kids.

He had tried to keep his head down and throw everything he had into making Evergreen Springs and his horse training operation a success, to create as much order as he could out of the chaos his selfish and stupid mistakes had caused.

Two months ago, everything had changed. First had come a call from his ex-wife. She and her current boyfriend were heading to Reno for a week to get married—her second since their stormy marriage ended just months after Ty's birth—and Sharla wanted him to meet her in Boise so he could pick up the kids.

Forget that both kids had school or that Cole was supposed to be at a horse show in Denver that weekend.

He had dropped everything, relishing the rare chance to be with his kids without more of Sharla's drama. He had wished his ex-wife well, shook hands with the new guy—who actually had seemed like a decent sort, for a change—and sent them on their way.

Only a few days later, he received a second phone call, one that would alter his life forever.

He almost hadn't been able to understand Sharla's mother, Trixie, when she called. In between all the sobbing and wailing and carrying on, he figured out the tragic and stunning news that the newlyweds had been killed after their car slid out of control during an early snowstorm while crossing the Sierra Nevada.

In a moment, everything changed. For years, Cole had been fighting for primary custody, trying to convince judge after judge that their mother's flighty, unstable lifestyle and periodic substance abuse provided a terrible environment for the children.

The only trouble was, Cole had plenty of baggage of his own. An ex-con former alcoholic didn't exactly have the sturdiest leg to stand on when it came to being granted custody of two young children, no matter how much he had tried to rebuild his life and keep his nose out of trouble in recent years.

Sharla's tragic death changed everything and Cole now had full custody of his children as the surviving parent.

It hadn't been an easy transition for any of them, complicated by the fact that he'd gone through two housekeepers in as many months.

Now he had his sister to take care of. Whether her ankle was broken or sprained, the result would be more domestic chaos.

He would figure it out. He always did, right? What other choice did he have?

He picked up a *National Geographic* and tried to

find something to read to keep himself awake. He was deep in his third article and the kids on to their second Christmas special before the lovely doctor returned.

She was every bit as young as he had thought at first, pretty and petite with midlength auburn hair, green eyes that were slightly almond shaped and porcelain skin. She even had a little smattering of freckles across the bridge of her nose. Surely she was too young to be in such a responsible position.

He rose, worry for his sister crowding out everything else.

"How is she? Is her ankle broken? How are the babies?"

"You were right to bring her in. I'm sorry things have been taking so long. It must be almost the children's bedtime."

"They're doing okay for now. How is Tricia?"

Dr. Shaw gestured to the chair and sat beside him after he sank back down. That was never a good sign, when the doctor took enough time to sit down, too.

"For the record, she gave me permission to share information with you. I can tell you that she has a severe sprain from the fall. I've called our orthopedics specialist on call and he's taking a look at her now to figure out a treatment plan. With the proper brace, her ankle should heal in a month or so. She'll have to stay off it for a few weeks, which means a wheelchair."

His mind raced through the possible implications of that. He needed to find a housekeeper immediately. He had three new green broke horses coming in the next few days for training and he was going to be stretched thin over the next few weeks—lousy timing over the holidays, but he couldn't turn down the work when he was trying so hard to establish Evergreen Springs as a powerhouse training facility.

How would he do everything on his own? Why couldn't things ever be easy?

"The guest room and bathroom are both on the main level," he said. "That will help. Can we pick up the wheelchair here or do I have to go somewhere else to find one?"

The doctor was silent for a few beats too long and he gave her a careful look.

"What aren't you telling me?" he asked.

She released a breath. "Your sister also appears to be in the beginning stages of labor."

He stared. "It's too early! The babies have to be too small."

Panic and guilt bloomed inside him, ugly and dark, and he rose, restless with all the emotions teeming inside him. She shouldn't have been outside where she risked falling. He *told* her she didn't have to go out to the bus to pick up the children. The stop was only a few hundred yards from the front door. They could walk up themselves, he told her, but she insisted on doing it every day. Said she needed the fresh air and the exercise.

Now look where they were.

"We're monitoring her condition and I've been in consultation with the best ob-gyn in the valley. We've given her some medication to stop her contractions and put the brakes on. It's been less than an hour, but so far it seems to be working."

He sat back down, relief coursing through him. "Okay. Okay. That's good. Isn't it?"

"It's still too early to tell. We have to keep her overnight up on the obstetrics floor to continue monitoring fetal activity."

"Sounds wise."

She paused for a long moment and he tried to sort through her silence for whatever else she might not be telling him.

"There's a chance she might have to stay longer. I just want to make you aware of the possibility. She's a complicated case—multiple births are always a little tricky. Add in an ankle injury that's going to make it tough for her to get around at home and possible premature labor, and her chances of needing hospital bed rest go up. I'm consulting with the ob-gyn but that's one of the options hanging out there."

Hospital bed rest. Damn. Could things get more complicated?

"Okay. Thank you for letting me know."

She glanced at the children, then back at him. "You're all welcome to go back and talk to your sister. I think she's feeling pretty alone right now."

He nodded and rose again. "Thanks. Kids. We can go back now."

"But, Dad! This one is almost over!" Jazmyn exclaimed. "Can't we wait ten more minutes to see the end?"

He fought the urge to roll his eyes. First she didn't

want to watch the show; now she didn't want to leave until she saw the end.

That just about summed up their life together. She was never happy with anything he did. If he made pancakes for breakfast, she insisted she wanted French toast. If he tried, in his fumbling way, to put her hair in pigtails, she told him she wanted a ponytail that day.

It was driving him crazy—and he had a feeling that was part of the reason both women he had hired to help him had lasted only a few weeks.

The doc gave him a sympathetic look. "If you'd like, I can stay with the children for a few minutes until the show is over while you have a moment alone with your sister."

Her thoughtfulness surprised him. In his experience, physicians weren't usually so solicitous. "It's just a TV show. She can catch it online later. I'm sure you have other patients to attend to."

"Right this moment, no. You actually caught us on a slow night. I've got to answer a few emails, which I can easily do out here while you talk to your sister for a few minutes."

He hated needing help. It was the toughest thing about being a single father, but in this case, he decided it would be stupid to argue.

"Thanks. The minute the show is over, you can send them back."

"No problem. I'll buzz you back. She's in room two."

She swiped her name badge across the door and he walked back into the emergency department. He found the room quickly. Inside, he found his baby sister looking pale and frightened, hooked up to a whole bunch of monitors.

He hurried over and kissed her cheek. "How are things?"

"I've been better." She shifted positions on the bed to try for a more comfortable spot, something that couldn't be easy given her advanced condition. "Did you talk to Devin?"

"Briefly."

"So she told you the ankle isn't broken."

"Yes. And that you're in premature labor."

"The beginning stages, anyway. So far the contractions have stopped."

"What happens if they start again?" He didn't even want to think about it.

"I'll probably be transferred to a bigger hospital in Boise with a higher level obstetrics department and larger newborn intensive care unit. Even if they don't start again, I'll likely be put on strict bed rest from now to the end of the pregnancy."

"Are the babies okay?"

Her mouth quivered a little. "They seem to be. They're not in distress or anything, at least for now."

"That's the important thing. That you're all okay."

Her eyes filled up with tears and her hands scrunched up the edge of the blanket. "Their lungs aren't fully developed yet. They're still so tiny. If they're born now, there's a chance they'll have to be on ventilators and might even have brain damage. Premature babies have all kinds of complications."

"Don't worry about things that haven't happened yet."

"I should have known I would screw this up, too."

He reached for her hand and gripped it in his, helpless and worried.

"You need to call Sean and let him know what's going on."

Tricia's mouth trembled slightly until she straightened it into a thin line. "No. Absolutely not."

"Trish."

"No. Don't go all big-brother protective and call him. Stay out of it. He made his wishes perfectly clear. He never wanted to be a father. He doesn't want these babies and he doesn't want me. If you call him, I'll never forgive you. I mean it."

Cole wanted to tear his hair out—or his brother-in-law's, at any rate. What he *really* wanted was the chance to take the man to some secluded canyon and beat the shit out of him for whatever he had done to devastate Tricia enough to walk away from their life together in California.

As tempting as it was to jump in his truck and drive from Idaho to California, violence wasn't always the solution. Cole would just end up in prison, which wouldn't help anyone.

Arguing with Tricia only served to make her dig her heels in harder, something she was very good at.

He sighed. "I'm only going to say this one more time, and then I'll let it drop. These are Sean's kids, too. However mad you might be at him, I believe he has the right to know what's going on with the three of you."

"Lecture duly noted," she said, refusing to meet his gaze. Feeling like an ass at the tremble in her voice, he squeezed her fingers.

"You'll be okay, kiddo, and so will those little lima beans in there. I have a good feeling about this."

She sniffled a little and gave him a watery half smile. "Devin is admitting me. I guess she probably told you that."

"Do you trust this doc? You said you know her from way back, but is that the most important thing here? I've been in my share of emergency rooms when I was on the circuit and I do know you have the right to be transferred by ambulance to a bigger hospital in Boise if you want another opinion, maybe from somebody who's watched a little more water pass under the bridge."

Tricia shook her head. "I don't want anybody else. I know she's young but I trust Devin. In fact, I'm going to ask her if she'll deliver my twins when the time comes, unless they end up coming early and I need a specialist."

"Why? You haven't seen her in years. You know nothing about her on a professional level."

"I'm not a complete idiot. Everybody who comes into the room raves about her, from the nurses to the receptionist to the ob-gyn we consulted." She held up her smartphone. "I also looked her up on Google, and she has excellent reviews online."

"And being married to a tech guy, you know you can certainly trust everything you read online."

"I trust my gut. That's the important thing."

He shook his head. "Sounds like you've made up your mind."

"I have."

The woman *had* been very kind to stay with the kids—which reminded him that he needed to find them before they became wrapped up in another show.

"Are you okay here? I'm going to go grab the kids and get them some dinner, and then we'll be back."

"You don't have to do that. I'll be fine tonight. Take the kids home to their own beds and I'll be in touch with you in the morning with an update."

"Are you sure? I don't feel good about leaving you here by yourself."

"I'll be fine. To be honest, after all this excitement—plus the medicine they gave me—all I want to do is sleep."

That didn't completely convince him, but he didn't know what else to do but take the kids home to preserve as much routine for them as possible. He couldn't spend all night in the waiting room with them, especially if Tricia didn't need him.

"You'll call or text me right away if anything changes, right?"

"Yes. Definitely."

"If you send me a list of what you need to be more comfortable, I can run it back tonight."

"Just my bag from the car." She gave him a sheepish look. "I've had an emergency hospital bag packed for weeks. Even before I came out here, I brought it with me to Idaho and grabbed it on impulse on the way out the door this afternoon. It's got my phone charger, a robe and some slippers and a couple of magazines I've been meaning to get to."

This didn't surprise him. Tricia was just about the most organized person he knew. It was what made her brilliant at her job as director of a nonprofit charity in San Jose.

"I'll grab your bag. If you think of anything else, call me."

To his alarm, she started to tear up again. "I will. Thank you, Cole. For everything. You've always been the one person I can count on in this world."

He managed not to snort his disbelief. She must be on some serious drugs if she could say something so ridiculous. He hadn't been around when she needed him. First he had been too busy partying on the circuit, then he had been paying the price for all that hard living. A good chunk of their relationship over the past decade and a half had been long-distance.

He couldn't repair all that he had done. If he had learned one thing in prison, it was the lesson that a guy could only fix what was in front of him. He leaned in and kissed her cheek. "You know I love you, squirt."

"I do."

"Your only job right now is to take care of yourself and those little spudnuts in there, got it?"

"Is that an order?"

"If that's what it takes. Just rest. I'll be back in a minute with your bag."

"Thank you."

She leaned back against the pillow, looking pale and fragile. Her foot was up on pillows and her big abdomen stretched the sheets.

He again fought the urge to find her SOB husband and knock some sense into the man. Barring that, the only thing he could do was bring her bag back and then take care of his children.

CHAPTER TWO

"THAT WAS A good show," the adorable boy declared when the closing credits to the animated Christmas show on the television started to roll.

His sister gave a dismissive shrug. "I guess. I thought the elf was kind of stupid. I mean, why didn't he just give the girl's letter to Santa in the first place instead of trying to answer it himself because he was trying to be such a big deal?"

"People can make all kinds of crazy choices in stories," Devin pointed out. "If Elvis had given the letter to Santa, the story would have ended there and he never would have learned to care more about helping other people than about how important he looked to them."

"Maybe."

Jazmyn looked doubtful, not particularly swayed by Devin's thoughtful analysis on the nature of elves in fiction and the character journey of this particular elf.

"When is Aunt Tricia gonna be done here so we can go home?" the girl asked. "We haven't even had dinner yet and it's almost Ty's bedtime. I'm okay, but

Ty is *starving*. He has to keep his blood sugar steady or he gets *crazy*."

"I do not," Ty protested.

"You do. That's what Mom used to say all the time, remember?"

"I guess." He looked upset at the reminder. From what she had seen, the boy was extremely sweet, with those big soulful dark eyes and endlessly long eyelashes. "I guess I *am* hungry."

"If your dad doesn't come out in a few moments, I'll grab some crackers and cheese for you. Maybe that will hold you over until you can get some dinner."

"But when can Aunt Tricia go home? Is she done with the 'tractions?" Jazmyn asked.

"Did she have to get a big cast on her leg?" Ty asked before she could answer his sister. "My friend Carlos broke his arm on a trampoline and had to get a big cast. It's camel-flage."

"Camouflage, you mean," Jazmyn corrected him.

"That's what I said."

"Your aunt has to stay the night so we can take care of her leg—which isn't going to need a cast but will probably be in a brace that she can take on and off. I'm not sure if we have one in camouflage but I can see."

"What about her babies?" the girl asked. "She's not going to have them tonight, is she?"

Devin hoped not. "I don't think so. They're a little too small right now."

"She's having a boy and a girl," Ty informed her. "The boy is going to be Jack and the girl will be named Emma. That was my grandma's middle name. I never met her because she died. Aunt Tricia said I can hold them anytime I want."

"I'm sure you'll be a big help."

"I'm going to. She said I could even feed them a bottle if I wanted."

"Lucky."

"You don't even know how to feed a baby a bottle," his sister said skeptically. "I do. I fed you when you were little."

Since Jazmyn was only a few years older than her brother, Devin doubted the veracity of that claim, but she wasn't about to call her on it.

"With two babies, there will be plenty of chances for everybody to hold them and feed them."

"Don't talk about food because I'm *starving*," the girl moaned dramatically.

"I'm sure your dad will be out soon to take you back to your house for some dinner."

"It's not *my* house," she muttered.

"It is *so*," Ty argued. "Dad said so. We live with him now."

"Not for long. Grandma Trixie says she's going to fight for custody so we can come live with her in California, just as soon as she finds us all a good place to stay."

Why would a grandparent think she could possibly win a custody fight against a parent? What was the background? Where was their mother, first of all, and why hadn't they been living with their father before now?

Cole's life seemed a mad tangle of complications.

"I don't want to live with Grandma Trixie. I like living with Dad," Ty said, his voice small. "We have our own rooms now, which we never had before, and a yard to play in and Dad says I can even get a horse of my own after I learn how to ride better."

"Who wants a stupid horse?" Jazmyn tossed her brother a disgusted look. "With Grandma Trixie in California, we could go to the beach every day, even in the winter, and maybe even see movie stars."

"I'd rather have a horse and live with Dad," Ty muttered. Devin had the feeling this wasn't the first time the two of them had engaged in this particular argument. To keep the peace, she opted for distraction.

"Let's go see if we can find some crackers and juice. Ty, why don't you give me a hand?"

The agreeable boy slid off his chair and followed her to the reception desk. "Hey, Brittney. My man Ty here is hungry and so is his sister. Any chance we could grab a few of those cracker packs and maybe some cookies from the food room?"

"Sure, Dr. Shaw." The young receptionist hopped up. "I should have thought of that. What a dope I can be. I'm sorry. Just give me a sec."

She smiled. "Thanks."

The receptionist hurried away. While she was gone, Ty became interested in the small Christmas tree on the desk, made entirely of inflated nonlatex gloves cascading down with an elastic bandage garland.

"Are those all balloons? Did somebody have to blow them all up?"

"I would guess so," she answered.

"I bet that took *forever.*"

"It's not that tough. Here, I'll show you." She grabbed a glove from the box tacked to the wall and quickly showed him how to bunch the end together and blow it up, then tie the end like a balloon. "And now look." She grabbed a Sharpie from the canister on the reception desk and doodled a face on it, with the thumb sticking out like a long nose, much to the boy's delight.

She might not be able to knit, but who said she wasn't crafty?

She had learned the fine art of glove creature creation during her first surgery, when she'd ended up staying ten days because of an infection. In the children's hospital in Boise, she had met Lilah, another teenage girl with cancer. It was Lilah, she remembered, who had shown her the trick of creating creatures from surgical gloves. They used to make them for the younger kids receiving treatment.

Lilah had lost her battle just a few months later.

Devin thought a silent prayer for her friend and for the others she had said goodbye to along her cancer journey.

"Can you make one for Jazmyn?" Ty asked.

"You bet."

In a minute, she had another inflated glove. This face she drew with long eyelashes and puckered lips. Ty quickly took it over to his sister just as the receptionist came out with a handful of treats.

The kids were eating crackers and cheese with

enthusiasm—pausing every few moments to bop each other on the head with their inflated glove creatures—when their father walked back into the waiting room.

She suddenly felt as if all the air had been sucked from the room, which she was fully aware was a completely ridiculous reaction to a gorgeous man.

"Hey, kids."

"Where's Aunt Tricia?"

Cole glanced at Devin, looking rather endearingly uncertain, as if he wasn't quite sure what to tell his kids. "She's sticking around here for the night. Dr. Shaw wants to keep an eye on her and the babies a little longer."

"Who's going to fix us breakfast and get us on the bus?" Ty demanded. "We don't even have Mrs. Lynn to help us anymore."

"I can do that just as well as Tricia or Mrs. Lynn."

"Aunt Tricia said you can't even make toast without burning it," Jazmyn informed him.

"Aunt Tricia talks too much," he muttered. "Between you and me, we ought to be able to handle things for a few days, don't you think?"

"I guess," she said doubtfully.

"Get your coats and gather up your things so we can take off," he ordered. "We need to get Aunt Tricia's bag out of the car, then grab some dinner so I can get you two to bed."

"Can we take these?" Ty asked Devin, holding out his inflated glove.

"Of course," she answered. "I'll warn you, they might start to lose air pretty soon."

When they were just about ready to go—mittens found, beanies adjusted—Jazmyn turned contrary.

"I need to use the bathroom," she suddenly declared. The girl was quite a character. She could have gone anytime in the past fifteen minutes but she had waited until she knew her father was in a hurry.

"Can't you wait until we get home?" Cole asked.

"No. I have to go *now*."

"Fine. Go ahead."

She headed to the ladies' room just off the lobby. "You need to go?" Cole asked his son. The boy shook his head, content to toss the rubber glove balloon into the air and catch it again.

"Thanks for keeping an eye on them," Cole said to her.

"No problem. They're fun kids. How old are they? I didn't have the chance to ask."

"Jaz is eight going on about thirty-six and Ty just turned six."

"Those are fun ages at Christmastime. Still young enough to believe in the magic and old enough to appreciate the wonder of it all."

"I guess. I'm not sure any of us is in the mood for Christmas this year," he said, his tone rather bleak.

Why? What was the story here? She wanted to ask but decided it wasn't her business. "You said you had a bag of your sister's?"

"Yeah. I guess she's had a hospital bag packed since before she came out to Idaho. She threw it in the truck before we left the house. Mother's intuition or something. Apparently it contains a few necessities like magazines and slippers."

"Handy."

"I guess." He looked around the empty waiting room, then back at her. "I've got to tell you, Doc, I'm still not convinced this is the best place for her and the twins. I can't help thinking maybe the smartest thing would be to pack her up right now and take her to a bigger hospital in Boise."

Devin ignored the little pinch to her pride. "I understand your concern. I told Tricia that's a decision she can certainly make. I will tell you, we have a state-of-the-art facility here, brand-new in the last two years, with every possible advanced fetal and maternal monitoring capability and a couple of excellent specialists in the area who will be taking a look at her tomorrow. If at any time your sister feels uneasy about the care she's receiving here, I would be the first to encourage her to transfer to a different facility. At this point, we're dealing with a sprained ankle and contractions that currently appear to be under control. I would advise against moving to another facility far away from her family, but that's, of course, her choice."

"Yeah, she was quick to remind me of the same thing," he said, his voice wry.

"Sisters. What can you do?"

He almost smiled but seemed to catch himself at the last minute as his daughter came out of the ladies' room, wiping her just-washed hands on her coat.

He unpeeled from the wall. "Thanks for keeping

an eye on them for me. Come on, kids. Let's grab the bag for Aunt Tricia, then take off back to the ranch before that snow gets any deeper."

Devin watched them walk outside, their faces colored by the blinking Christmas lights around the front door as snow swirled around them.

"I can't believe how much snow has already fallen," Brittney said, looking out after them.

Before Devin could answer, Callie appeared. "There you are. We just got a call from Dispatch. Paramedics are on their way to the scene of a three-car accident and they're warning us to get ready for multiple injuries."

So much for her relatively quiet evening.

She put the very sexy cowboy and his cute kids out of her mind so she could focus on the job at hand.

She didn't have the chance to check on Tricia again until several hours and two more weather-related accidents later.

Devin's friend had been moved to a room on the obstetrics floor, the third floor of the hospital, where each room had big windows offering lovely views—in daylight, anyway—of the Redemption Mountains and the beautiful unearthly blue waters of Lake Haven.

On a quick break, Devin took the elevator up and headed to the obstetrics nurses' desk. She found Tricia's chart and saw that the contractions appeared to have stopped. Dr. Randall, the ob-gyn, had made a visit a short time ago and Devin sighed when she read his recommendation. As she had feared, Dr. Randall agreed with her and thought this was one of the rare cases when hospital bed rest was indicated.

That wouldn't be easy for anyone—especially not Tricia.

Thinking she would just take a peek inside to see if her patient was sleeping, she cracked the door only a little. A light was on above the bed, she discovered. Tricia sat upright in the bed with her leg propped on a couple of pillows, hands clasped over her distended abdomen.

When she spied Devin, she gave a small smile and quickly tried to wipe away the tears on her cheeks.

Devin didn't give another thought to the peanut butter and honey sandwich she had planned to eat during the break. Her patient was in distress and that was far more important.

She pushed the door open and walked inside. "Oh, honey. What's wrong? Are you having pain? How's the ankle?"

Tricia shrugged. "It hurts, mainly because I don't want to take any heavy pain medication that might harm the babies. But at least it's not broken. Mostly I'm upset because this isn't the way I planned to spend the last few weeks of my pregnancy. Alone, on bed rest in a strange hospital."

"I'm so sorry."

Tricia sniffled and Devin handed her the box of tissues that was just out of reach on her bedside table. She grabbed one and wiped at her eyes. "So you heard?"

"I was just reading your chart."

"Dr. Randall thinks I should stay here on hospital bed rest for the next week so they can continue monitoring things. I'm dilated to a three and twenty percent effaced, which makes the risk of premature labor high, and now I can't even walk to the bathroom on my own. The stupid ankle is complicating everything."

"I know it's hard but this might be the best thing for all of you. You want to keep those little ones inside there as long as possible, trust me. In just a few weeks, they'll be considered full-term and the risks of neonatal complications drop considerably."

"I know. But I don't have to like it. It stinks."

"You won't get an argument from me. I get it, believe me."

She didn't, really. She could understand and empathize on a clinical level but she didn't really know what it was to be pregnant and frightened. That was something she would never be able to appreciate, except theoretically.

The ache in her chest was as familiar as it was unwelcome.

"I'm sorry I bothered you," she said quietly. "Sleep is really the best thing for you and those kidlets."

"I was sleeping until a short time ago, but then I had a bad dream that woke me."

Devin tried to lighten the mood. "I hate that. A few nights ago, I dreamed I was the grand marshal of the Lake Haven Days parade but instead of riding on a float, I had to do cartwheels the entire parade route, all the way down Lake Street in front of everyone in town. My hands were killing me, even in the dream."

As she hoped, Tricia smiled a little at the ridiculousness of Devin's subconscious. "The mind is such a strange thing, isn't it?"

"You said it, sister." Devin slipped into the visitor's chair next to the bed.

She felt a comfortable kinship with the other woman, though they had been separated for years and hadn't stayed in touch. Some friendships were like that. Despite time and distance, coming together again was like slipping on a favorite shirt you misplaced for a while in the back of your closet.

"Is it still snowing out there?" Tricia asked. "I spoke with my brother before I fell asleep and he said they passed a couple of slide-offs on the way home. He said they already had four or five inches on the road up to Evergreen Springs."

"We've had weather-related accidents all night. This is the first chance I've had to slip away to check on you. Your brother and the children made it home safely, though?"

"Yes. He said it was slick and they slid a little, especially going up the driveway, but nothing serious."

"That's a relief."

Tricia was silent, her fingers tangled in the edge of the nubby hospital blanket. "I hate that I've complicated everything for him. As if everything wasn't tough enough already—now he has to worry about me, too."

"Why are things tough?"

Tricia made a rough sound. "I could paper the walls with all the reasons, starting with the kids. Jazmyn and Ty have only been with him a few months and they're all still trying to find their way together."

"Is that right?" She didn't want to be nosy but she couldn't deny she was curious about the situation.

Tricia sighed. "Their mom, Cole's ex, was killed in a car accident just after her third marriage."

"Oh, no. Those poor children." Perhaps that explained some of Jazmyn's surliness and the shadows in poor little Ty's gaze.

"I know the kids miss her. My heart breaks for them. I don't think Ty, at least, really gets what's going on, but Jaz was super close to her mother and she's devastated. It's been so tough for all of them. I'm sad for the kids but I can't honestly say I'm sorry Sharla is dead."

Devin blinked a little, surprised by the other woman's rancor. "Okay."

"I know that makes me sound like a terrible person but I don't care. She was a vindictive witch who did her best to keep Jaz and Ty away from Cole as much as possible, unless it was convenient for her to dump them off on him. She hopped from man to man, town to town, and put him and those kids through hell."

"That doesn't sound like a good situation for anybody."

"It wasn't. I hope things will be a little easier for all of them now. Maybe they can have some kind of stable home life for the first time, at least after Cole finds a housekeeper who will stick around for longer than a few weeks. You don't know anybody looking for a job, do you?"

"As a housekeeper?" Devin asked. "I don't, but I can certainly ask around."

"He needs a nanny more than a housekeeper, really. He just can't keep up with the ranch and the house and the kids by himself. He's hired a couple of people to help but neither of them really clicked with the kids. Jaz can be…moody and difficult sometimes. As for Ty, he's the sweetest thing, but he can be energetic when he's in a mood. Neither of them has ever had any kind of structure or discipline. I've been helping him out these past weeks since the last housekeeper left before Thanksgiving. I don't know how he's going to juggle everything on his own without me."

"I'm sure he'll figure it out." Cole Barrett struck her as a man used to taking care of business. She ignored the ridiculous little flutter in her stomach as she thought of the man. "You need to let your brother worry about his home life. That can't be your concern."

"I can't help it. I stress about him and the children. If he wasn't so darn stubborn, the solution to the whole problem is right there at the ranch, staring him in the face. But that would be too easy and require my inflexible brother to bend a little. I mean, Dad is right there on the ranch, living fifty yards away, but Cole will gnaw off his own leg before he asks Stanford to lift a finger."

"I take it your brother and father don't get along." The man really *did* have a tangled mess of a home life.

Tricia sighed heavily. "That's an understatement. I'm not saying Cole doesn't have his reasons for being angry, but people can change, right? Dad is trying."

Devin didn't quite know how to answer that, since she didn't know any of the particulars, so she remained silent.

After a moment, Tricia winced. "Sorry. You didn't come in here to be bored by my family drama."

"I'm not bored. I just wish I could help somehow."

"The housekeeper is the critical need, especially with me stuck here. They're going to be eating frozen pizzas and cold cereals until I have these babies. He's the kind of man who will never ask for help. He'll just muddle through as best he can."

She knew more than a few of those. "I'll put the word out. It might be tough to hire someone right before Christmas but I'll ask my sister if she can think of anybody. McKenzie is the mayor of Haven Point and she seems to know everything that goes on."

"Thank you. Seriously, Devin. Thank you. I'm so glad you were here when Cole made me come."

She smiled and rose. "I need to head back downstairs. Is there anything else I can do for you?"

"You've done so much already." Tears welled up in the other woman's eyes again and Devin squeezed her fingers. This was a tough situation for anyone, especially when she was pregnant with twins and appeared to be alone.

Tricia hadn't said anything about her husband,

though she still wore a wedding ring. Devin took a chance and though it wasn't her business as a physician, she wanted to think their old and dear friendship gave her a little more leeway.

"Have you been in contact with the babies' father? Does he know what's going on?"

Tricia reached for another tissue. "No. He won't care, anyway."

"Ah. I'm sorry I brought it up."

"Sean and I are…estranged, I guess you could say. It's such a mess."

"I didn't mean to distress you, honey. Forget about it."

"No. You should know what's going on. It's a long story but the core problem is he's angry about the pregnancy. We have always been that couple who told everyone who would listen that they didn't want children. We were both adamant about it. This was an oopsie of epic proportions…and wouldn't you know, I'd get pregnant with twins?"

Devin forced a smile, though she felt that familiar little ache in her chest again.

"As soon as I found out I was pregnant, my whole mind-set shifted," Tricia said, "and suddenly I loved and wanted Jack and Emma desperately, but Sean never came around. I thought he might eventually, but we had another big fight just before Thanksgiving. He couldn't come to the last ultrasound. This is after weeks of him being too busy to come to other appointments. He was supposed to come out here with me, too, for the holiday, but at the last minute he volunteered for a business trip. It was the last straw, you know?"

She didn't, but again, she nodded.

"It was plain to me things would never change. I decided I couldn't raise my children in an atmosphere where they felt unwanted, even for a moment. I know what that's like and I couldn't put my children through that, so I decided to stay with Cole and the children, to have the babies here and stay at Evergreen Springs until I figure out what to do now."

She sniffled a little and wiped at her eyes. "Now here I am in the hospital with a sprained ankle. I've made such a mess of things."

Devin rubbed her arm. "You're in very good hands here, my dear. We will take great care of you and your babies. I promise."

"What about Cole and the kids? While I'm in here resting on my butt, he'll be scrambling to do everything on his own. He's a dear, dear man but he's in way over his head with those kids of his. He can barely boil water. They'll be eating peanut butter and jelly sandwiches for every meal."

Devin took her friend's hands. "Your concern right now has to be keeping those babies safe and healthy and doing what you can to heal that ankle. I need you to promise me you won't worry. It's not good for any of you. We'll find someone to help your brother."

"You know, I believe you." Tricia rested back on the pillows, some of the strain easing from her features. "That was always one of the things I loved best about you, Dev. If you said you would do something, you did it. You always kept your word."

"You have to believe me about this. Your brother will be fine. We'll make sure of it."

She wasn't sure how, she thought as she bid Tricia good-night and left the room. She didn't even know the man, but she had promised her friend.

Cole Barrett would receive help, whether he wanted it or not.

CHAPTER THREE

WHEN DEVIN FINALLY parked her SUV in the garage and let herself into her house on the lakeshore, it was nearly midnight and most Haven Point residents lay tucked in their beds while the snow continued to fall and the winds blew.

She flipped on the lights of the kitchen, a little light-headed with exhaustion. Her day had started with clinic hours at her practice beginning before 9:00 a.m. Barring those few moments of knitting with Greta, she hadn't had time to take a breath all day.

Why, again, had she ever wanted to be a doctor?

Oh, yes. Because she wanted to think that some days she was actually making a difference, helping others as she had been helped by so many caring professionals.

Seamus, the friendlier of her two cats, wandered in and rubbed against her leg in greeting.

Devin picked him up. "Hello there, handsome. Anything exciting happen around here? What kind of trouble did you and Simone get into without me?"

He let out a long meow, the tattletale. Both of her cats were rescues from the shelter but Simone had been with her only a few months, a replacement for her dearest and oldest friend, Trina, who had been with Devin since she was a kitten.

The newcomer and Seamus adored each other, which was great, but so far the other cat hadn't warmed up to Devin.

She was working on it, though. She pulled the kibble out of the pantry and shook the container. A moment later, Simone peeked shyly around the corner. She was still trying to persuade the cat to come closer when her phone rang.

To Devin's great relief, it was her sister, not an emergency call tugging her back to the hospital.

"Hey, Kenz," she answered. "What are you doing up so late?"

"I could say the same for you, Dr. Shaw. I was letting Rika and Hondo back inside after their last trip out for the night and saw you drive past. Tell me you've been on a hot date."

She snorted. When was her last hot date? Nothing came immediately to mind. She really needed to do something about that but the dating pool in Haven Point wasn't very deep at the moment. The town was changing, though, especially now that Caine Tech was developing a new facility on the edge of town at the site of the old boatworks, which had once been owned by the family of McKenzie's fiancé.

"You know me. I have to fight them off with a scalpel."

McKenzie laughed. "You would, if you stood still long enough. Have you been working all day?"

"I covered Pat Lander's shift in the emergency

department after work. His grandson had a Christmas concert over in Star and he didn't want to miss it. Nobody else was available. What are *you* doing up so late?"

"Ben flew in for the weekend," she answered. "We went to dinner at Lydia's place in Shelter Springs and stayed later than we planned. I just checked my email and saw you sent me something about calling out the troops. What's up?"

Devin slipped off her shoes and sank into her favorite chair in the family room, with wide windows looking out on the lake. Right now she saw only snow drifting past the window but she could imagine it on a summer afternoon with the water gently lapping the dock and clouds rippling past the mountains.

"I wanted to take a couple of quick freezer meals—soups, casseroles, whatever—to a single dad in the area who apparently isn't very skilled in the kitchen."

"Oh? Anybody I know?"

This was always a tricky situation. Privacy rules demanded she not discuss her patients, not even when that patient had been a friend to both of them. But how did she let McKenzie know what was needed when she couldn't give specifics?

"Cole Barrett," she finally said. "Do you know him?"

"Are you kidding? Yum. Tricia's brother, right? The sexy rodeo cowboy who lives up at Evergreen Springs. I've bumped into him a few times having breakfast when I'm grabbing coffee at Serrano's. Not a big talker, by the way, but he *was* one of those on the front lines of the sandbagging during the big flood."

Earlier in the summer, a dam upriver from Haven Point on the Hell's Fury had become unstable. The town avoided significant damage, mostly because the town's mayor—who just happened to be her sister— had quickly mobilized everyone to evacuate and put protective measures around homes in the flood zone.

"Wait a minute," McKenzie said after a moment. "Cole Barrett is a single father? You're kidding. I had no idea the guy had a family. I don't think I've ever seen him with kids."

"Apparently his ex-wife had custody of their son and daughter but she died a few months ago so the kids have come to live with him."

"Oh, the poor kids. This is a terrible season to lose a parent."

If they had been together in person, Devin would have given her sister a tight hug, suddenly remembering her sister had personal experience in that department. She and McKenzie were half sisters, actually, and McKenzie had come to live with their family when she was ten, after her own mother died. That had been around the holidays, too, she remembered, more determined than ever to help Cole and his children through this rough time.

"He needs a housekeeper. Do you know anybody in town who might be looking for a job?"

"I think everybody who's in the market is applying at the new Caine Tech facility. I can check with a few people. Anita knows everything," she said, referring to her assistant at city hall. "She might have some ideas."

"Thank you. Meanwhile, Tricia has been in town helping him out but she can't right now." Devin chose her words carefully, mindful again of patient privacy. "I was thinking it would be very neighborly if we called out the Helping Hands to fill up his freezer with a few things he could fix in a pinch while he's handling things on his own."

McKenzie spearheaded a loosely organized group of women who gathered regularly to provide service to Haven Point residents who might be struggling.

"That's a fabulous idea. I'll send out an email right now. When would you like me to have people drop off their meals?"

She hadn't thought that far ahead, to actually delivering the meals. That would necessitate seeing Cole again, something that suddenly gave her ridiculous butterflies.

Her tired brain took a moment to scan through her schedule for the next day. "Why don't we say midmorning tomorrow? That way everybody can see the email first thing and check their freezer inventory. I've got yoga class at the senior citizen's center that won't be done until ten. Let's use the store as a central drop-off place, if you don't mind. I can pick everything up after yoga and take it up to Evergreen Springs. I thought I would make up a spinach lasagna, a chicken and rice casserole and the Gruyère mac and cheese everybody seemed to like at the last potluck."

"Ooh. That sounds delicious. I wish I had a big bowl of it right now."

"I'll save you some," she promised.

"I was already thinking about throwing together a big batch of burgundy beef stew in the slow cooker tomorrow. Ben loves it and I'll have plenty of extras for Cole. I'll just cook it on the stove instead. It's always better reheated anyway, once the flavors have time to meld."

"Thanks, Kenz."

"I'm actually glad to have the chance to do something for Cole. He worked nonstop last summer when the Hell's Fury flooded and then disappeared before I ever had the chance to say thanks. I don't think I saw him even take a break for a sandwich. It will be nice to feel like we're paying him back a little for all his help."

"That works."

"And maybe if we're nice enough to him," McKenzie went on in a voice that was growing in enthusiasm, "he won't feel like he has to be such a hermit up there on the mountain. Sexy cowboys hanging around downtown for the tourists to see can only be good for our reputation, right?"

Devin laughed. "You can be the one to tell the man you want to pimp him out for the good of Haven Point."

"He wouldn't have to go bare-chested or anything. I would be happy if he just walked up and down Lake Street in his Stetson, tipping it every now and then to the tourists with a random 'ma'am' or 'howdy.'"

She heard a deep voice on the other end—Ben, she assumed. McKenzie said something to him Devin couldn't hear, then came back laughing.

"Okay, apparently Ben thinks that's not one of my better ideas. We'll keep it on the back burner for now."

"That's a good place for it. Way, way back," Devin said with a laugh. "I'll be by tomorrow to pick up the food."

She ended the connection, deeply grateful for her sister. McKenzie had come into the family through difficult circumstances but Devin couldn't imagine her world without her sister's quirky sense of humor, her creative mind and her deep sense of compassion and loyalty.

Seamus wandered in again and pounced onto her lap. Simone peeked her head around the edge of the door frame, then slunk into the kitchen toward her food bowl with mad ninja skills, as if she were trying to become invisible by being one with the maple heartwood floor.

"Hey, kitty, kitty," Devin said softly. Simone gave her a wary look, ate a little food, then darted back out of the room.

She petted Seamus for a moment, listening to the quiet sounds of the house where she had been raised—the whoosh of the furnace clicking on, the creak of old joists, the wind moaning under the eaves.

Some people might think it was weird that she still lived in her childhood home. Not only did she still live in it, she had used her inheritance from her father to purchase it from her mother and sister after she decided to come back to Haven Point to practice and went into partnership with Russ Warrick.

The sprawling house was too big for one person,

but she didn't care. She loved it, anyway. How could she not, right here on the lakeshore with a beautiful view of the steep and jagged mountains reflecting in the water?

It had always been a place of refuge. In the midst of all the chemo and radiation and fear—and then later, during the stress and pressure of medical school, residency and internship—this had been her go-to happy place.

She had done a few things to it since she purchased it. The kitchen was all new and she had taken out the old carpet and installed wood flooring throughout the house. She had taken out a couple of walls between two of the smaller rooms on the west side of the house and made one large master suite for herself with vaulted ceilings and huge windows.

It was her retreat, her sanctuary. She headed there now, accompanied by Seamus. Devin flipped the switch to turn on the Christmas tree, one of two in the house that McKenzie had decorated for her.

She was so tired she decided to forgo her usual routine of yoga stretches before bed and just changed into pajamas and sank into her bed. If she was going to help Cole Barrett and his kids, she had a feeling she would need all the sleep she could get.

HE HAD BROKEN a grand total of thirty-two bones in his body during his rodeo days but none of those injuries compared to the sheer sadistic agony of stepping on one of Ty's LEGO pieces, even in stocking feet.

Cole bit back a curse but let it slip out anyway

when his other foot stepped down on a colored pencil that jabbed at his foot through the sock.

Too bad he didn't drink anymore, because right now he could really use a whiskey instead of the glass of water he had just about spilled all over the floor.

His house was officially a pigsty. After only a few hours of the kids at home on a Saturday morning without Tricia or his housekeeper, toys, discarded backpacks and cereal crumbs were scattered everywhere. Did they just grab bags of their belongings out of their rooms and run through the house tossing things right and left?

And how did they seem to have so much stuff, anyway? They had come to him with hardly anything. Sharla's transient lifestyle had precluded them owning much besides some clothes and a few toys.

He reached down and picked up a mini brick figure of Darth Vader before the bad dude could slice off his toe with his plastic light saber.

"I think this guy is yours," he said to Ty as his son headed in with another handful of dry cereal—which possibly explained the crushed bits on the carpet.

"I almost broke my foot on a couple of your other toys. Sorry I broke your creation."

Ty winced. "I forgot to pick them up. Sorry. Should I get them now?"

"That would be helpful. And do you remember we talked about only eating in the kitchen and dining room?"

"I forgot that, too."

"One more thing. Remember the rule about snacks?

If you want something to eat, you need to ask me first, and if I say yes, you should put it in a bowl so we don't trail pieces all over the floor for other people to step on."

"Okay," he said with a put-upon sigh.

The poor kid probably felt as if he'd gone from living in Disneyland with no rules and all the junk food he could want to doing hard time in Alcatraz.

Cole mustered a smile. "Thanks."

"I told him he didn't need any more cereal, because he already had breakfast and would only ruin his lunch, but he didn't listen to me," Jazmyn said in that know-it-all tone that could sometimes grate on his last nerve.

"I don't mind him having a snack but we all need to work together to keep the place clean. Speaking of which, I believe I asked you to clear the breakfast dishes off the table."

"I was drawing something," she answered. Apparently she thought obeying her father was optional—or at least negotiable.

He wasn't Sharla and the rules at Evergreen Springs were very different from what they were both used to.

He had made the mistake of letting things slide for a while after they first came here, when they were both reeling from their mother's death.

They were still having a tough time of it—he had a feeling they would for a long time—but he was beginning to realize they needed structure and order to help them feel secure and stable here with him.

"It's a very lovely picture," he answered. "You are an excellent artist, Jazmyn."

"Thanks."

"Now you need to do what I asked and clear the table, unless you would like to lose the colored pencils for the rest of the day."

She narrowed her gaze at him and opened her mouth as if to argue, but something in his expression stopped her. Wise girl. Instead, she gave a little huff and started clearing things off with dramatic, jerky movements.

He didn't know what to do with her. She didn't want to be here. She told him continually how she couldn't wait until she lived with her grandma Trixie. Sharla's mother was threatening a custody battle, and while he didn't think she would have a leg to stand on, he knew too well how quickly the system could turn on a guy.

Trixie didn't help the situation at all by constantly telling Jazmyn she wanted his daughter to come live with her in California.

When she was younger, Jazmyn had adored him and thought he could do no wrong. Eight years of her grandmother and mother poisoning her against him had altered their relationship. He didn't know how to fix things, especially when she could be so frustrating and fought him about even the most basic things, like brushing her teeth or helping out with minor chores.

He had trained plenty of horses and dogs but was discovering training kids was a little more complicated.

She was a tough cookie, his little girl. In a lot of

ways, she had been forced to raise herself because of circumstances—particularly her selfish, immature mother with repeated substance abuse problems and the string of men she brought in and out of the kids' lives.

Jazmyn had been through far too much in her short eight years on the planet. It was no wonder she had become a bossy, difficult little thing.

For now, she seemed to be willing to do something he asked and he decided to enjoy it while it lasted. He returned to his laptop and was deep in the new accounting program he was trying to figure out for the ranch when the doorbell rang.

"Who could that be?" Ty asked, rushing to the door before Cole could even push his chair back from the table.

He really needed to have a talk with the kid about stranger danger and taking a few basic precautions, like waiting for his dad to answer the door. He didn't want to make his kids paranoid but Cole knew better than most that there were nasty people in the world. He'd lived among the worst for eighteen months.

At least Coco, the old ranch dog who lived inside these days, had padded after him. She was half-blind but she would still go to the wall for everybody she considered part of her pack.

He headed after both of them just as his son opened the door for Devin Shaw.

Cole was struck again by how lovely she was, with her appealing smile, green eyes sparkling in the sunshine and all that delicious creamy skin, a little pink from the cold.

A few random snowflakes spangled the blue-and-silver beanie she wore and the jaunty matching scarf. She looked bright and vibrant and very different from the scrub-wearing professional he had seen at the hospital.

He had just a moment for purely masculine appreciation before the questions began to fly in his mind. What was she doing here? Was Tricia all right? Had there been some kind of complication? He had talked to his sister earlier in the morning but maybe the situation had changed.

No. If there had been a problem, Tricia would have called him. Not only that, but he had a feeling Devin wouldn't be so calm right now, nor would she be giving such a friendly smile.

"Hi."

"Hi, Dr. Shaw," Ty said. "Did you see all that snow?"

She crouched down to talk to him at his level. "I sure did. I just drove through it on the way up here from town. It's pretty deep. With snow like that, there's only one thing to do. You have to build a snowman."

Ty's face lit up. "Yes! We should! Jaz, don't you think we should build a snowman?"

While Cole was busy trying not to stare at Devin, Jazmyn had wandered out to see who was at the door.

"It's too cold," Jazmyn answered, though Cole didn't miss the sudden spark of excitement in her eyes. She was so contrary she even argued with herself and didn't want to admit what she really wanted.

"If you dress warmly, you'll be so busy having fun, you won't even feel the cold," Dr. Shaw assured her.

"Can we, Dad? Can we?" Ty asked.

He didn't know how to answer. He didn't want to disappoint his son but he had ranch accounts to finish and then a call scheduled in fifteen minutes with a new client who wanted to discuss a possible lucrative new contract. The vet was supposed to be dropping by sometime that afternoon to take a look at one of the horses he was training who seemed off his feed.

A little resentful of Dr. Shaw for showing up on the doorstep and giving him one more thing to feel guilty about, Cole opened his mouth to tell Ty they could try to build one later in the afternoon but she spoke before he could.

"I've got a few minutes," she offered. "And I'm particularly good at snowpeople. I would love to help you build a snowman, if your dad doesn't mind."

What was he supposed to say to that? He couldn't send her on her way without sounding like even more of a jerk.

"I'm sure you didn't drive all the way up here just so you could build a snowman with my son," he said.

She smiled. "No. I would just consider that a bonus. Actually, I came out to bring you something."

He gazed blankly at her. "You did?"

She opened the front door and pointed to a large cardboard box outside on the porch.

"What is it?" Ty asked.

"Is it a puppy?" Jazmyn asked. "I really want a puppy."

"We have a dog," he answered, pointing to Coco, who had eased her tired bones down onto the rug in the foyer.

"She's old and she doesn't ever want to play," Jazmyn answered. "*And* her breath stinks."

"It's not a puppy," Dr. Shaw assured him. "Stinky or otherwise."

"Is it a Christmas present?" Ty asked.

"I guess you could call it that. A Christmas present from lots of different people."

"Can I see what it is?"

"Go ahead."

Ty opened the flaps, peered inside, then eased away with a confused look. "It's just bowls and stuff."

"What is it?" Jazmyn asked, pushing her way forward. If there was anything interesting happening within her orbit, Jaz wanted to be part of it.

"Dinner," she answered cheerfully. "Several dinners. And maybe some lunches, too."

He frowned, eyeing the box warily. "What are you talking about?"

She shrugged, but if he didn't know better, he would say she looked a little embarrassed. "I hope you don't mind, but your sister told me a little about your situation."

"My situation," he said stiffly. How much had Tricia told her?

"She said you recently lost a housekeeper. With her in the hospital now and likely to stay there for at least a few weeks, she's concerned about you and the children."

"I've got things under control," he muttered. One look into the living room mess would certainly prove that for a bald-faced lie.

"I'm sure you do," she answered. "But everybody can use a little help and you've got your hands full. My sister helped me put the word out to our sources that we have a neighbor in need and this is the result."

He gazed down at the box filled with containers. "Food. You brought food."

"These are ready-made meals that can go in your freezer or fridge. A few soups, some casseroles, even a lasagna in there. All you have to do is heat them, no prep required."

He couldn't quite wrap his head around what she was saying. "Who did you say this came from?"

"Lots of people. When somebody needs help in Haven Point, people love the chance to step up."

People he didn't know had fixed meals for him and his kids. How was he supposed to react to that? In all his life, he wasn't sure anybody had ever done something like this for him before.

"I know it's not much," she said at his continued silence. "But it should get you through a week or so. They're all really kid-friendly meals. We tried to make sure of that. I believe you should be able to find a thing or two your kids will like."

"Food? That's the present? That's weird," Jazmyn said.

"Is there any mac and cheese?" Ty asked. "That's my favorite."

She smiled. "As a matter of fact, I made some for you myself this morning."

She made it? Cole couldn't quite process the idea of a busy physician spending even five minutes preparing a meal for his family.

"Wow. I don't know what to say," he finally answered.

"You don't have to say anything. Everybody was happy to help. Most of my friends already had a meal in their freezer or just made extra this morning of whatever they were going to make for their own family's dinner. Oh, and it helps that I'm very good friends with Barbara Serrano, whose family owns the diner in town. She sent over several things in there. I think I saw a meat loaf, some chicken alfredo and some of their fabulous pasta *e fagioli* soup."

All of those sounded delicious. His kitchen skills were limited to burgers on the grill, pancakes and a pretty good omelet, which meant the kids—Jaz in particular—would likely be launching a rebellion after another day or two.

"In fact," Dr. Shaw went on, "so many people offered something that I've got another box in my truck. Do you think you have freezer room? Don't worry if you don't. I can take it back to my place for now and then come back with another load in a week or so."

He had been so careful around the people of Haven Point—never rude but not exactly friendly, either. It was easier to stick up here on the ranch, to do his business over the phone or outside Haven Point. That way, people didn't ask questions and he didn't have to get into uncomfortable explanations. Even so, when he went to town, he wondered if people were whispering about him. Ex-con. Washed-up. Disaster.

Now they could add struggling, out-of-his-depth single father to the mix.

Despite all his efforts to keep people in town at a distance, somehow they still had been willing to do this for him and for his kids. It defied comprehension.

He decided gracious gratitude was the only option available to him. "I have room," he finally said, his voice gruff. "Thank you. I'm...overwhelmed."

That she had been intuitive and compassionate enough to spearhead the effort to help him out was the most stunning facet of the whole thing.

"You're welcome." She smiled again and the warmth of it seemed to seep right through his skin. "Why don't I put these in your freezer while the children get their winter gear on. I'll entertain them for a little while out in the snow."

"Yay!" Ty exclaimed. "I'm gonna get my boots on right now."

"What about you, Jazmyn?" she pressed. "We sure could use your help. I bet you know all about making snowmen."

Somehow she also knew just the right button to push with his daughter.

"I am pretty good at rolling the balls," Jaz said. "I'll go get my coat."

She chased after her brother toward the mudroom, leaving him alone with Devin.

"You'll have to forgive me for being just a stupid cowboy here but...why?" He gestured to the box of food. "I don't quite get it. You're probably very busy with your patients and such. You don't have time to go around making house calls to everyone in need, bearing casseroles and lasagna."

"Not everyone. No."

"So why us?"

"Tricia is a friend," she said simply. "She said you could use the help but that you would never ask. This is our small way of letting you know you don't have to. Ask, I mean."

"I… Thanks."

"You're welcome. Now, I just need you to point me in the direction of your freezer."

"There's a large chest in the garage that's pretty empty except for some steaks and roasts."

A cattle ranch usually wasn't scarce on beef. He could grill a steak just fine and had no problem with burgers but he didn't know the first thing about how to cook a roast. One more thing he was going to have to figure out, he supposed.

"There's another box in the back of my SUV. I'll go grab that one."

"No. I can do it. Just wait here."

He shoved on his boots left by the door and headed out to her vehicle. On his way, he caught movement out of the corner of his gaze and spotted a figure in a blue parka clearing the sidewalk at the foreman's cottage fifty yards away.

His jaw hardened just as Stan caught sight of him. His father lifted his hand in a wave and even from here, Cole could see the flash of his teeth as he smiled that damn hopeful smile.

He ignored his father, as he had been doing since Stanford showed up so unexpectedly a few weeks ago, and turned back to Dr. Shaw's SUV. The box was large, filled to the brim with more containers. This was at least a month's worth of meals for him and the kids.

Again, he was aware of that warmth seeping through him like the water from the hot spring above his ranch cutting through the frozen landscape.

Amid all the stress with Tricia in the hospital and struggling so much to figure out things with the kids, it would be a relief beyond measure not to have to worry about what he would feed them each night.

In another life, his pride might have pinched that people thought he needed this kind of help but he decided he couldn't afford that kind of pride under the circumstances. He would take this for what it was, a kind gesture from people in town.

He carried the box back up the steps but neither Devin nor the other box of food waited for him. He headed toward the garage and found her standing over the big chest freezer, trying to find room for things while Ty stood at her elbow, handing her packages.

Jaz, he noted, was nowhere to be seen.

"Thanks," she said when he carried the box toward her—just as if he were doing *her* the huge favor.

"Sure."

She pointed to a container she had left in the box. "That's the pasta *e fagioli* soup from Serrano's along with some of their famous breadsticks. It was made fresh this morning and isn't frozen. You only need to heat up the soup and cook the pasta in it and warm the bread sticks, too, and you'll be set for tonight. Instructions are on it. I'll put that in your refrigerator. The rest of this is easily labeled with instructions so you should know what to do. If you can't figure something out, you can call me and I'll track down instructions for you. The trick is to toss one of these in your refrigerator the night before you want to eat it and it should thaw enough to cook the next day."

"Got it."

She bent over the chest freezer and he couldn't help checking out her very shapely ass—then he felt like a jerk for ogling her when she was doing him such a huge favor.

The freezer wasn't as big as he thought—either that, or she had more food than just a few weeks' worth. When the freezer was filled to the brim, she still had a couple of containers that wouldn't fit.

"What are the chances you might have room in your kitchen freezer for these?"

"We can probably find a little space."

"Excellent. Lead the way."

He took her back to the kitchen, where the breakfast dishes waited in the sink.

She didn't say anything about it, just headed for the side-by-side refrigerator and moved a few things around until she found room.

"Done," she declared after the last plastic container had been stowed in the freezer. "That should at least keep you from having to eat McDonald's for every meal."

"I like McDonald's," Ty protested.

She smiled and placed a hand on his head. Something about the sight of that slender, pale hand on his son's dark hair made his chest feel uncomfortably tight.

"McDonald's is a once-in-a-while treat, not for every day," she said, then deftly changed the subject before he could argue. "So are we building the world's greatest snowman or what?"

"Yes! Jazmyn went to get her book that has a picture of a snowman in it. She wants to build one like that, she said. I'll go tell her to hurry it up."

"You do that."

Once more, he was alone with Devin—not a good situation when he had suddenly become aware of a fierce urge to kiss that color from her cheeks.

She was so pretty and soft and he had spent the past half decade forced to wade through everything ugly and hard in the world.

"You don't have to do this. The snowman thing, I mean," he said. "They'll live if I can't get to it until tomorrow. Or they could always fumble through on their own."

"I want to," she assured him. "As long as you don't mind, that is."

"Why would I mind?" he asked. "You're doing something fun with my kids."

"Well, with one of them, anyway. We'll see if Jazmyn will cooperate."

"If Ty is doing something fun," he said drily, "you can bet Jazmyn will come out to show you all the ways you're doing it wrong."

She smiled, a little lock of auburn hair slipping out of her beanie. He found his sudden urge to twist it around and around his finger quite appalling.

The silence between them was suddenly thick and rich as his grandmother's Christmas toffee. She gazed at him for a long moment, then swallowed hard and shifted her gaze away. If he wasn't mistaken, the color rose a little higher over her cheekbones.

He was almost relieved when his cell phone rang just then.

"This is the call I've been waiting for. It's going to take a few minutes, I'm afraid, and as soon as I'm done, I need to head down to the barn to check on a few things. When you're done playing around in the snow, just send the kids down there. They know the way."

She swallowed again as she nodded. "I'll do that. Thanks."

He grabbed his cell phone and headed to the ranch office just off the family room, cursing himself for a sex-starved idiot and vowing to put the lovely doctor out of his mind.

CHAPTER FOUR

As she watched Cole walk away with his phone at his ear, Devin took an unsteady breath and leaned against the countertop of his comfortable kitchen.

Holy ever-living wow.

Cole Barrett might just be the most gorgeous man she'd ever met in person, with all that sun-burnished skin, the firm jawline, that indefinable air of danger that seemed to stir and seethe around him. He had the sort of rough and rugged masculinity that made a woman want to whimper.

Too bad he didn't have the personality to match.

He seemed cool, unapproachable and completely humorless. Maybe even a little arrogant.

That wasn't necessarily a fair assessment, she corrected herself. He had been grateful enough for the food she had delivered from the Helping Hands and had even cracked a joke or two during their conversation. Those moments seemed few and far between, though, and her overall impression was of a stiff, unfriendly man who didn't like her much.

He hadn't smiled once. She had been watching for it.

Was that his natural mien or did she bring out the worst in him somehow?

"I'm ready," Ty sang out. "Where are you?"

Devin forced herself to move from the kitchen and followed the sound of the boy's voice to the foyer. He wore a red-and-blue parka that looked a size too big and a pair of gloves that didn't match each other.

"He should wear a scarf," Jazmyn said. "And you need to take another scarf out for the snowman. That's what they wear, you know."

"Good idea." Devin couldn't help being amused by this girl with her strong opinions and her obstinate nature. She wanted to hug her but she had a feeling Jazmyn wouldn't appreciate the gesture. "It sounds like you know all about snowpeople. It's a good thing you're coming with us to show us what to do."

"I can't find my gloves so maybe I'll just watch."

"I saw them in the mudroom behind the hamper," Ty said, probably foiling his sister's master plan to stand by and supervise.

"We'll start rolling and you can come out when you're ready," Devin said.

"Okay."

As she and Ty headed for the door, the ancient-looking collie climbed slowly to her feet and followed after them.

"Can Coco help us?"

"Is this Coco? Hi there, sweetheart." Devin scratched the dog's head. She adored dogs and had always wanted one but her mother had claimed to be allergic when she was young and then she had become too busy with medical school to make it practical. Independent cats were a little more forgiving of the brutal schedules of medical residents and interns than a dog.

Fortunately, her sister had a fabulous dog, a beautiful cinnamon standard poodle named Paprika, and she let Devin hang out with her and take her for a walk whenever she needed that exuberant canine affection.

This dog had gray hairs around her mouth and moved with the slow care of many old creatures. She had kind eyes, though, and Devin fell for her as hard as she had for these two motherless children.

"Coco is my dad's dog. She was my dad's grandpa's dog before that. Dad says she's about as old as the moon and the stars."

She smiled at the charming phrase, words she never would have expected from a man who seemed so stiff and somber.

"Hello, Coco. Want to come help us?"

The dog headed straight for the door. Outside, she walked gingerly down the three porch steps and curled up in a little patch of sunshine at the bottom.

Devin wanted to lift her face to it, too, even though it was weak and pale.

The view from up here was spectacular, she had to admit. The ranch house at Evergreen Springs was perched on a hillside overlooking town, with a view of the entire lake and the towns of Haven Point and Shelter Springs up at the northern end of the lake.

She loved living right on the lakeshore. From her bedroom window she could watch geese peddle in for a landing and osprey dive for fish and sunrise over the Redemption Mountains reflected on the shimmering waters of Lake Haven. Even so, there was something to be said for stepping back—in this case *up*, into the foothills—to gain a fresh perspective. The lake looked stunningly blue against the new white snow around it, especially contrasted with the dark green of the firs and pines surrounding it.

She drew in a deep breath of crisp air scented with pine and snow, with stray hints of hay and livestock.

She had a million things to do on this, the first of a rare few days off, but right now she couldn't imagine anywhere else she would rather be.

"Why aren't we building the snowman?" Ty asked, a little frown furrowed between his brows.

Devin snapped herself back to the moment. "Sorry. I was just enjoying the view you've got here. It's beautiful, don't you think?"

He looked down at the lake and the towns. "I guess. I like it here but Jazmyn said she'd rather live by the ocean than a dumb lake that's too cold to swim in most of the time."

"Did she?"

He nodded. "But Dad said he's traveled all over the country when he used to be in rodeos and he's never seen anything, anywhere, as pretty as our ranch."

Cole was turning out to be full of surprises. Maybe there was more to him than the taciturn rancher who couldn't be bothered to crack a smile.

"Dr. Shaw, how do we build a snowman?"

"First of all, you don't have to call me Dr. Shaw.

Call me Devin, okay? People who build snowmen together ought to be on a first-name basis. Second of all, you really haven't done this before?"

He shrugged. "We never lived in a place with snow before. That I can remember, anyway."

She found that rather sad, as she loved each changing season. But then, people in warm climates didn't have to shovel snow or scrape windows. Everything in life had trade-offs.

"Should we get started?"

"Yes!"

Jazmyn bounced down the steps as Devin was demonstrating to Ty how to craft the perfect snowball, the start of every snowman.

The snow was the ideal consistency, wet enough to stick together, but not so heavy it was hard to work. She crafted the first large snowball until it was too big to hold in her hands, then set it down on the ground.

"Okay. This is the fun part. Start rolling it around and around."

Cole took up the challenge and in just a moment, the snowball had doubled in size.

"How's that?"

"It's still not big enough for the bottom ball," Jazmyn declared. "I'm stronger than you are. Maybe I better do it."

"If we all three work together, we can make it even bigger," Devin told her. "We have to figure out where we want to end up. Where do you want the snowman to stand?"

Ty stopped, his cheeks flushed pink from the cold

and the exertion. "How about right there, by the front porch, where we can see it from the window?"

"No. that won't work," Jazmyn said.

"Why?" he demanded.

"Because that's where we're going to put our Christmas tree, remember? Aunt Tricia promised we could put one up this weekend."

"Oh, yeah. I forgot."

Devin didn't have the heart to tell either of these children their aunt wasn't coming home this weekend to put up a Christmas tree. She wondered if Cole had told them yet that Tricia would probably have to stay in the hospital until she delivered her twins.

"We're going to cut down our very own tree," Ty informed Devin. "We were going to do it last weekend except Dad didn't have time. He had a horse 'mergency."

"Our mom liked a fake Christmas tree. It was white with pink lights and it was soooo pretty," Jazmyn said.

"Aunt Tricia said we can't put up an artificial Christmas tree here," Ty said.

Jazmyn sniffed. "I don't know why not. I want a white tree with pink lights but Aunt Tricia said Evergreen Springs always has to have a real tree. It's even in the name. Christmas trees are evergreens—did you know that?"

"I did." Devin smiled, her heart aching a little at the sad note in Jazmyn's voice when she talked about her mother. Deep compassion seeped through her for these children whose world had been tossed around as if they were pinecones floating in the fast current of the Hell's Fury.

Personally, she thought a white tree with pink lights didn't sound appealing, but she supposed it was like the difference between living somewhere like Haven Point or choosing a warmer climate. Everybody had personal preferences, which was what made the world such a crazy, jumbled place of both beauty and tragedy.

"Well, there are *tons* of evergreens at Evergreen Springs," Jazmyn informed her. "Just look around."

"There's a whole *forest* of them," Ty added, grunting a little as he tried to keep rolling the ball that was now up to his chest.

"I wish we had a tree already but Dad hasn't had time," Jazmyn said with a little note of disgust in her voice.

"He got four new horses to train this week and maybe two more coming next week," Ty answered.

So they didn't only raise cattle here at the ranch, apparently. Cole Barrett sounded like a busy man. Still, that was no excuse for not giving two grieving children as happy a Christmas as possible.

That was the missing element at the house, Devin suddenly realized. She had seen no sign of Christmas anywhere. No stockings hanging over that beautiful hewn-log mantel over the river-rock fireplace in the great room, no evergreen garlands twining down the staircase, no candles or bells or wreaths.

And no Christmas tree.

The holiday was now a little less than two weeks

away. Busy or not, Cole would have to find time to give this to his children.

What would he do now, without his sister here to help? She could only imagine how overwhelming he must be finding this, suddenly having custody of two needy, emotionally fragile children.

Had he even bought gifts for Jazmyn and Ty?

Tricia probably would have done a few things to bring a holiday mood to the house but considering her marriage was in trouble and she was pregnant with twins, perhaps she hadn't quite had the energy.

Not her business, Devin reminded herself. She had done her kind deed for the day, gathering freezer meals for him in an effort to take one thing off his plate until he could hire a housekeeper. She couldn't jump in and start decorating his house.

Why was she so drawn to help him?

The children, she told herself. It was all about the children. Cole Barrett could sit here in his cold, cheerless house for all she cared, but these children needed more.

"Do you have a Christmas tree?" Ty asked her, his breath coming in puffs as they pushed the big ball across the yard one more time, working together to pat on more snow as they went.

"I do. I have a couple of them, one in my bedroom and one in my family room. They don't have very many decorations on them. I have two cats named Seamus and Simone, a tiger-striped and a black cat, and they like to knock off the ornaments."

"You don't have a little boy or a little girl?" Ty asked.

Devin forced a smile, ignoring the familiar crampy ache around her heart. "No. I'm afraid not."

"But you have two cats," Jazmyn said. "I'd like to have a cat. If I did, I would name her Penelope and call her Penny."

"Sounds like you've given it some thought."

"I have. I'd like a cat *or* a puppy." She went on about the time she, Ty and their mother had lived in an apartment building and the lady next door had four cats and let Jazmyn come over sometimes to pet them and help give them food and water. From there, she chattered about how easy school was for her because they were behind the school where she used to go, about her favorite TV show, about the trip to Disneyland her grandmother had apparently promised her.

Whenever his sister stopped to take a breath, Ty interjected his own occasional commentary—about the new brick set he wanted for Christmas, about the horse his father said he could get someday and about his new friends at school.

In the process, they finished the midsection of the snowman and worked together on the final ball.

"That is the perfect snowman head," Jazmyn declared. "It's not too square and not too tall."

"I agree. Can you help me lift it up?"

The two of them worked together to heft the large ball onto the top of the snowman and pat a little more snow in to anchor it in place. Then it was time for the finishing touches.

"What a good idea you had to bring out a scarf. That's just what he needs," Devin said, which made Jazmyn preen. Devin wrapped the scarf around, even giving it a jaunty, complicated knot.

"We have to put on a face now! I'm going to go see if there's a carrot in the refrigerator."

"Good thinking. While you're doing that, we'll look for some sticks for the arms and something to use for eyes and a mouth."

She and Ty easily found sticks as well as an abundance of pinecones perfect for crafting the snowman's face and buttons down his front. She was lifting the boy up to wedge in a couple of pinecones for his eyes when Jazmyn returned from the house.

"No carrots," she said in a tone of deep disgust. "All we had were dinky baby carrots and that would just look stupid. But I did find an orange plastic cup. I thought that might work."

"Nice save." Devin smiled. "I think that should do very well."

"And look what else!" She pulled a battered black cowboy hat from behind her back. "This is the perfect hat for a snowman who lives on a ranch like us."

"As long as that's not your dad's best hat."

"He never wears it. He has a different one. I think this is an old one."

She could only hope so. Cole could always take it down if he didn't want it on the snowman. With a mental shrug, Devin pointed to the cowboy. "You'd better do the honors and put on the finishing touches."

Looking much less surly than she had when they

started, Jazmyn reached as high as she could to shove in the nose but she couldn't reach the top so Devin scooped her up and held her while she positioned the cowboy hat at a jaunty angle.

"There. Perfect."

"It's the best snowman *ever*," Ty declared.

"I don't know if it's the best one *ever* but it's the best one I've ever built," Jazmyn agreed.

Devin fought a smile. Beneath her contrariness, Jazmyn was actually a very sweet girl. She simply had strong opinions and wasn't afraid to share them. That wasn't a bad trait at all, only one that perhaps needed tempering. She needed to learn that her viewpoint didn't necessarily trump all others.

"We should build a friend for him," Ty said.

"Looks like he already has some." Devin pointed to a couple of finches who had fluttered to a landing atop the snowman's hat.

Both children giggled and they stood still for a moment, watching the birds hop around the hat, while the beautiful view of the lake and valley stretched out below them.

"Can we build another snowman?" Jazmyn asked. "That way he won't have to be alone here when the birds fly away and it gets dark."

"It can be smaller. Maybe like a big brother and a little brother," Ty said.

"Of course. Now that we know how to do it, we should be able to make one in a snap."

They had finished the bottom two balls when she noticed a man come out of the small house not far from the main house. He picked up a snow shovel from the porch and started working on the small driveway and walkway, all of which looked mostly clear.

He seemed to be watching them all intently. When Jazmyn spotted him, he waved. She returned it kind of halfheartedly, then dropped her hand quickly.

Even from here, she thought the man's shoulders slumped a little.

"Who's that man?" she asked Jazmyn.

"Oh." The girl shifted her gaze guiltily. "That's our grandpa Stan. Don't tell my dad I waved at him, okay? We're not supposed to talk to him, never ever *ever*. We're supposed to pretend he's invisible."

Ty glanced down at the little house. "Dad says if we ignore him, maybe he'll go away, like a stray dog."

"But then he said we shouldn't say that because it's not very nice to stray dogs," Jazmyn added.

She remembered what Tricia had said the night before. *I'm not saying Cole doesn't have his reasons for being angry, but people can change, right? Dad is trying.*

What problem did Cole have with his father? It must be something intense if he warned his children away from even waving at the man.

This appeared to be yet another tangled strand in the knotted, complicated life here at Evergreen Springs.

They started in on the head and were rolling it in the last untrampled patch of snow when Cole headed around the house. He paused for a moment, watching them with an inscrutable expression on his features.

He wore a ranch coat and a black Stetson—much nicer than the one on their snowman. Devin told herself that little jerky skip in her heart rate was only because of the exertion and the cold.

"You're not done yet? I thought you'd be all wrapped up out here."

"Almost," Jazmyn said. "We decided to make two snowmen."

"They're friends," Ty added.

Devin smiled. "You're just in time to help us put the head on. That's the hardest part."

He didn't look thrilled at the job but she had to give him credit for at least pretending to get into the spirit of the thing. He lifted up the snowman's head and set it atop the other two stacked balls. "There you go. Looks great. I see you used my old cowboy hat."

"I hope that's okay," she said.

He shrugged. "It's so old, it's a wonder any of the stitching still holds. I'm not sure why it was still hanging around. I thought I threw it away ages ago."

"We need another hat," Ty said suddenly. "I want to find one for this snowman."

"You pick the hat and I'll find another scarf," Jazmyn ordered.

Her brother acquiesced—Devin had a feeling he did a lot of that—and the two of them raced into the house.

The ancient border collie lifted her head and watched them go, then went back to sleep while a few more finches fluttered atop the cowboy hat of the bigger snowman.

Devin was ridiculously aware of Cole. She had no idea why she was so drawn to this rough, taciturn rancher; she only knew she didn't like it. At all.

"Thanks for spending a little time with the kids. They seemed to enjoy it and it helped me get a few things done without having to stop every few minutes to deal with some crisis."

"We had a good time," she said. "I think it helps make the place look a little more festive for the holidays, don't you?"

"Um, sure."

She thought about keeping her mouth shut, but the kids had mentioned a Christmas tree several times while building the snowmen. It was obviously something that mattered to them and she wasn't sure their father quite grasped how important it was.

"Jazmyn and Ty were telling me that you always cut a live Christmas tree here at Evergreen Springs."

"Yeah. It's on the list. Things have been a little crazy around here the last few weeks. We were planning to go today but with Tricia in the hospital, I'm not sure when we'll get to it."

"Is that something I could help you with?"

CHAPTER FIVE

COLE GAZED DOWN at the soft and pretty doctor. Her cheeks were rosy from the cold, which ought to clash horribly with her auburn hair. Instead, she somehow looked fresh and sweet and adorable.

He let out a breath. He did *not* understand this woman. First she brought boxes of food for him, then she spent an hour out building a snowman with his kids. Now she was offering to help him cut down a Christmas tree.

"Have you ever cut down a Christmas tree before?" he asked, eyebrows raised.

"Me? No. Heavens, no. My mom always insisted on an artificial tree, though I think one year my dad bought a real one out at the tree lot south of town, just for the smell. How hard can it be, though?"

"Harder than you might think," he answered. "It's not just about cutting down the tree. We could be up there and back in a half hour, as long as we find the right one quickly. But then the whole thing always seems to turn into an all-day thing, with setting it in the stand so it's straight, then finding the lights, checking them for dead bulbs, hanging them on the tree, finding the box in the attic that has the ornaments, then hanging those, too, just so."

He shrugged. "With the new horses that have come in the last few weeks, I just haven't had the time to spare."

"I understand. But can I be blunt?"

He couldn't help his wry response. "Judging from our short acquaintance, I'm going to go with yes."

She made a face. "*May* I be blunt, then."

This was the part where she was going to tell him what a terrible, neglectful father he was. Yeah. He knew all that.

"The children need a Christmas tree," she said, confirming his suspicions. "This year, more than ever."

"They told you about their mother?"

"Tricia told me last night. I'm so sorry."

Did she think he mourned Sharla? He felt the loss only for his children's sake. "Then you have to understand the way things are right now. Jazmyn and Ty are still grieving and lost, and they don't want to be here with me right now. Whatever you might think, a Christmas tree is not going to be some secret healing balm to make us one big happy family."

"It's not about the tree," she insisted. "It's about the process of cutting it down with them, about helping them build new traditions while still providing the comfort of continuing with old ones."

He wanted to tell her she was crazy but her words had the resonance of truth. He had to do something about Christmas for the children. Yeah, none of them was much in the mood for Christmas but they needed to go through the motions if they had any chance of returning to a place of normalcy and healing.

"Okay. I get your point. I need to make time, even though it's tough. Fine. I'll take them to cut a tree. I've got an hour or so before the vet is supposed to be here. We can do it in that time if we leave now. Maybe we can find time to decorate it tomorrow or Monday after school."

She pursed her lips again, giving him a wild desire to lean down and nibble on them. What the hell was wrong with him? Didn't he have enough on his plate right now without tossing in inappropriate lust for a curvy little doctor with kissable lips and a tiny smattering of freckles over her nose?

"I'll tell you what. If you cut the tree down, I'll stick around and decorate it with the kids. You won't have to do anything. You can go back to your horses or your ranch accounts or whatever you need to do."

He frowned. "Nobody told me we've become the Haven Point charity project for the month."

"You can look at it that way and be all grumpy and suspicious. Or you can simply say thank you."

She was right. He was being an ass. She was being more than nice and he was fighting it every step of the way.

"This whole needing-help gig is tough for a guy like me. I'm not real crazy about it."

"I get it. They say the first step is the hardest."

He couldn't help himself. He chuckled. It wasn't much of a laugh and sounded a little rusty to him, but she stared at him as if he'd just sprouted stick arms like the snowmen and started waltzing with one of them.

After a startled moment, she smiled, too, and he felt a sharp kick to his gut. Oh, she was lovely. In the sunlight, amid all the fresh snow, she looked as bright and pretty as a gleaming Christmas angel ornament.

Looking at her reminded him of the same feeling he had when he was doing morning chores and walked out of the barn to find a brilliant winter sunrise over the Redemptions—breathless, awed and a little humbled that he had been lucky enough to see it.

"Just think," she said. "Give your kids an hour of your time right now and then you don't have to think about the tree again until you take it down after Christmas, except for watering it."

He released a long sigh as the kids came running back out of the house. He had a million things to do for Christmas. Tricia had made a to-do list for him after Thanksgiving and she had even picked up a couple of presents for the kids but he still had the bulk of their shopping to do. He planned to go online after they were in bed so he could order a few more gifts.

The Christmas tree had been a huge part of his to-do list. Dr. Shaw was right. Kids needed that sort of thing. He used to love going with his grandfather up to the thick evergreen forest above the house to pick out a tree. Even after he'd grown older and tried to pretend it was a pain in the neck, he still enjoyed it.

He would love to be able to check that off—especially if she was sincere about helping him decorate.

He still didn't get why she wanted to help him and his struggling little family, but only a stupid man would turn down a pretty woman offering to take on a task he had been dreading.

Cole was plenty of things, but he wasn't stupid. Most of the time, anyway.

He released a breath. "All right. Looks like we're going to cut down a Christmas tree. I'll go get my chain saw."

LIFE COULD TAKE such surreal turns sometimes.

Devin couldn't quite believe she was sitting in a pickup truck beside Cole Barrett—a man she had met less than twenty-four hours earlier—driving up a snowy road on his ranch on her way to help him pick out a Christmas tree.

His tough pickup was equipped with a plow and seemed to have no trouble cutting through the six inches of fresh powder as they drove through a stand of bare aspens, with their fragile white trunks.

As they drove higher, the aspens gave way to a pine and fir forest. She could see a dozen trees that would work for a Christmas tree, but he obviously had a specific destination in mind.

"How long is this going to take?" The fun and sweet Jazmyn who had helped them build the snow-people had reverted to Cranky Jazmyn, finding fault with everything.

"A little longer," Cole answered. "We try to take each year's tree from a different area so we're not leaving bare spots in the forest."

"This is dumb." The girl pouted. "Why can't we just go to a store and buy a tree like everybody else does?"

"What's the fun in that?" Cole said. He was obviously trying to be cheerful, which Devin found rather touching, considering he had been reluctant to do this in the first place. "When you cut your own, you'll have the freshest, most beautiful tree in town. Just wait until you smell it."

"I was hoping we could have hot chocolate after we built the snowman," she groused. "My mittens are wet and now I'm freezing to death."

Oh, the drama. Devin had to smile. "We can have hot chocolate while we wait for the tree to dry out a little before we hang the decorations. And if you take your mittens off and hand them to me, I'll try to warm them a little on the heater up here."

Jazmyn grumbled a little more but handed up her mittens, which Devin held in front of the vent blowing hot air from the engine compartment.

"Can I use the chain saw?" Ty asked.

Cole gave a rough chuckle that seemed to shiver down her nerve endings. He glanced in the rearview mirror at his son. "I think we might need to work our way up to that, but we'll see."

A moment later, he pulled the pickup truck into a little clearing surrounded on three sides by thick forest. The other looked down to the lake.

She climbed out, speechless at the vista spread out below them. The view from his ranch house had been lovely enough but it was positively stunning at this higher elevation. She could see the entire lake in all its turquoise glory.

"Wow. What an incredible view!"

"Isn't it?" Cole said from beside her. "This is one of my favorite places on the whole ranch. It's a good place to sit and ponder."

She sent him a sidelong glance. What sort of things did he ponder up here? For all his gruffness, she had a feeling he was a much deeper thinker than he would like people to believe.

The man fascinated her, pure and simple.

She wanted to know more about him. What had happened to his rodeo career and his marriage? What were the shadows she occasionally glimpsed? Why had he basically cloistered himself away up here on his beautiful ranch, making little effort to weave himself into the fabric of the social life in Haven Point?

None of her business. Devin reined herself in sharply. This man and his secrets were none of her business. This silly crush she was developing was ridiculous and embarrassing.

Coco had gone back inside the house where it was warm. Instead, Cole had brought along one of the outside ranch dogs—a funny-looking red-and-white dog he called an Australian shepherd. The dog hopped down from the back of the pickup truck the moment Cole lowered the tailgate.

He raced to the children and licked them as a couple of magpies chattered at them from the trees.

Devin watched one of them take flight, then noticed something a few hundred feet away through the trees. "What's that steam coming up over the trees there?"

Cole's eyes took on a secretive look, his mouth lifting a little into what was almost a full-fledged smile that she found every bit as breathtaking as the view. Silly her.

"It's the second-best part about this spot, next to the view. Come see."

He led the way, tramping down snow in his big, heavy boots to make a pathway for them to follow. They were still on the road, she realized, just farther than he had cleared. The sky was a glorious blue here in contrast to the new snow, which reflected shimmery diamond-bright sunlight.

Snow drizzled down from the fringy branches of the evergreens they passed. Even with him blazing a trail, the way was a little difficult, uphill around boulders and fallen trees.

The air smelled of snow and pine with something else underlying it, a strange metallic scent in the air. She heard the sound of trickling water ahead of them somewhere and the air here seemed warmer somehow, moist and alive.

Cole finally stopped. "Here you go."

All the clues came together when he stepped aside, revealing a magical treasure.

"You have a hot spring!" she exclaimed.

The steaming pool was about thirty feet by forty feet, surrounded by rocks that had obviously been brought in to protect it. A small log hut stood beside the pool and a few wooden benches clustered around the side.

"This is Evergreen Springs, where the ranch gets its name."

Oh, it was glorious. She wanted to wade into the water right now. "Have you had the water tested? Is it safe? What's the mineral content? What about bacteria? Algae growth?"

He looked surprised at her interest and a little overwhelmed at the barrage of questions. "An old rodeo buddy is now a geologist at Boise State. He samples it every couple months or so for me, in exchange for me letting him use it when he wants to. It's completely safe. The predominant minerals are calcium, magnesium, selenium and sodium."

"This is amazing! You have no idea."

These kind of mineral hot springs used to dot the entire area. Like Taos, New Mexico, or Sedona, Arizona, the Lake Haven region was considered a healing place by native peoples for generations before Europeans ever stumbled onto it. Early Native American tribes, mostly Bannock, Shoshone and Paiute, would bring their injured and sickly to the lake to rest and recover.

Devin knew that in the Victorian age, a few intrepid settlers tried to capitalize on that reputation by creating a retreat community around the regional mineral springs with their purported healing properties, similar to Hot Springs, Arkansas, or Steamboat Springs, Colorado, but those efforts floundered for various reasons.

Shelter Springs—the first town on the lakeshore—had prospered anyway by drawing in tourists and businesses alike, while Haven Point had struggled in recent years after the town's most prominent business, Kilpatrick Boatworks, closed its doors. Many downtown businesses were shuttered as a result, though the town was now seeing a revival thanks to Devin's sister, McKenzie, and her fiancé, Ben Kilpatrick, along with Devin's friends Aidan and Eliza Caine.

Because of her own particular medical journey, Devin was fascinated by Lake Haven's reputation as a place of healing and refuge. She had studied the history and knew that a geothermal shift in the earth's crust after a major earthquake in the sixties had dried up many of the hot springs.

To find a hot spring here in this sort of pristine condition was for her more exciting than if he'd offered her a cave filled with gold bricks.

"We go swimming there," Ty said. "It's fun. Dad says it always has warm water, even in the wintertime."

"We can't get any in our mouths. It's not safe to drink," Jazmyn warned.

"How hot does it get?"

"The water stays between 104 and 112 degrees Fahrenheit year-round," Cole said.

"It flows into the Hell's Fury?"

"Eventually. First, it meets up with a couple of other tributaries before making its way to the big water."

"This is amazing. Do you have any idea what a rare find this is these days?"

He shrugged. "That's what Jake—my geologist friend—tells me. It's been here forever, as far as I know. My grandfather was the one who lined it with all the smooth rocks. He said it worked wonders for his arthritis and used to soak here at least a couple times a week. I just know it's a great place to soak during haying season or whenever you have stiff muscles."

It would be magical on a winter night lit by lanterns around the edge, with the steam curling up in the air while a light snowfall drifted down. Or on a summer night, for that matter, with a sweet breeze blowing and stars spangling the sky.

She was suddenly filled with envy. "You should consider yourself very fortunate."

"You're welcome to come out and try it sometime."

The invitation sounded warily offered and she sensed it hadn't been easy for him, which meant even more to her.

"Thank you! I would *love* that."

An idea seemed to have planted itself in her brain as she thought of her yoga class that morning and the dear people she had come to love. As soon as the idea came, she dismissed it. If he was reluctant to invite *her*, he probably wouldn't be crazy about a bunch of senior citizens, even if they were darlings.

She was admiring the handiwork—the smooth, natural stone steps into the water and the charming little clapboard warming hut when Jazmyn's impatience spilled over.

"Are we going to find a tree or just stand here in the cold snow all day looking at the dumb hot spring?"

Cole's mouth pressed into a line. "We're looking for a tree. We have to pick the right one."

"It shouldn't be too hard." Jazmyn looked around. "There's only like a million of them here."

"You can't just cut down any old tree. Keep your eyes peeled for the perfect one. Remember, it still has to fit inside the house."

"Ooh." Ty made an exaggerated face of disgust. "Peeled eyeballs. That's gross."

"That just means be on the lookout," Cole said. "We're looking for one that's not too big around or too tall."

He led the way back toward where he had parked the pickup truck. On the way, they found and rejected several for various reasons until Jazmyn stumbled onto one she immediately fell in love with.

"This is it," she exclaimed, her sour mood forgotten. "It's beautiful. The perfect shape and the perfect size. We *have* to get this tree."

Cole tilted his head one way, then the other. "I think you're right. This one looks just right. Are we agreed, then?"

"Yay!" Ty said. "Can I cut it down?"

"It's kind of tough, since I have to go pretty low to the ground. I'll tell you what. I'll cut this one down but you can help me haul it back to the pickup. It's a big job and I'm going to need somebody with muscles."

"I've got big muscles." Ty lifted his arm and made a fist with his mittened hand. Devin assumed he flexed but it was impossible to tell beneath his many winter layers.

"I'm counting on it, kid," Cole answered as he pulled goggles and ear protectors out of the chainsaw case.

"Okay, now you'll have to cover your ears and step back," he ordered them. Devin tugged the children back a little, where they could still see. A moment later, Cole fired up the chain saw, sending a few birds in nearby trees scattering into the air. In no time, he cut through the narrow trunk like a butter knife through peanut butter.

Jazmyn clapped her hands with excitement but Ty suddenly looked upset.

"Will the tree grow back?" he asked when Cole took off his ear protectors and joined them, the chain saw now silent.

"That one won't, but we always plant a dozen new saplings for every tree we cut down. You can come up here and help me in the spring."

"Okay," he said, his tender sensibilities appeased.

"Now what?" Devin asked.

Cole shrugged with a half smile that made her insides shiver. "Now we haul it back to the truck, knock off as much snow as we can and take it home."

While she carried the chain saw, Cole and Ty pulled the tree through the snow with a rope Cole had tied around the trunk. Jazmyn trudged along beside her, her brow furrowed a little as if she were deep in thought.

Just before they reached the pickup truck, Cole

raised the tree vertically and tapped the trunk hard on the ground several times to knock off as much snow as he could before he lifted it into the bed.

"So that's that. Now we just have to get it home so you all can decorate it."

"Yay!" Ty said. "We'll finally have a Christmas tree tonight!"

Jazmyn said nothing. Something was obviously bothering her as she hadn't said a word since Cole cut down the tree, Devin suddenly realized.

When she finally spoke, her words were a surprise. "Dad," she began in a hesitant voice, "can we cut down a tree for Grandpa Stan?"

He jerked around and stared at her as if she had just sliced through his pickup truck with the chain saw.

"It doesn't have to be a big one," she said. "Even a little tree would be better than nothing, wouldn't it? He can't get one himself. I bet he doesn't have a truck with a plow or a chain saw of his own to cut one down. I think we should get one for him, don't you?"

"Why would we want to do that?" Cole asked, his voice as hard as the granite boulders scattered around the mountainside.

Jazmyn drew in a shaky breath, looking nervous. "Last week when you gave money to the guy in the army coat with the sign outside the grocery store, you said he needed a little bit of help. You said we should help people who are having a hard time whenever we can. I think Grandpa Stan is having a hard time. He always looks sad."

"Some people's misery is entirely of their own design," he muttered, his mouth in a tight line.

"So we're not supposed to be nice to everyone?" Jazmyn asked. She seemed genuinely confused and Devin could tell Cole was having a tough time trying to work his way through this parental quandary.

How did he teach his children about compassion and kindness to others while keeping them from a man Cole didn't want in their lives?

She wanted to say something but knew this wasn't her decision. She had no right to intervene.

He finally gave a deep sigh. "Fine. We'll cut a tree down and leave it on his porch. The smallest one we can find. You're right, it's a nice thing to do and I'm proud of you for thinking of someone else. But you're still not allowed to talk to him."

A moment later, Cole picked out a tree close to where they parked. It was a little bare on one side and had a few spindly branches but Devin wasn't about to point that out to him.

"Will this do?" he asked Jazmyn.

She nodded, and he cut it down quickly with the chain saw and carried it with one hand back to the pickup truck.

"What about you?" he asked Devin. "I should have thought to ask before. Do you need a tree?"

She shook her head, touched that he would ask, even belatedly. "I'm good. I already have a couple of artificial trees that have been up since before Thanksgiving. My sister makes me decorate early. If I don't have everything up by the first of December, she'll come over and do it herself."

He gave a low sound that was *almost* a chuckle. "Sisters can be such a pain, can't they?"

"Yes," Ty muttered under his breath, too low for his own sister to overhear.

Devin tugged his hat, filled with affection for all of them.

As they loaded into the pickup truck and took off back down to the ranch house, the children were more animated than she had seen them, talking about how they wanted to decorate the tree.

Devin sat back and listened, warm air from the heater seeping through her coat to warm her chilled bones.

That wasn't the only thing warming her, she suddenly realized with a great deal of apprehension. Here with this troubled little family, she was discovering a dangerous, seductive sense of belonging.

She would have to be very, very careful not to lose her heart to all of them.

CHAPTER SIX

COLE DROVE CAREFULLY down the snow-covered dirt road back toward the house, trying fiercely to ignore his growing awareness of the woman who sat beside him.

She smelled delicious, that fresh, sweet, flowery scent he had noticed before. Being trapped in a pickup truck cab with her was more distracting to his driving skills than the kids bickering in the back.

It was increasingly tough to keep a lid on this attraction, especially when he kept catching all these random impressions—the soft line of her throat, the gentle curve of her ear, the creamy skin, dotted here and there with pale freckles. Those freckles made a man want to go on a solemn quest to unearth every one she had, one at a time.

He swallowed, his hands tightening on the steering wheel, aware of how very long it had been since he had spent this much time in the company of a female who wasn't related to him.

When he came back to the ranch, everything had been such a mess. First he'd had to throw his energy and time into fighting Sharla and her vindictive efforts to keep the kids from him. In between court battles, he had been trying to clean up the ranch's tangled finances left by his grandfather's death.

When the hell was he supposed to find time to date in all that chaos?

Once upon a time, horses, women and whiskey had been the only things that mattered to him. Not necessarily in that order. He had partied hard in every aspect of his life. On the circuit, buckle bunnies were eager to show a good time to any cowboy in the money—and despite being half-drunk most of the time he had been hell on wheels on the back of a bucking bronc.

He could stroll into any bar west of the Mississippi and walk back out ten minutes later with the sexiest woman in there, if he wanted. And he had wanted, plenty of times. That's how he'd met Sharla, after all.

He had even been stupid enough to be flattered after that first weekend together when she showed up at his next PRCA event and then the one after that. Before he quite knew how it happened, she was traveling with him to every event on the circuit and a few months later, she changed his life forever when she told him she was pregnant.

He had put the womanizing aside after he married Sharla, figuring that one of them ought to at least *try* to keep the vows they made.

He didn't go to bars these days. After he dried out and came back to Haven Point, he had tried to go with a couple of his buddies a few times to watch a football or basketball game, but he'd learned that sitting there nursing a soft drink wasn't quite the same. The funny thing was, when he was sober, the women trying their best to pick up a cowboy in a bar all seemed brassy and hard.

He was going to blame that long, self-imposed drought for this sudden ache in his gut, this yearning for the softness of a woman's touch. He could suddenly imagine it only too well, her breathy sighs, that luscious auburn hair tangled in his fingers, her small, competent hands sliding over his body—

"Weren't you going to drop off a tree for your father? You're about to drive past his house."

Devin's low voice interrupted the completely inappropriate direction of his thoughts. He drew in a sharp breath, aware he was half-aroused. Fortunately, things subsided quickly. Nothing like a conversation about his father to take the wind out of his sails, so to speak.

"His *temporary* house," he said, his voice short. "Stan is only here to be a pain in the ass."

He glanced in the backseat and was relieved that the kids were too busy arguing about who was better at building a snowman to notice his verbal slip. He was doing his best not to swear around them, though it seemed to be a harder habit to break than getting loaded every night.

"Sometime you'll have to tell me the story there," she said.

He glanced over and saw she looked genuinely interested.

"It's not a pleasant one," he answered as he maneuvered the vehicle around and pulled back in front of the house.

"I gathered as much."

As much as he would like to keep driving and find something else to do with the little spruce he had cut down, he couldn't forget what Jazmyn had said.

You said we should help people who are having a hard time whenever we can. I think Grandpa Stan is having a hard time. He always looks sad.

Damn, it was hard being a parent, having to eat his own words sometimes. The whole thing would be much easier if he didn't have to put his money where his mouth was.

He didn't want to be decent to his father. As far as he was concerned, Stanford Barrett didn't deserve so much as a handful of pine needles from him.

They could always find someone who deserved the other Christmas tree far more than the jackass who'd sired him, but Cole was afraid Jazmyn might have something to say about that. She would push and push until he caved.

If he stood his ground and refused to give his father the tree, she might end up thinking he expected her and Ty to be decent only when it suited their purposes—not the message he needed to impart to an impressionable girl who had spent her first eight years in an environment of chaos and mixed signals.

Though he wasn't crazy about Christmas in general terms, it *was* supposed to be the season of giving, of hope. How hard could it be to do this one simple thing and give his father a stupid Christmas tree?

He released a heavy breath, furious all over again that Stan had put him in this position by showing up out of the blue right before Thanksgiving, as if they were one big happy family.

As if he didn't have enough to stress about, between his grieving kids and his troubled—and heavily pregnant—sister.

What he hated most about the situation with Stan was Cole's own helplessness to fix it. He couldn't kick him out, as much as he wanted to—at least according to his attorney. His grandmother's will gave Stan a quarter share of the ranch, just like Tricia. While Cole had the biggest share, his attorney warned him he didn't have the right to refuse occupancy to Stan except in the main house.

Stan didn't appear to want to go anywhere. Cole couldn't figure out how in the hell he thought he could saunter back onto the ranch and pick up with the children and grandchildren he had abandoned, just as if the past twenty-plus years had never happened.

Needles quivered as he yanked the four-foot tree out of the truck bed and hauled it up to the porch. Cole shoved it against the side of the house and stomped back down the steps without bothering to knock.

He made it to the bottom step when he heard the squeak of the screen door and then his father's unwelcome voice.

"What's this?"

He wanted to ignore the man—that was the pattern of their relationship, after all, the one Stan himself had established—but he forced himself to turn around. "It's a Christmas tree. What does it look like?"

Stan looked stunned, his eyes that were so similar to Cole's clouded with confusion.

"We were cutting a tree for our place and my observant daughter commented that you didn't have one," Cole said gruffly. "She wanted us to cut one for you and I was too tired to argue with her. That's all. Let's get one thing straight. This was for Jazmyn, not you. It's not a peace offering or an olive branch or whatever damn thing you want to call it. It's just me trying to keep my daughter happy."

Stan looked at the pickup truck and Cole did his best to harden his heart against the wistfulness he saw on his father's expression.

"She's right," Stan said. "I haven't had the chance to get a tree yet. Please tell Jazmyn thank you for thinking of me."

He wanted to tell his father to go to hell, that he wouldn't tell Jazmyn anything, but that would just make him look small so he nodded curtly and made his way back to the pickup.

"What did he say?" Jaz asked eagerly once he climbed inside.

"Thanks," he muttered. "He said to tell you thanks. That was it."

He shoved the truck in gear and drove back to the ranch house without looking back, aware the whole time of Devin's sidelong glances.

He had told himself all these years that he didn't care what his father did, that he felt nothing for the man. A few weeks in the same zip code as Stanford revealed that for yet another lie.

He cared.

After all these years, the pain of that abandonment felt as strong and real as the day his father dumped him and Tricia on people they barely knew and drove away.

More than anything, it pissed him off, especially when he'd been forced into the position of fighting with everything he had just to stay in his own kids' lives.

He put away the anger for now and focused on finishing the task at hand, dealing with the kids' Christmas tree.

Everybody piled out as soon as he pulled in front of the house.

"I need to go find the tree stand," he said. "I think it was in the garage last I checked. Go ahead inside and warm up while I go hunt it down, then we'll haul the tree inside."

"Hurry, okay?" Jazmyn said. "I can't wait to see it all set up."

Always the little boss. He refrained from rolling his eyes as he headed for the garage. When he finally located the tree stand on one of the shelves—the last place he remembered seeing it, since he hadn't bothered with a tree since his grandmother's death two years earlier—he carried it into the family room, where they always set up the tree, then returned to his pickup truck. He pulled the tree out of the pickup bed, then gave the trunk several hard smacks down on the driveway again to shake off as much remaining moisture as he could from the branches.

A few moments later, he had to enlist Devin's help guiding the trunk of the tree into the tree stand and then holding the trunk straight while he tightened the screws.

It was a strange and unsettling domestic scene that seemed to add to the growing connection between them.

There was no connection between them, Cole reminded himself harshly. How could there be? She was the kind, compassionate, respected physician and he was an ex-con recovering alcoholic. Better to push her away now, while he still could.

"The branches are still pretty wet," he said once he was satisfied the tree was straight and wasn't going to tip out of the stand. "It probably needs to dry out for a while longer before we string any lights or decorations on it. Don't worry about sticking around. I'm sure you've got things to do. The kids and I can hang the ornaments on tonight or tomorrow."

"Oh! I wanted to decorate it *now*!" Jazmyn complained.

"I don't mind waiting," Devin assured him. "I don't have anything planned today, which is a minor miracle. I wanted to go check on your sister later, even though I've handed her care over to Obstetrics, but that's the only thing on my plate."

"It might be an hour or more and I'm supposed to be meeting the vet down at the barn in about twenty minutes."

"No problem. I'm good here with the children. While we wait for the tree to dry a little, we could make a few other decorations to hang on the tree and around the house. Snowflakes, paper chains, that sort of thing."

"Oooh!" Jazmyn lit up at that idea. "Great-grandma had a whole box of shiny paper and markers. I found them in the closet in my room. We can use that! Come help me carry them down, Ty."

She marched out of the room with her brother close behind. Cole really was going to have to do something about her bossiness and about Ty's too-amenable nature. If things continued in this manner, neither of them would be destined for a happy life.

As soon as the children left the room, he turned on Devin. "Okay. Tell me. Why are you doing this? Giving up a whole Saturday to help me and my kids? First the food and now this. You don't even know us."

Her cheeks were a delicate pink but he didn't know if she was blushing or if they still held color from the cold outside.

"Originally, I helped you because Tricia asked me to, then because I wanted to after I spent a few minutes with your children. Now—" She paused with an embarrassed-sounding laugh. "What would you say if I offered you a proposition?"

It didn't take much for his brain to jump into an instant fantasy of the two of them ripping up the sheets, of covering her mouth with his and touching those lush little curves and losing himself inside her…

He jerked himself back to the moment, quite certain that wasn't what she meant.

"A proposition. What's the fine print?"

"Okay, maybe not a proposition. Let's call it a barter of sorts."

Again, his imagination flashed into overtime. But while he could list many things he wanted from her, he couldn't come up with a single thing he might have to offer in return.

"A barter of *what* sort?" he asked warily.

"Without Tricia here, you're going to need help with the kids. Believe it or not, I have an unusually light docket for the next few days, since I'm scheduled to work straight through the holidays. I can step in for a couple of days to help you out with the children after school and in the early evenings until you can hire someone."

On the surface, the idea was tempting. Under ordinary circumstances, this was a relatively slow time of year on the ranch, when he could work around the children's school schedule and take them down to the barn with him.

He could still do that, try to juggle everything, but right now he had several horses in various stages of training and he just simply wasn't finding enough hours in the day to finish everything.

He had planned to register the children in the after-school program at the school but Jazmyn was already complaining about how boring it was likely to be and begging him to let her babysit for her brother—which wasn't happening anytime soon.

It would be wonderful if he could put at least one worry out of his mind, knowing the children were cared for after school for a few days. He had a feeling this wouldn't be that easy, that she would attach strings that were likely to strangle him.

"And in exchange? What do you want out of the deal?"

She gave him a winsome smile. "You grant me and a few of my patients access to Evergreen Springs. The actual spring, I mean, not the ranch in general."

Yeah. Always check the fine print.

"No," he answered bluntly.

She blinked a little. "Why not? It's the perfect solution."

"For you, maybe," he retorted. "I don't want a bunch of strangers wandering around the ranch, poking their noses into my business."

"Oh, for heaven's sake. Nobody will wander anywhere or poke anything! I teach a yoga class of a dozen senior citizens with varying stages of age-related conditions. Lovely people, each of them. They're not interested in your business. Though, to be fair, I have a feeling Eppie and Hazel might be."

He didn't know who Eppie and Hazel were or why the thought of them seemed to amuse Devin so much.

He frowned. "I don't care about your yoga class. The answer is still no."

"You haven't even heard the question!" she exclaimed. "At least not all the reasons I want to use your mineral spring."

"Does it matter?"

"Maybe. I believe there are inherent healing properties to the mineral waters around the lake—or at least palliative properties. You've got one of the only free-flowing natural mineral springs left. If some of my patients could just soak in it even a few times, I believe they would see improvements in mobility, flexibility and comfort."

He found the water soothing, certainly, both physically and mentally. But healing? That he didn't quite buy.

"That would be very nice for them, I'm sure. But they're not doing it at my ranch."

"Why not? We would completely stay out of your way—I promise! You won't even know we're here."

"Who's going to plow the road to the spring? And how are they going to get up there? It takes a pretty sturdy four-wheel-drive vehicle in the snow."

"I can plow it," she answered.

"With what?"

"I've got a truck with a plow. I traded it for some medical work a few winters ago."

"Seriously?" He gave her a long look, trying to imagine this delicate-looking woman driving a big, beefy pickup truck.

"Believe me, it comes in very handy for a small-town doctor in the rural Idaho mountains. I've become something of an expert. I could plow the road and a couple of the older gentlemen in the class have four-wheel-drive vehicles and are very used to driving on these mountain roads in winter. We can get up there. That's not a problem."

She seemed very earnest about it. He didn't want to come across as a jerk but he had enough to deal with right now without worrying about a bunch of strangers wandering around the ranch.

"It's not maintained at all," he tried again. "What you saw is all there is. Just the one changing hut, heated by a woodstove."

"That's okay. I'm not looking for some sort of fancy resort. It's about the water, not the amenities."

She gave him a steady look. "Anyway, a couple of those delicious casseroles in your freezer came from some of the kind ladies in my yoga class. Letting them soak away their arthritis pain in your hot spring would be a very small way to repay them for their efforts on your behalf."

He snorted. "What kind of reasoning is that? I didn't ask anybody to fill up my freezer with delicious casseroles. While I'm grateful for it, I'm not sure it puts me under any contractual obligation."

She gave a rueful smile. "It was worth a try, wasn't it?"

He thought of all she had done for him and his family in the past twenty-four hours. Her concern and care of his frightened sister topped the list but she had been showing him kindness after kindness since then.

Now she was offering to help him out of a bind with Jazmyn and Ty after school for a few days. Would it really be a big deal to let some of her patients come out and soak in the spring?

"You said a few times," he said.

Her vivid green eyes lit up as she must have seen the weakening of his resolve. "Yes. No more than three."

"Fine. Two or three times. That's it. Don't get any ideas that you can wriggle your way into making it a regular thing after the holidays."

"I wouldn't dare."

With that smile and her eyes bright with excitement, she was just about the prettiest thing he had ever seen. He knew he was staring but he couldn't seem to help himself. Something about her just seemed to reach through all his careful defenses. He was having a tough time resisting her—which was stupid, since he could never let this attraction go anywhere.

For a moment, he wondered what it would feel like to be the sort of man who deserved a woman like her, then his kids came pounding down the stairs, both carrying large boxes.

"We looked *everywhere* and brought down every craft thing we could find," Jazmyn announced. "Scissors, stamps, paper, glue. We brought *everything*."

Devin, her color a little pink, looked away from Cole and focused on the children. "Perfect. I think we can find a place to use it all."

"Can I put some Christmas decorations in my room?" Ty asked.

"I don't know. We'll have to see what we can find and what we need in other places of the house."

"I want a Christmas tree of my very own," Jazmyn said.

He should have thought of that and cut a small sapling for each of the kids. He would do that next year, he resolved.

Assuming they all survived this Christmas together and then the next twelve months.

"This should all be perfect." Devin pulled off her coat and set it over one of the kitchen chairs. "Set everything on the table and we'll take a look and see what we've got to work with."

"I carried the biggest box because I'm the oldest," Jazmyn said, which, of course, didn't sit well with her brother.

"Only because you stole it out of my hands."

"It doesn't matter who brought down the bigger box. The important thing is that now we can get busy," Devin said. She glanced over at Cole. "Where will we find the lights and ornaments for the tree?" she asked.

"In the attic, in a bunch of red boxes marked Christmas. I'll carry them down."

"We can do that. Don't worry about it."

He gave her a look. "My house. My Christmas decorations. I'll get the boxes."

She rolled her eyes but turned her attention to the craft supplies the children had brought down.

When he carried the last box down and set it in the family room near the tree, he headed back into the kitchen to find Jazmyn cutting out snowflakes from shiny paper and Ty frowning in concentration as he cut out strips for a paper chain garland.

"That should be it. I have to go down to the barn. The vet finally texted that he's on his way."

Devin smiled and he forced himself not to stare again like some creepy stalker dude.

"We might be a while," he said. "Just bring the kids down when you're done here. They can hang out at the barn. I put a little TV and DVD player with movies in the tack room or they can always play with the barn kittens. They like that."

"I can stay for a while," she said. "I'd like to head over to the hospital to check on a couple of patients around seven, but I'm free until then."

When she was here with his children, looking so soft and adorable, it was tough to remember she had a high-powered career and went around saving lives. "You don't have time to decorate my Christmas tree and hang snowflakes in my windows. I can't ask this of you."

"If you'll recall, you didn't ask. I offered. I wouldn't have offered if I didn't want to do it. This is going to be a blast. Don't worry about us. We're going to be busy decorating for at least a few hours, anyway. In fact, now that you've done all the heavy lifting, you'll probably only be in the way—isn't that right, kids?"

Ty smiled and even Jaz giggled a little. It was a sound he didn't hear very often from his daughter and the sweetness of it seemed to curl through him like a sparkly ribbon.

"Go," she said when he hesitated. "We're just fine. I'm happy to stay and help. I *want* to, actually. We put all the work into cutting down the tree and I don't want to leave until I see it all decorated. Right now, I can't imagine anything I would rather do or anyone I would rather be doing it with."

This time, both kids giggled and Ty even leaned

into her arm a little bit. They had responded to Devin in a way they hadn't to anyone else—certainly not the two housekeepers they'd gone through. Even with Tricia, they had been a little bit standoffish, maybe because she had been preoccupied with her failing marriage and her pregnancy.

If Devin Shaw wanted to help him out with the children so he didn't have to worry about them for a change—if she wanted to keep them entertained here at the house, where they were warm and comfortable and relatively content—he didn't see how he could refuse.

"Fine. I appreciate it. I don't know why you're helping us, but I'm...grateful."

"You're very welcome," she answered with a soft smile, and it took every ounce of self-control he had fought to develop over these past few years not to step forward and kiss that sweet mouth.

Instead, he shoved on his hat and grabbed his ranch coat, then headed out, hoping the December air would cool his overactive imagination.

CHAPTER SEVEN

"Oh, wow. Look at this."

Devin gazed into the box she had just opened, where a delicate crystal angel had been carefully nestled in tissue paper after some prior Christmas.

The angel had flowing gold robes and a kind-looking face. Both Ty and Jazmyn paused their rummaging through boxes for ornaments to admire her.

"Oooh! She's pretty," Ty exclaimed.

"That should definitely go on top of the tree," Jazmyn declared.

The girl reached into the box to take it out and Devin bit back her words of caution. Jazmyn was actually being very careful with everything they found in the boxes.

"I wonder if that was our great-grandma Barrett's."

"That's a pretty good guess," Devin said. She had a feeling Cole wasn't big on buying crystal angel tree toppers—or any ornaments, for that matter.

The Christmas decorations they had found seemed to span many different eras and styles—though apparently the children's great-grandma Barrett was quite fond of crocheting and knitting. They found homemade crocheted Christmas tree skirts, ornaments, stockings. There were even a knitted Mr. and Mrs. Santa Claus and a reindeer, which Jaz fell in love with and wanted in her own room.

Devin guessed that Cole's grandmother had created them all. She must have had plenty of time for handiwork during the area's notoriously harsh winters. Devin painted a cheerful mental picture of the woman sitting by the fire, keeping her hands busy while her husband watched television.

"Look," she said, pulling out another smaller container from the same larger box where she had found the angel. "Here's a sister to the other angel. That might work on top of your tree."

Much to Jazmyn's delight, they had found a trio of small, skinny pine trees in varying sizes among the decorations. She claimed the largest, naturally, about four feet tall, for her own room.

"Is there one for my tree?" Ty asked.

Devin shook her head. "I haven't seen one yet, kiddo. But look. Here's a star tree topper. Do you want that one?"

"Okay."

He was such an easygoing, agreeable young man. Devin supposed that was a good thing, considering his sister was just about his exact opposite in personality.

"Do you think the big tree is dry enough for the lights yet?"

"Probably a little while longer."

For nearly two hours, they had been busy making ornaments and going through the boxes to see what they had to work with.

Devin didn't consider herself much of a decorator but already the few things they had set out around the house seemed to have made an improvement.

The ranch house at Evergreen Springs was beautiful, with classic lines and a comfortable, homey feel. It was a little old-fashioned and cluttered with dusty knickknacks she couldn't imagine Cole ever buying.

Likely he hadn't done much to the place since he inherited it from his grandmother. He really needed someone to come in and refresh the whole place. New curtains, a fresh coat of paint, a bit of new furniture.

Devin's friend Eliza Caine sprang to mind. The Christmas before, Eliza had swept into Snow Angel Cove, the huge rambling lodge owned by billionaire tech genius Aidan Caine, and turned it into a warm, beautiful home.

While built on a much smaller scale, Evergreen Springs reminded her of Snow Angel Cove. The lovely home could use the same attention as Snow Angel Cove, skills Devin certainly didn't have.

"Since we're still waiting on the big tree, can I take these ornaments to my room and decorate my tree?"

"Sure. Let's do it."

"Then mine," Ty insisted.

"Absolutely."

Devin carried up both slender trees while the children hauled the boxes of ornaments. She set Ty's down in the hallway for now and followed Jazmyn into her room.

"Oh. What a great bedroom!" she said.

Jazmyn looked around with considerable pride at

the comfortable space that held a double bed covered in a gauzy canopy and a purple quilt. "Aunt Tricia helped me find a new bedspread and curtains. This used to be her room and her bed. When she got here at Thanksgiving, she said it looked too old and dingy for me. We ordered new stuff and everything came in the mail this week."

"I love it! Where do you want to put the tree?"

Jazmyn pointed to the small space near her bed. "That way I can see it before I go to sleep," she said.

Devin mostly supervised as the children hung the few ornaments Jazmyn had picked out along with some of the snowflakes she'd cut out. Finally, Jazmyn placed the miniature angel on top.

"Let's see how it looks. Ty, turn off the lights."

Her brother obediently went to the doorway to flip the switch. Though afternoon sunlight still filtered through the curtains, the colored lights on the tree lit up the room and the angel glowed gold.

"Oh," Jazmyn breathed. "It's beautiful."

"I especially like the angel," Devin said with a smile.

They stood for a moment, admiring their handiwork, then Jazmyn finally spoke, her voice subdued.

"Do you think our mom is an angel?"

Devin caught her breath at the unexpected question. How was she supposed to answer that? She had her own religious and philosophical views—reinforced by her time as a physician where she balanced science with the unexplainable—but she didn't know what position Cole took on the matter and she didn't want to overstep. "It helps to think she is, doesn't it?"

"I guess." Jazmyn's eyes glimmered in the lights from the tree. "I miss her a lot."

"Oh, honey." Devin caught her small frame in a hug, then felt two other little arms trying to span both of them when Ty came over to join in the embrace.

Her throat felt thick and tears burned in her own eyes. These poor children. She was a grown woman when her father had died and she still missed him every single day, though he had been gone for several years. Losing a loved one left an empty space in the heart reserved just for that person. She couldn't imagine losing a parent when she was only a child, before she was old enough to store up wonderful memories to last a lifetime.

"I'm so sorry, my dears. I'm sure you do miss her. It hurts when we lose someone we love, doesn't it? I'm afraid there's really nothing anyone can say to make that hurt go away. It does help to remember how very lucky you are to have a dad who loves you, who's trying his best to help you through this tough time."

Ty nodded but she noticed Jazmyn didn't say anything. Obviously, the relationship between Cole and his daughter was a tense one. It made her sad for both of them.

"Can we do my tree now?" the boy asked after a moment, with the resilience of the young that she fiercely envied.

"Yes. Let's do it. After that, the big tree will probably be dry enough for us to decorate. By then, we're going to be experts at tree decorating."

Ty raced across the hall. His room also had fresh

curtains and what looked to be a new quilt, this one in red, white and blue.

"I never had my very own Christmas tree in my room before," Ty said.

"Last year, we didn't even have a Christmas tree," his sister added. "We didn't even have a house. We had to stay in a dumb hotel because we didn't have anywhere else to live."

"We got to go swimming there, anytime we wanted. It was fun. And Santa found us anyway, even in a hotel," Ty said.

She brushed a hand over his hair, admiring him for being able to find the good in a tough situation.

"He did," Jazmyn conceded. "He had to put our presents on the floor around a lamp, I guess because we didn't have a real tree that year. The year before that, we had a white one with pink lights, though, the kind my mom liked. That's when we lived with Carlos. Or was it Len? I can't remember."

"I don't know. I was only four," Ty pointed out. "I wasn't even in school."

The picture they painted of life with their mother wasn't a very pleasant one, but then Tricia had intimated their mother had been a mess.

Devin had to hope things would be better for them now, since they had been reunited with their father. Despite his abrupt nature and the secrets she sensed about him, Cole seemed a decent man who seemed genuinely concerned about his sister and about his children.

They all deserved a wonderful Christmas together,

this chance to create new traditions and begin building their lives together.

"Well, you have two beautiful trees in your rooms now. Let's go check the big tree your father cut down. Keep your fingers crossed that it's finally ready for the lights."

SHE COULD THINK of worse ways to spend a snowy Saturday, Devin thought an hour later as she wound the last of the lights around a branch of the tree. The heavenly tart aroma of fresh-cut pine soaked through the whole room, so delicious it almost made her want a real tree of her own.

On the other hand, *she* would also be smelling like a Christmas tree for days, with pine sap all over her hands, and her fingers had been poked about a dozen times by needles. She hadn't realized what a pain stringing lights on a tree was, especially since most of the artificial kind these days came prelit.

She wasn't sure the smell compensated for all the hassles. She could always just buy a pine-scented air freshener.

Cole had been right on the money about the tree's size. It fit perfectly in front of the big window, not too tall and not too bushy.

"How does this one look?" Ty asked from the newspaper-covered coffee table. He held up the ornament he was making with Jazmyn's help in some empty clear balls she had found in the boxes.

"I put some glue in it like you said and some glitter."

"Wonderful," she assured him. It appeared as if a

glitter gun had exploded all over the newspaper but she wasn't going to mention that.

"What about mine?" Jazmyn asked, not to be outdone.

"You're both very skilled. Now we need to start hanging them on the tree. Are you ready to decorate?"

"Yay!" Ty exclaimed.

"Great. We should put on music. I don't know why I didn't think of it before."

She had noticed Cole had a docking stereo station for a phone similar to hers—what did he listen to? She had to wonder—and a moment later she found a children's Christmas music station on a radio app she had on her phone. Soon the children were singing along to "Rudolph the Red-Nosed Reindeer" and "Jingle Bells."

Devin wrapped the ribbon garland around the tree, then left the children to hang the ornaments as she headed into the kitchen to heat up some of the pasta *e fagioli* soup Barbara Serrano had sent along.

"This is the prettiest Christmas tree *ever*," Jazmyn said when she returned from the kitchen to help them hang the rest of the ornaments.

"It really is," Devin said. She stepped back to take a look and had to smile. Against the snowy backdrop through the window, the tree glowed with colorful lights and ornaments. Just about every branch had two or three things hanging from it. It looked jumbled and off balance and completely charming.

The entire house looked festive and bright, a far cry from what it had been a few hours earlier. They had found some artificial greenery for the big mantel in the great room and stockings now hung beneath it—one for Cole, Tricia, Jazmyn and Ty and two tiny baby stockings for Tricia's twins.

They had found more greenery and fairy lights to twist down the banister of the staircase and Devin had been thrilled when she found two brand-new spools of tartan ribbon in the boxes. She tied bows everywhere and gathered candles from every corner of the house for a centerpiece on the table.

Paper snowflakes fluttered everywhere and the paper chain garland Ty had worked so hard to make was strung around the front door entrance.

The place was still cluttered and a little old-fashioned but it looked much better than it had before, if she did say so herself.

"Are we ready to put the big angel on top?" she asked.

"Can I do it?" Ty asked.

"You're too little," Jazmyn said. "You can't reach."

"It's pretty fragile," Devin told him. "Plus I'm not sure you can reach the top from the ladder. Why don't I put it up and then you can turn off the lights in here so we can see how it looks."

"Okay," he said, ever cheerful. She climbed the ladder while Ty hurried to the light switch.

"Wait until I'm done," she cautioned, envisioning herself falling right onto the tree in the darkness.

She carefully set the angel on the top branch, fastening the clips that kept her in place, then eased away. "How's that? Is she straight?"

Jazmyn tilted her head one way, then the next. "I think so. What do you think, Ty?"

"Yep. Can I turn off the lights yet?"

"Let me get down from the ladder first."

Devin stepped down and folded away the ladder she had rounded up in the garage for their decorating efforts.

"Okay. Hit the lights."

Ty complied and the room was suffused in a warm, multicolored glow from the tree.

"Oh," Jazmyn exclaimed. "It's *so* beautiful."

"I agree," Devin murmured. "Good work, you guys."

"I wish my mom could see it," the girl said sadly.

Devin couldn't help it. She put an arm around the girl and pulled her close. Ty, not to be left out, came on her other side and they stood that way for a long moment, looking at the tree and listening to "Away in a Manger" on the radio.

They were still standing there when the front door opened and Cole walked inside. He took in the scene—the tree, the decorations, the Christmas music and the three of them standing together. She thought she saw something raw and hungry flash in his gaze but it was gone in a moment. Cole looked around the house with mock amazement.

"Wow. Did I wander into the wrong house by mistake?"

Ty giggled. "Nope. This is our house. It looks like Christmas, doesn't it?"

"It does, indeed." He gave a full-fledged smile to

his son, the first one she had seen from him. It made him look younger, somehow. Softer. Ty beamed back and even Jazmyn looked happy for the moment.

Something stirred in Devin's chest, a wistful yearning to belong to this little group.

"Wow. You three have been so busy," he said.

"I made all the snowflakes," Jazmyn informed him. "Ty wanted to make some but he can't cut good enough."

Ty huffed out an annoyed breath and Devin fought the urge to reprimand the girl. Somebody needed to have a long talk with Jazmyn about being more aware of other people's feelings. If her negative attitude went unchecked, she was going to grow into a bad-tempered teenager and a miserable adult.

She wasn't the girl's parent, though. It wasn't her place to reprimand her about anything when her father was there.

"He's working on it, though, aren't you, kiddo? Ty filled all the balls with glitter. He did an awesome job with that. You've got two very creative kids here."

He hung his hat and coat on the hook by the door and slipped out of his boots, looking rumpled and gorgeous and very, very tired.

"I'm sorry I was gone so long."

"We only just finished, so really, your timing was perfect. Is everything okay?"

He sighed. "Not really. One of the horses I'm training has turned up lame and the vet is stumped as to what the problem is or how to fix it. No obvious sign of trauma or heat. We've ruled out abscess but don't know what else might be going on. I have to contact the owner and see what she wants me to do from here."

"How frustrating. I feel for the vet. So much of medicine, for people, at least, is trial and error. It must be even worse when the patient can't explain where it hurts."

"Right. That definitely adds to the frustration. Anyway, thanks for sticking around so long. That would have been a long time for the kids to hang out down in the barn."

"No problem. I was glad to help. I should probably take off, though. There's soup warming up on the stove and those fresh bread sticks from Serrano's on the counter for your dinner."

"That sounds great. I'm starving."

"You have to leave?" Ty sounded disappointed.

"I'm sorry, kiddo. But I had a great day with you and I'm sure you can't wait to show your dad your own tree."

"What do you kids say to Devin for helping you decorate?"

"Thanks," Ty said. He reached out and gave her a big, earnest hug around her waist. She hugged him back. For some ridiculous reason she didn't understand, her throat felt tight and a little achy, especially when Jazmyn came over and gifted her with one of her sweet, genuine smiles.

"I love the tree in my room and I had fun making the snowflakes. Thanks, Devin."

"You're very welcome, my dear." She hugged the girl, too. "I'll see you next week."

"Okay. Dad, can we watch *Phineas and Ferb*?" Jazmyn asked.

"Just for a minute," he answered.

The kids both raced to the TV room off the kitchen and Devin headed to the entryway for her coat.

"I really appreciate what you've done here," Cole said. "The house looks terrific. I honestly don't know when I would have found the time to deck the halls appropriately. And you were also right—the kids need this. I should have made time earlier. Thank you."

"You're welcome, Cole. It was my pleasure. Seriously. They're a delight."

He looked doubtful about that but nodded, anyway.

"Oh. I almost forgot. I had a phone call earlier from my sister and we might have found a solution to your nanny-housekeeper problem."

"Oh?"

She started to put on her coat and after a pause, he stepped forward to help her into it. The air seemed to shift as he moved behind her, smelling of leather and horses and big, tough cowboy, and her stomach suddenly felt shivery and odd. She swallowed, ordering her hormones to behave.

"You probably know my sister, McKenzie, is the Haven Point mayor and she knows everyone who knows everyone. She and I were talking about possibilities and came up with one. Letty Robles. We talked to her and she expressed tentative interest."

"Oh?"

"McKenzie and I both think she would be *perfect*. She's been a widow for a few years and used to teach third grade at the elementary school until she took early retirement to care for her husband in his last months. She's a vibrant, active sixtysomething who I think would be wonderful. If I had children, I would want her to help me with them. There's just one catch."

"Isn't there always?" he said wryly.

"Not an insurmountable one, just a little inconvenient. Right now she's on a trip to Disneyland with her kids and grandkids and won't be back for a couple of days. She gets back in town on Tuesday and said she would love to help you after that, if you can cobble things together until then. Also, she wanted to be clear that you don't have to make a lifelong commitment at this point. You can test-drive each other until after Christmas or Tricia has her babies and see how things work.

"She said she can be here Wednesday morning for an interview and if you're happy, she can start Wednesday when the kids get home from school."

He gave a rough, disbelieving laugh. "You *have* been busy."

She smiled. "I can multitask. So Monday, I'll plan on picking up the kids after school. I may have things to do in town but they can come with me and help me out, if you and they don't mind."

"I'm sure they'll be thrilled to be with you again. I don't know what to say, Devin. I'm going to be so deeply in your debt, I'll never climb out."

"I'm glad to help," she assured him. "Seriously, they're a delight. I hope you know what a lucky man you are."

She hadn't meant to say that last part. He gave her a curious look but let the matter drop, to her relief.

"Maybe we'll see you at the hospital later," he said. "I was going to drop in and check on Tricia tonight."

"Maybe."

She would do her best to make sure that didn't happen, Devin thought after she said goodbye and walked into the wintry evening.

Right now she was feeling entirely too vulnerable and exposed. She needed a little time away from him *and* his children to remind herself of all the reasons she could never be a permanent part of their lives.

CHAPTER EIGHT

"So what do the doctors say? Anything new?" Cole asked his sister the next evening,

Tricia shifted restlessly on the hospital bed. "Nothing has changed from yesterday when you stopped by. The babies are both fine and so am I."

"No new contractions?"

"Not a one, but the threat of premature delivery is still very real. I'm still dilated and effaced."

Yeah, he didn't want to go in that direction while talking to his sister.

"Everybody's crossing fingers and toes that the contractions don't start up again or I'll have to be transferred to the hospital in Boise, where they have a higher level newborn ICU," she went on.

"Has it been horrible here?" he asked.

"Not really. I mean, is this the way I wanted to spend the last few weeks of my pregnancy? Um, no. But the food is at least halfway decent and I've got my laptop to stream movies and TV and all the books and magazines I could want to read on my tablet. Everyone has been so nice to me, from the nurses to the lab rats."

"That's good."

"I'd rather be back at Evergreen Springs."

"You should see our house right now," Jazmyn told her. "Our Christmas tree is so pretty."

"That's what you said yesterday. I still can't believe Devin spent the day helping you put up a tree and decorate it."

He couldn't quite believe it, either, but he saw proof of it every time he turned around at the ranch house.

"I like her," Ty said with that sweet smile of his. "She's nice."

"I think so, too," Tricia said, smiling back at him. "Tell me what else you've been up to."

The kids proceeded to chatter to their aunt about going down to the barn with him that morning, about playing with the cattle dogs and going for a short horse ride around the paddock and about how Christmas was less than two weeks away now.

They sounded almost happy. It hit him with more than a little shock. When had that happened? They had both seemed so lost and sad since coming here after their mother died. He couldn't be naive enough to think they were done with mourning, but maybe they were beginning to find a few things to like about living with him.

"Want to play a game?" Jazmyn asked. "Dad made us bring some. He thought it might keep you from being so bored."

"Did he?" Tricia gave him a surprised look. What? Wasn't he allowed to be thoughtful once in a while. "I'd love to play a game."

"Here," he told his daughter. "Trade me places so you're close enough to play. Ty, come over here."

The children brought chairs close to the bed and Cole headed to the leather recliner in the corner of the hospital room.

"Okay. Here's what you do," Jazmyn began.

The leather recliner was comfortable, probably designed for fathers who didn't want to leave after the excitement of watching new life come into the world. Cole leaned back and closed his eyes, letting the conversation wash over him.

He must have dozed off for a minute or two. He was deep in a dream where a certain beautiful doctor was leaning over him with a stethoscope to check his suddenly racing heartbeat when something— a subtle shift in the atmosphere, a scent, a karmic warning—woke him.

She was there, he realized, standing in the doorway wearing a skirt and white tailored blouse that made her look deliciously crisp and professional.

She was gazing not at her patient but at him. When his sleepy gaze met hers, she quickly looked away, back at the trio playing cards on the bed.

"I'm sorry. I didn't realize your family was here, Tricia. Sorry to interrupt."

"You didn't," his sister assured her. "We were just hanging out."

"I was beating Aunt Tricia and Ty at UNO. It's our favorite game."

"It's a good one," she agreed as Ty scampered

down from his chair and headed over to give her one of his tight hugs.

"Hi, Devin," he said with clear affection. Apparently their time together the day before had cemented some kind of bond between them.

Her face softened as she looked down at his son and Cole found himself wishing she would look at *him* with that kind of sweet affection. "Hi, bud. How's our snow guys?"

"They haven't melted, even a little."

"Whew. Good thing it's still cold, then."

She smiled, then ran a hand over Jazmyn's hair. "And how's my favorite snowflake cutter?"

"Fine, I guess. I was watching a show but didn't get to finish it before we had to leave."

Cole sighed. She had bellyached about having to leave her show through the entire drive from the ranch to the hospital. As his grandmother used to say, she was the kind of person who would complain if you hung her with a new rope.

"You recorded it," he reminded her, yet again. "You can pick it up right where you left off when we get home."

"*And* Grandma Trixie said she wanted to call us on Skype tonight. Maybe she tried to do it while we were gone."

"Your grandmother has my cell number," he answered patiently. "Every time she wants to talk on Skype, she calls or texts me first. Since I haven't heard from her today, I think we're good."

Jazmyn adored her grandmother and thought

Trixie could do no wrong. As far as Cole was concerned, his ex-mother-in-law was very much like her daughter—unreliable, self-absorbed and full of promises she would never deliver.

"I thought we were having fun playing UNO," Tricia said.

"We were." Jazmyn at least had the grace to look a little embarrassed about complaining. He decided to take that as progress.

"I'm sorry to interrupt the big game. I'll let you get back to it. I'm here checking on another patient and just wanted to see how you're doing. I'm going to be around the hospital for a while. I'll let you all visit and stop back before I leave."

She waved at them all and left, taking the scent of flowers with her. The room seemed colder without her, somehow. Cole dismissed the fanciful thought. It wasn't possible for one person to brighten up a room simply by walking into it. Was it?

He was left to mull that as they finished the game. Just as Tricia was sliding the cards back into their tin, her cell phone on the little tray next to her bed rang with a distinctive, romantic-sounding ringtone.

Her features looked wistful and sad for just a moment before they hardened.

"Phone!" Ty bellowed, reaching for it.

"Don't answer it," she answered calmly. "Here. Just hand it to me."

His son picked up the phone and set it next to his aunt, who turned off the ringtone with every appearance of nonchalance, but Cole didn't miss the way her hands trembled a little.

The kids didn't seem to think anything unusual about that, which made him wonder if she had done this at the ranch before she came into the hospital. Instead, Jazmyn pulled out some paper and crayons from the pack she had brought along, announcing she was going to draw her aunt the best Christmas picture ever. Ty, of course, objected, saying *he* was going to draw the best picture. Soon they were fighting over the red and green crayons, not paying any attention to the adults in the room.

"Was that Sean?" he asked, after making sure the children were occupied.

"Yes."

"And you're still not taking the man's calls? Really?"

"What's the point? He knows where I am."

"Does he know you're in the hospital?"

Tricia's mouth tightened. "I'm handling this in my own way. You need to stay out of it and let me."

Which meant she hadn't told him. Cole frowned at his sister. "These are his babies, too. Take it from a man who's had to fight tooth and nail to be allowed to spend time with his kids. You need to let him know what's going on."

"This isn't the same situation," she argued. "You loved your kids. You wanted them in the first place."

"Not at first," he argued quietly, again making sure the children in question couldn't hear. "I was scared as hell when Sharla told me she was pregnant with Jaz. Becoming a father was never in the master plan—if I'd been sober enough back then to come up with a master plan, anyway."

"Scared or not, you did the right thing. You never would have made Sharla feel it was her fault she got pregnant. You stepped up and filled the role. I don't think Sean is capable of doing that and I can't raise my children in a situation where they *ever* feel unwanted by their father. I won't do it."

She sniffled a little and grabbed a tissue off the table beside the bed and Cole squeezed her fingers, fighting the urge to pound both her bastard of a husband and their bastard of a father for creating this insecurity in her.

"He hasn't been to a single prenatal class or appointment. Did you know that?"

Cole shook his head.

"Not only that but whenever I would try to talk to him about the babies—to have him feel them kicking or ask him to pick out furniture or *anything*—he froze. I know he has reasons why he didn't want kids. I was fine with that when I married him, since I didn't want them, either. I didn't plan these babies but when I found out I was pregnant despite the precautions we took to keep that from happening, everything changed for me. I loved them from the moment I saw that plus sign on the pregnancy test."

Children did have a way of changing your world perspective.

"I kept thinking Sean would come around eventually but he never did. He just kept pulling further and further away from me. When he volunteered to take that last business trip right before Thanksgiving when he knew I was scheduled for an ultrasound, I knew it was the last straw. He didn't want these babies and he didn't want me anymore. I couldn't stay there under those conditions."

This was more than she'd told him since she arrived about the reason she had left her husband. He wanted to tell her to give the man a chance to step up but it sounded as if she had given him seven months' worth of chances.

"I'm sorry, sis. You know I'll help you as much as I can. You can stay at Evergreen Springs as long as you need. Forever, if you want. It's a good place for kids to grow up. It took me a long time to see that."

She sniffled into her tissue, gripping his hand with hers. "Thank you. That's incredibly sweet of you but I'm not ready to make any permanent decisions yet. I just want these babies to make it here safe and healthy. We'll come home to the ranch and I'll figure things out after that."

"Take all the time you need. Thanks to Devin, I've found someone to help with the kids. If it works out, she might be able to help you with the twins, too."

"Devin did that?" Her eyes widened.

"And more."

"Oh, she's a sweetheart, isn't she?"

"Yeah," he murmured. "She is."

He tried to sound casual but something in his tone or his expression must have alerted his eagle-eyed sister. Her gaze sharpened and he could feel himself flush, hoping she wouldn't notice.

The last thing he needed was for his baby sister to figure out he was entirely too drawn to her lovely doctor.

"We should probably be going." He stood up. "Kids, are you about done?"

"I just finished." Jazmyn proudly held up her picture of a Christmas tree with wrapped packages beneath and red ribbon curling around the branches.

"Oh, that's beautiful."

"I drew a snowman," Ty said, handing over his picture of three similar-sized circles stacked up with a black hat on top.

"Wonderful," she said.

"We made two with Devin yesterday, a big one and a little one," he informed her.

"Did you? Sounds like you had lots of fun with her."

"She's nice," Ty said.

Again, Tricia sent Cole a searching look. He gave her a steady look back. She didn't need him to tell her all the reasons why a woman like Devin would never be interested in someone like him.

"We'll have to take a picture of you two in front of the snowmen and email it to Aunt Tricia. For now, leave your pictures here and grab your things. We need to go scare up some dinner."

They obeyed without argument, for once—small miracle—and he kissed his sister's cheek and told her they would try to stop in again the next night.

When they walked out, he immediately spotted Devin at the nurses' station. She looked crisply professional, with her auburn hair contained in a braid and little dangly green earrings in her ears and her stethoscope around her neck. He just wanted to stand and look at her all day.

She smiled when she saw them. "Hi! Did you have a good visit?"

Ty nodded and skipped right over for another hug, which she gave him with a surprised little laugh. "I drew a picture of a snowman like we builded. Can we make another one sometime?"

"Maybe," she answered. "Not today, I'm afraid. It's almost dark and I'm still working."

"We're going to McDonald's if we're good," Ty announced. "We might even be able to play in the play area."

Yeah, he was a crappy parent. With all the delicious meals she had brought over, he was still taking his kids out to McDonald's. It was the easiest choice when they'd been gone for a big part of the afternoon.

"That sounds fun," she said. "I wish I could go with you. But I'll see you after school tomorrow, right?"

"Yay!" Ty said, and even Jazmyn looked happy about seeing her again.

"Are you sure?" Cole asked. "You've done more than enough."

"Absolutely. I only work until three and it's no problem at all to pick them up at school. I'm looking forward to it and to be honest, I need their help."

"With what?"

"Some friends and I are making some crafts to sell

at the Lights on the Lake Festival next Saturday. We could use some little fingers to help us."

"Child labor, huh?"

She grinned. "Not at all. We pay salaries in candy canes and hot cocoa."

His laugh stole out of nowhere, taking him by surprise. It had been a long time since a woman made him laugh as Devin did. He wasn't sure how to feel about that—or about the way her gaze flickered to his mouth, then quickly away while a blush crept over her cheekbones.

He cleared his throat. "I, um, would be very grateful for your help tomorrow. I've got to run to Boise and I'm not sure if I'll be back before school gets out."

"Is it the horse who was having trouble yesterday?"

"Partly," he said, choosing his words carefully. "The farrier came out this morning and found a sneaky abscess both the vet and I missed. We've got a plan of treatment now. I just need to pick up some medicine in Boise. That's one of my errands, anyway."

He didn't tell her the other big item on his list. Some things were better left to himself.

"Well, don't worry about the kids. I'll pick them up after school and then take them back to the ranch for you after we're done making ornaments, when they're all hopped up on sugar."

"Thanks for that," he said with another laugh.

"You're welcome."

He tilted his head, knowing he shouldn't enjoy looking at her so much.

He wondered what the pair of nurses who were

pretending not to pay any attention to their inter-
change would do if he tucked a strand of auburn hair
that had slipped from her braid behind her ear, leaned
forward and covered her mouth with his own, as he
had been longing to do since the moment he met her.

To keep from making that disastrous move, he
shoved his hands into the pockets of his coat. "You
take care of my sister, you decorate my Christmas
tree, you find me a new housekeeper, you watch over
my kids after school. You can stop anytime now, or
I'll never be able to repay you."

"We made a deal," she reminded him. "I'm hon-
oring my end and I fully expect you to do the same."

Oh, right. His stupid agreement to let her friends
use the hot spring at the ranch. He sighed, knowing
he was well and truly trapped.

Possibly in more ways than one.

"Right. I'm planning on it."

"What about Wednesday afternoon? Does that
work?"

"You don't waste time, do you?"

She shook her head. "Life is too precious to waste
a minute of it. It's a lesson I learned a long time ago."

From becoming a physician or from something
else? He wanted to ask but this didn't seem the right
moment, with Ty tugging at his arm, more than ready
for his Happy Meal.

"Wednesday should be fine. I'll let the school
know you have permission to pick up the kids. I guess
we'll see you tomorrow, then. Come on, kids."

With his children close behind, he headed for the

elevator, trying to ignore the silvery anticipation curling through him like a Christmas tree garland at the idea that he would see her again soon.

CHAPTER NINE

THEY WERE LATE.

Devin glanced at the clock in her SUV as she scored a good parking space along Main Street, just half a block from her sister's store.

"You can leave your backpacks here. We probably won't need them inside."

"Ty has math homework to do," Jazmyn informed her.

"We'll only be hanging out here an hour or so, then we'll head out to the ranch. He can do his homework after we're done here—and so can you."

The girl didn't look very thrilled at the reminder that her brother wasn't the only one with homework on the agenda.

"What are we doing here?" Jaz asked as they reached the door. "This is a flower store."

"You'll see."

She pushed open the door of Point Made Flowers and Gifts to a cacophony. Through the doorway into McKenzie's workroom, Devin could see the place was packed.

Rika, McKenzie's standard poodle, was apparently the greeter for the day. She padded over to them and licked Devin's hand, then turned her attention to the children. Ty giggled. "Can I pet her?"

"Go ahead. She's very friendly."

The children were busy giving Rika the love when McKenzie, with apparently supersonic hearing, came out in response to the door chimes.

"Hey, it's my favorite doctor—and she brought little friends."

"I'm not little," Jazmyn said in a note of deep offense. "I'm eight years old. I'll be nine in five months. Ty is six and he won't be seven until September."

Her sister smiled at this information. "You're absolutely right. My mistake. You're not little. Hi there. I'm McKenzie. Dr. Shaw is my sister."

She held out a hand, which the girl shook solemnly. "I'm Jazmyn. This is my brother, Ty."

"Welcome to you both. Are you here to help?"

"Help do what?" Ty asked.

"I'll show you. Come on back."

McKenzie led them all to the workroom, which looked like barely organized chaos. It wasn't a full contingent of the Helping Hands but about a dozen women were there, busy with various craft projects. The room smelled of pinecones, hot glue and Spanish moss.

"Hey, Devin," Barbara Serrano said. "How did your food rescue work out the other day?"

"It was wonderful. Thank you, everyone, for answering the call. Once he got over his shock, Cole Barrett was so very grateful."

"He's that sexy rodeo cowboy, Iris Barrett's grandson, isn't he?" Hazel Brewer asked.

"Er, yes." She spoke quickly to keep Hazel and her sister from making any of their usual spicy commentary in front of the children. "He was in a bit of a bind and really needed the help. I'm so grateful you all were so willing to step up."

"You bet. Next time we'll be glad to take it up there ourselves for you, won't we, Eppie?"

Her sister giggled and Devin refrained from rolling her eyes. She loved them dearly but sometimes they made even *her* blush.

"These are his children. This is Jazmyn and this is Ty. They're here to help us. What can we do?"

Jazmyn was quickly put to work threading hanging ribbon through ornaments, while Barbara pulled Ty over to help her pour rice into sachet warming bags.

These were last-minute projects for the booth the Helping Hands always had for the Lights on the Lake boat parade and festival. The annual event was a highlight of the holidays in Haven Point, when boat owners decorated their watercraft with Christmas lights and proceeded to make their way from the Haven Point marina to Shelter Springs.

Everyone in town turned out for the event, which included food, music and a gift boutique. The proceeds from the Helping Hands booth went to various organizations throughout the town. This year they were again donating their proceeds to the library's literacy program.

Devin settled into an empty chair between Samantha Fremont and Megan Hamilton and started sewing closed the bags Ty was helping to fill. When finished, they could be microwaved for moist, comforting heat scented with calming lavender and chamomile. They could also be frozen for use as cold packs.

While knitting was her Waterloo, she loved to sew and didn't do nearly enough of it. Stitching up her patients didn't count.

As she worked, she sat back and listened to chatter about the new tech facility Ben Kilpatrick and Aidan Caine were opening in town and the ripple-effect development going on everywhere. Samantha's mother, Linda, was ecstatic that the building she rented for her clothing store was scheduled for a renovation and complete face-lift starting in the spring.

All the while, Devin kept a careful eye on the children, who seemed to be having a wonderful time. Jazmyn was getting along like a house on fire with Linda, which Devin didn't necessarily think was such a great thing, since Linda had a notoriously sour personality. Jazmyn was already headed that way. She didn't need any more encouragement.

Devin was a fast hand sewer—probably thanks to those patients—and after less than an hour, she had a nice stack of finished rice bags in front of her. She had finished so many that she was running out of work room on the crowded table.

"Where are we putting these?" she asked.

Samantha pointed to some boxes against the wall and Devin rose with her arms full.

"I'll show you," McKenzie said.

Her sister apparently had an ulterior motive. As soon as Devin carefully set the finished rice bags in an empty box, McKenzie cornered her.

"Okay, Dev," she said in an undertone. "Spill. What's the story?"

She straightened. "What do you mean?"

"Is something going on with you and Cole Barrett that I should know about?"

Devin glanced over her shoulder to where the children were busy ten feet away and not paying her any attention.

"No!" she said in a low tone. "I barely know the man. Why would you ask?"

McKenzie made a face. "Oh, I don't know. First I get a call asking everybody to provide meals for him. Next thing I know—at least according to the interesting conversation I just had with his daughter—you spent all day Saturday hanging out at his ranch and helping him decorate. Now you bring his children here to help us wrap things up for the bazaar. What is this sudden involvement with the man and his family?"

Ugh. She adored McKenzie but her sister was entirely too protective of her. She didn't need McKenzie jumping into overdrive, thinking she had to watch out for her.

"Nothing," she protested. "Aren't we supposed to be the Helping Hands? That's what I was doing. The man was in a bind and I stepped in when I saw a need."

"And decorating his Christmas tree?"

She glanced over at the children. "I feel sorry for

those children. They lost their mom just a few months ago and now their aunt is in the hospital and their father seems a little bit overwhelmed. I just wanted to help. What's wrong with that?"

"You always care about your patients and their families," her sister said, "but I've never seen you get this emotionally involved so quickly. Babysitting, Dev. Seriously? I mean, you haven't babysat since high school."

"I'm not babysitting," she protested. Exactly. "We're just hanging out. I brought the kids here because I figured we could always use more help and I thought they might enjoy it."

"Are you sure it has nothing to do with their hot rodeo cowboy of a dad?"

Devin could feel her face heat more than one of the microwaved rice bags. Darn this red hair and her light complexion. "Absolutely positive," she insisted. "I feel sorry for the man. That's it."

The words sounded hollow, even to her.

McKenzie studied her so long that Devin squirmed. "He's been in trouble with the law. Did you know that?"

Shock washed over her. "I... No. In Haven Point?"

McKenzie shook her head. "Before he came back. I don't know any details. I only know a few years back, he came into the Mad Dog to watch a basketball game or something when I was there with Wyn. She was a little tipsy and mentioned how hot he was and that she would love to buy him a drink and see where it led, except he was on parole and she didn't need the complications and didn't want to have to explain herself to Chief Emmett."

Wynonna Bailey was a police officer in Haven Point. She wasn't the sort to make up a story like that.

On parole. She couldn't seem to think around the words.

He had struck her as a dangerous man but not in the sort of way that might get him in trouble with the law. Was that why his wife had kept his children away from him?

What had he done?

And was this the reason he kept himself so isolated up at the ranch? He had lived in Haven Point for at least a couple of years but kept to himself for the most part. Did it have anything to do with his criminal past?

Tricia hadn't said a word, but then Devin supposed that wasn't something a person just shared in casual conversation. *Oh, by the way, my brother is on parole. Isn't that interesting?*

What had he done?

"Is Wyn coming this afternoon?" she asked, trying for a casual tone.

"Don't think so. She's on duty."

Rats. She suddenly wanted to pin down her friend and see if she could shed a little light on the mystery that was Cole Barrett.

Maybe she would have to go track her down after her shift was over...

Devin caught herself when she realized the direction of her thoughts. His history with the law wasn't her business. He was still a struggling single father with two grieving children who needed all the attention and love they could find.

"Just be careful, sis," McKenzie said.

"I appreciate the warning but it's not necessary. I've been taking care of myself for a long time."

"I worry about you. You know I do."

On impulse, she reached out and hugged her sister. "I'm fine. The scare this summer was just that. A scare. Everything checked out. The cancer hasn't come back and it won't. The doctors are quite sure of it. I can't live my life in fear, Kenz. I've done too much of that."

"It's one thing to let go and live a little. It's completely another to buddy up to an ex-con when we don't know anything about the man. Maybe I'll have Ben do a little digging around and see what kind of digital footprint the man has out there."

"You will *not*." She frowned. "Seriously, Kenz. Back off. I'm helping Cole out because he's going through a tough time right now. That's as far as it goes. Whether he has a…questionable past or not, he and his children need help. I won't turn my back on him."

McKenzie opened her mouth to argue but Megan Hamilton came over with an armload of ornaments.

"Where are we putting these?"

"Right here," McKenzie said, pointing to one of the empty boxes.

Devin took the chance to escape her sister's interrogation, though as she returned to sewing up the rice bags, she couldn't help feeling that her life seemed as tangled as the thorniest knot of thread.

"WHAT TIME IS my dad going to be back?" Jazmyn asked a few hours later from her spot at the kitchen table at Evergreen Springs.

The kitchen smelled delicious—cinnamon from the cookies they had made mingling with the savory scents of the chicken casserole she had put in a few minutes earlier.

"He texted me about an hour ago and said he was leaving Boise. I would imagine he'll be here soon. Let's see if you can both surprise him by having your homework done before he gets here."

"Mine's almost finished." Ty beamed at her.

"That's because you have easy subtraction problems that even a baby can do," Jazmyn retorted. "Mine is multiplication, which is so hard."

Ty didn't say anything, simply returned to his homework, and Devin tried to figure out whether she had the right to call Jazmyn out on her mean behavior. Ty adored his sister and she said such hurtful things, always demeaning his efforts or trying to make her own seem more grandiose.

Devin understood she was lashing out in her pain and confusion over losing her mother. Ty had lost *his* mother, too, and deserved compassion and encouragement from his beloved older sister, not this constant barrage of criticism.

Devin wanted to pull her aside privately and talk to her about the harm she could be doing to her brother through this constant comparison she did between the two of them but she didn't think that was quite her place. Her only role here was to help Cole out in return for using his hot spring, not to offer parenting help—especially when she had no actual experience to draw from, only instinct.

She would have been a good mother.

The thought pushed its way into her consciousness, more harsh and nagging than Jazmyn could ever be.

She tried to ignore the familiar pinch of pain, the ache in her chest at unrealized dreams. Most of the time she didn't think about it these days but sometimes the hard reality sneaked out of nowhere and smacked her hard.

At those times, she wanted to shake herself and add in a good face slap or two, along with an order to snap out of it and stop the pity party.

Just because she lacked the necessary equipment to bear a child didn't mean she couldn't ever be a mother. Maybe she couldn't have children in the traditional way but she could always adopt or foster a child.

"I'm done!" Ty said five minutes later.

"Oh!" his sister exclaimed. "Not fair! I was almost there. I only had one problem left."

"Hurry and finish and then we can find a game to play while we wait for your father," Devin said.

Jazmyn was writing the last number down when the doorbell rang.

"Somebody's here," Ty said, eyes wide.

"I wonder who it is," Jazmyn said. "Maybe it's a delivery. I love deliveries."

"Who doesn't?" Devin smiled as she headed for the door.

But it wasn't a familiar brown truck or an express delivery. Instead, a tall older gentleman with silver hair and a rugged face very similar to Cole's stood in the doorway.

He had a little pudgy yellow Labrador puppy next to him on a leash and the dog yipped in greeting.

Though she had seen him shoveling snow the other day at quite a distance, she still knew exactly who this man was—Cole's father.

He blinked a little in surprised wariness. "Oh. Hi. I was looking for Patricia."

Had neither sibling told their father Tricia was in the hospital on bed rest with her twins? Was the rift so great between them?

Something else that wasn't her business, Devin reminded herself.

"She's not here right now. May I help you?"

"I…I'm not sure." He looked taken aback and she had the distinct impression he had geared himself up to talk to Tricia and didn't quite know how to respond now that he had learned she wasn't home.

Both children crowded into the doorway with her to see the newcomer and Ty spoke first.

"Hi. You're my grandpa. I'm not supposed to talk to you."

Pain flashed in the older man's gaze. "True enough."

"Is that your dog?" Jazmyn asked.

The puppy yipped again, as if he knew they were talking about him. He was really quite adorable, with big eyes and a Christmas-red shiny collar.

"Yes. This is Buster."

"He's *so* cute. Hi, Buster. Hi there. Hi." She sank down onto the floor of the entryway and the dog wriggled with joy at finding a new friend and began licking her everywhere he could reach while she giggled and scooped him into her arms.

"I want to hold him. Can I hold him?" Ty asked. He knelt down beside his sister and before Devin knew it, their grandfather and his puppy named Buster were inside the house, with the door closed behind them to keep out the cold December air, while the children laughed and wrestled the puppy with total exuberant excitement.

Devin watched them, too caught up in their joy to summon the energy to put a stop to it, even though she knew that was probably the wisest course. After a moment, she turned to their grandfather. "Well played, sir."

"Don't know what you're talking about." The man arched an eyebrow and she didn't miss the mischievous glint in blue eyes that reminded her so much of his son's. If Cole had it in him to be playful, he would probably look like a younger version of his father.

She snorted. "You think a puppy is your clever way of squeezing the toe of your boot in the door. It's tough to say no to an adorable face like that, as your grandchildren just amply demonstrated, and you think you can slip inside right along with him."

He gazed down at the children giggling at the dog as he jumped from one of them to the other, trying to lick them both. She didn't miss the satisfaction there.

"Maybe I just wanted a puppy. I needed *somebody* to talk to in that little cottage."

What was the story here? Why was the man living in the foreman's cottage and completely estranged from his family, so much that he had to resort to this sort of desperate tactic? She thought of that little wave he had offered to Jazmyn when he was shoveling snow and the dejected set of his shoulders as he watched them and she couldn't help a little trickle of sympathy for him.

He obviously wanted a relationship with his son and grandchildren, but she had no idea what he had done to anger Cole.

"Puppy or not," she murmured, "I'm fairly certain you're not supposed to be here."

"You know who I am." He spoke as a statement, not a question.

"Only that you're Cole's father. And that you're not his favorite person."

He laughed without humor. "An understatement of rather epic proportions."

He held out a hand with a little glint in his eye. Something told her this one could be a charmer when he set his mind to it. "Stanford Barrett. My friends call me Stan."

The little yellow Labrador puppy had started sniffing in all the corners of the entryway as he investigated this new space, with the children following around behind him, giggling the whole way at his antics.

Stan Barrett had gone all out, apparently, even willing to take on responsibility for a pet in an attempt to sneak into his grandchildren's lives. So far, it was working.

"I'm Devin Shaw. I'm a friend of the family." It wasn't precisely a lie. She was friends with Tricia, anyway.

"Devin Shaw. Are you related to Haven Point's very pretty mayor?"

"She's my sister. And she is. Very pretty, I mean."

"A few weeks back, I met your sister when I was having breakfast at the diner. She introduced herself and asked if I was a tourist or new in town. We had a good chat. She was very kind."

"That would be my sister." Her sister tried her best to make everyone who came to Haven Point feel welcome.

"You must be the doctor, then."

"That's right."

"I'll have you know, she highly recommended your services, if I need a physician while I'm in town to refill my meds or anything."

What sort of meds did he need? The man appeared in the best of health but she certainly knew looks could be misleading. "That's good. If you can't get a referral from your own relatives, I figure you must be doing something wrong."

He gave her a half smile and seemed content for a moment just to watch his grandchildren with that wistful, sad sort of look in his eyes. Again, she felt that stirring of sympathy.

"Will Patricia be back later?" he finally asked.

She paused, uncertain what to tell him. If Tricia or Cole wanted him to know about her early labor and her bed rest situation, wouldn't they have told him?

Helpful, as always, Jazmyn took the decision out of her hands. "Aunt Tricia is in the hospital."

The news clearly alarmed Stanford Barrett. His mouth sagged and his slightly stooped shoulders straightened. "What? What's wrong?"

"She was going to have the babies too early," Jazmyn said. "They wouldn't have been able to breathe right, my dad says, so now she has to stay in the hospital for a few more weeks so Dr. Shaw and her other doctor can keep an eye on her."

He stared at Devin, his expression one of shock and concern. "When did this happen? Is she all right? Are the babies okay?"

"Friday. Yes. And yes. But I can't tell you any more."

Really, she shouldn't have even told him that much. Sometimes the privacy restrictions of her job felt heavy and cumbersome, though she understood why they were necessary.

She gave him a stern look. "I need to inform you, just in case you were thinking about rushing down to the hospital, the last thing Tricia needs right now is a lot of drama and agitation."

He suddenly looked older than he had when he walked in with the puppy, his features pale and a little pinched. Was he ill, as well? she wondered.

Could that explain this urge to reconnect with his son and daughter and grandchildren—both present and as yet unborn.

"No drama. I get it."

"Was there a message you'd like me to pass along to her? I'll probably be swinging past the hospital tonight before I go home. I can let her know you stopped by and she can contact you at her convenience."

He looked momentarily grateful at the offer but shook his head. "No. I only wanted to show her some baby pictures of her I found. I thought she might like to see them, to compare what she looked like to her babies. Maybe I'll try to stop by the hospital tomorrow. Don't worry. I'll leave the drama at home."

That seemed a kind enough gesture, at least on the surface. He seemed like a man trying to make amends for whatever harm he had caused his children but it wasn't her place to make that judgment call.

She glanced at the old-fashioned grandfather clock in the foyer.

"For what it's worth, your son is supposed to be home in about ten minutes, on his way back from Boise."

She thought of the brevity of Cole's message and almost smiled. Did he work hard at being so parsimonious with his words or was it a skill that came naturally?

"Message received," Stan said. "I'd better take my puppy and go."

"The puppy really is a nice touch," she said. "It seems to be working."

He shrugged. "You know what they say about desperate times."

"I love your dog," Jazmyn said, as if to reinforce that his desperate measures had paid off.

"Me, too," Ty said. He smiled at the man with traces of his sweet shyness.

"Can we play with him sometime or maybe take him for a walk?" Jazmyn asked.

Stanford smiled with genuine delight and Devin had a sneaky feeling that was exactly the outcome he wanted.

"I don't know about that. But if I happen to see you walking past the cottage after school one day, I might just send him out at the exact same time to play in the snow for a few moments. How about that?"

Jazmyn sent him a sly look of perfect understanding. Devin had the funny feeling the two of them were eerily similar.

This was quite obviously a sneaky, underhanded way of getting to his grandchildren without his son's involvement and she was quite sure Cole wouldn't approve.

She should stop it now, especially considering she had no idea what Stanford had done to earn his son's enmity. While she might instinctively like the man and feel sorry for him, she didn't know the real story and had to trust Cole had good reasons for keeping his father away from his children.

At that moment, she heard the crunch of wheels on gravel and an approaching vehicle engine.

"That sounds like Cole. You'd better go," she said.

He nodded and scooped up the dog with one arm. "See you later, kids."

"Bye. Bye, Buster."

"Bye, buddy," Ty said, trying to get in one more stroke of the dog's fur.

Stanford gave Devin a grateful smile that made her feel uncomfortably as if they were somehow in collusion. He slipped out the front door just as she heard Cole come in through the mudroom.

They returned to the kitchen as he was hanging his Stetson on the hook, leaving his streaky brown hair rumpled. He wore Wranglers and a Western-cut dark green shirt that made him look rough and masculine and completely gorgeous—if she were the sort of woman who went for the rugged cowboy type.

Which she wasn't, she reminded herself, a little weakly.

"Hi, Dad," Ty said.

He looked up and smiled at his son with sheer, unadulterated love that made something inside her melt. There was something so unbelievably sweet about a tough man who adored his children.

"Hey, kiddo. Hi, Jazmyn."

His gaze lifted from his children to her and she thought for a moment she saw something raw and hungry there before he blinked and it was gone. Her stomach jittered with nerves suddenly and she had to force herself to remember what McKenzie had told her. He had been in trouble with the law and had been on parole.

The man was trouble in cowboy boots, all the way around.

"Something smells good."

"We made snickerpoodles," Ty said. "They are *good*."

"Snickerdoodles," Devin corrected, mustering a smile. "And I took the liberty of taking out one of the casseroles I brought over the other day for dinner. A chicken and rice dish that is one of my sister's specialties. It should be just about ready."

"Sounds good," he said.

Jazmyn held back and didn't rush to greet her father as Ty did, though Devin sensed she wanted to.

"Dad, I'm all done with my homework and so is Ty. Can we watch the Rudolph show tonight after dinner?"

"I don't know why not. We still probably need to read, don't we?"

"Yes. But I can do that at bedtime."

"We saw a puppy named Buster," Ty informed his father. "He's so cute."

"Oh, yeah?" he said as he snagged a cookie off the cooling tray. "Where did you see a puppy?"

Jazmyn pinched him hard. Ty opened his mouth to yell at her, then seemed to realize what he had done and a look of horrified guilt crossed over his adorable features.

"Um. Somebody brought it. I forget who."

Jazmyn huffed out a disgusted sound while she rolled her eyes and Devin stepped forward.

"You should tell your dad. Neither of you did anything wrong. You don't need to hide anything."

"But we're not supposed to talk to…someone who has a puppy."

"He came to the house. You couldn't ignore him," she said. She turned to Cole. "Your father was just here. He has a very cute yellow Lab puppy named Buster. The children loved playing with him for only a moment. The puppy, I mean. Not your father."

As she would have expected, his jaw hardened and he glared at her. "You let him in?"

"I'm sorry," she said with a steady look. "I must have missed the note by the door listing everyone who should be barred entry."

"My father would be at the top of that list," he said. "In fact, his name would probably be the only one on it. And serial killers. Stan Barrett and serial killers."

At least his father wasn't a serial killer. She could scratch that worry off the list. "I'll keep that in mind next time," she answered.

"What did he want?"

"He was looking for Tricia. Apparently he has some of her baby pictures and thought she might like them before she has her own babies."

He glowered. "Did you tell him she's in the hospital?"

She hadn't exactly told him, Jazmyn had, but she wasn't about to throw his daughter under the bus.

"He knows, yes. I did tell him she doesn't need drama right now. I don't know if that will keep him away from the hospital, though."

"Thanks for that, at least."

She wanted to ask him what the antagonism was

between him and his father, but not with his children looking on.

"Your dinner is just about ready," she said. "I'll just get out of your hair so you can get to it."

"You're leaving?" Jazmyn said.

"You should stay and have dinner with us," Ty said. He slipped his hand in hers and she felt another chunk of her heart crumble for this sweet little boy who had so much love to give.

"We've kept Dr. Shaw long enough," Cole said. "She's a busy woman and has things to do."

She had plenty to do, but nothing as appealing as spending time with them.

"Please, can you stay?" Jazmyn asked, a surprising plea in her voice. While Ty had been affectionate from the start, Devin hadn't been sure at all if Jazmyn had warmed to her.

Cole also looked startled by Jazmyn's eagerness. He gazed from Devin to his daughter and back again. "You're welcome to stay, if you've got a little time to spare," he said.

"That casserole of McKenzie's is my favorite and I *am* starving," she said. "I would love to stay."

Maybe she would have the chance to ask him all the questions racing through her brain about his past and his tangled relationship with his father.

Or maybe she could just indulge this ridiculous little crush she had going on for a few moments longer, before she put it to rest once and for all.

CHAPTER TEN

DR. SHAW COMPLETELY baffled him.

He appreciated her help—heaven knew, he couldn't do everything on his own right now and would have been lost without her—but for the life of him, he couldn't figure out why she had taken such an interest in his family.

She had to be a very busy woman, with an active medical practice and what he gathered was a big social circle in Haven Point. What incentive did she have to help a man she barely knew?

He didn't like mysteries and Devin Shaw seemed like one big tangled ball of unanswered questions. Every once in a while, he caught a glimpse of something in her gaze, a shadow of something he didn't understand.

Maybe he would have an easier time figuring her out if his stupid brain could fire on more than one or two cylinders in her presence. He felt tongue-tied and stupid, just a big, dumb cowboy.

This crazy lust sizzling through him didn't help the situation at all. When he walked into his kitchen earlier and had seen her standing there, all soft and pretty and big-eyed, desire had kicked and bucked through him, just like a mad bronc through the gate.

He had never hungered for a woman with this raw force before.

Good thing his kids were there as a buffer between them, to remind him that he had far too many problems right now anyway and didn't need to add unrequited lust to the mix.

Casserole wasn't his favorite thing—yeah, he was a bit of a Neanderthal and preferred a big, juicy steak to anything where the bits were all jumbled together—but he had to admit, this one was pretty good. It had some kind of crusty, herby topping and a creamy, silky sauce that wasn't half-bad.

He was on his second helping, listening to Jazmyn and Devin talk about some town festival coming up that weekend and some craft thingy they must have worked on together for it when Devin suddenly set down her fork and turned to Ty.

"Are you feeling okay?" she asked, her brow furrowed with concern. "You're not eating. Don't you like the casserole?"

"I'm not hungry," Ty said in a small voice.

Cole frowned. Maybe it was just the low light over the table but he thought the boy looked a little pasty.

Devin must have agreed. She placed a slim hand on the boy's forehead. "You feel a little warm. Does your head hurt?"

"No. Just my stomach."

"Do you feel like you need to throw up?"

"Oooh. Gross!" Jazmyn exclaimed.

Ty shook his head but in midshake he switched to a nod. An instant later, he gagged a little, looking definitely green around the gills.

"Oooh! That's disgusting!" Jazmyn shrieked. "Don't throw up, or I will, too."

While Cole sat there like a stupid lump—there was that half-functioning brain again—Devin scooped up the boy and raced to the downstairs bathroom in the hallway. A moment later, they heard the unmistakable sounds of Ty losing whatever he had eaten for dinner.

Unfortunately, it brought back too many memories of his drinking days. Why the hell had he ever found it appealing to get loaded, knowing what would come later? He had wasted far too much of his life as a selfish, immature ass, thinking he could drink away the emptiness inside him.

"Let's get these dishes cleared away," he said to Jazmyn.

He had to give his daughter credit. For once, she stepped right up and helped him carry the empty dishes to the sink. She even rinsed them and loaded them in the dishwasher.

Only after she scooped the remaining casserole into a smaller plastic container and set it in the refrigerator without saying much of anything did he notice she was looking a little pale, too.

"You're not going to be sick on me, too, are you?" he asked.

"No," she said. "I feel fine. What about Ty? Will he be okay?"

"He's just got an upset stomach," he answered. "Maybe he ate a few too many snickerdoodles."

"He only had one. That's all Devin would let us have before dinner."

She still looked nervous and he rested a reassuring hand on her slender shoulder. "He'll be fine," he said quietly. "Remember, Devin's a doctor. She'll take care of him.

For once, she didn't push him away. He almost thought maybe she even leaned into his hand a little. Progress in tiny steps, he told himself.

"If you want to go watch the show you were talking about earlier, I can finish up in here."

"Okay," she said in a small voice.

"Do you need my help finding it?"

"No. I'm not a baby," she snapped.

Ah. There was his prickly daughter again. She headed into the TV room, though he saw her send a couple of worried looks to the bathroom on her way.

Cole waited in the hallway, feeling helpless in every damn part of his life. A few moments later, Devin emerged alone, leaving the door ajar. Behind her, he could hear water running and steam escaped with her. Strands of hair had escaped from her ponytail to curl enticingly around her face from the humid air, a fact he immediately chided himself for noticing.

"Is he still throwing up?" he asked.

She gave him a slight smile "I think we're done. He's having a warm shower now. We could use clean pajamas and underwear in here."

"I'll grab them," he said. He headed into the laundry room, where most of the clean clothes were still in baskets. It was all he could do to wash a few loads after the kids were in bed—forget about folding and putting them away at this point in his life.

He found a pair of pajamas with Ninja Turtles on them and a clean pair of Ty-sized briefs. When he returned to the hallway outside the bathroom, he saw Devin inside, wrapping Ty in a big bath towel.

The boy rested his head on her shoulder as if he was too tired and miserable to summon energy for anything else. The sight of her there, kneeling on his bathroom floor and embracing his sick kid, did funny things to his insides, things he didn't want to identify.

"Here you go," he said gruffly.

She took the briefs and pajamas from him with a soft smile, then helped Ty into them.

"Let's get you up to bed," she said.

"I'm not tired," the boy protested, already half-asleep.

"I've got you, kiddo."

He picked up the boy—this sweet child he loved so dearly, even though he was 99 percent sure Ty possessed not a shred of Cole's own DNA—and carried him up the stairs. He pushed through the doorway. Devin moved ahead of him and pulled away the covers of the bed so Cole could set him down between the sheets.

"How's your tummy now?" Devin asked.

"I don't know. Okay, I guess. I didn't eat my dinner."

"If you're hungry, we can bring up some toast or some crackers."

"No," he said, his eyes drooping.

"Just get some rest, then," Cole said. "I'll leave your door open so I can hear you if you wake up and start feeling sick again."

Ty nodded and gave a sleepy smile, then closed his eyes the rest of the way. Cole stood watching him for a moment—the veins through the translucent skin of his eyelids, the easy rise and fall of his little chest in his pajamas—and tried not to give in to the panic crawling through him.

He didn't know what to do in these situations. Tylenol? Antacids? What did you do for a kid who was throwing up? He didn't know the first thing.

He had a feeling Devin suspected some of what was racing through his mind. Out in the hallway, she reached a hand out and touched his arm, just for a moment, but he wanted to lean into her as Ty had done.

"Do you mind if I stick around a bit to keep an eye on him?" she asked. "I think he just has a stomach bug. He was a little warm, nothing too unusual, but I'd like to make sure he doesn't suddenly spike a fever."

Relief swamped him and he wanted to kiss her. At least he wouldn't have to figure out the illness on his own. "I would appreciate that very much. Thank you."

"I won't stay long. I've got to head back to the hospital to check on a few patients."

She led the way downstairs just as Jazmyn came out of the TV room to see what was going on.

"Is he still throwing up?" she asked.

Devin shook her head. "No. He's sleeping now."

He could almost see his daughter's busy little mind trying to work the angles.

"I'm worried about him," Jaz finally said solemnly. "I know it's close to my bedtime but I think I should stay up awhile longer, just to make sure he's okay."

Oh, she was a tricky one. "Yeah. Nice try," he growled. "Time for your shower now. Go on."

She drew in a breath for an argument and he braced himself for what was coming. Jazmyn rarely obeyed anything he said.

A good horse trainer had to establish a rapport with an animal, a relationship of trust while still having a firm hand. Yeah, he knew kids weren't the same as horses but he believed some of the principles held true.

Over the past few months, he had failed on all counts when it came to his daughter. At first, he had let her get away with some of her negative behavior because he knew she was grieving for her mother. Now she seemed to have established a bad pattern and both of them knew he wasn't the one in control.

He was going to have to make some changes but not tonight with the lovely doctor looking on.

Much to his relief, Devin once more stepped in to avert the impending crisis. "If you hurry and shower before I have to leave for the hospital, maybe I can read *Sparkle and the Magic Snowball*. It's quickly becoming my favorite Christmas story."

Jazmyn's eyes lit up. "Do you have it? My teacher read that one in class and I *loved* it."

"You're in luck," Devin said. "I have a copy on my tablet. It's not the same as flipping the pages and seeing all the beautiful illustrations but it will do in a pinch."

Jazmyn looked delighted. "Yay! I'll hurry."

She practically galloped up the stairs, leaving Cole to gape after her.

"How do you do that so easily?" he asked.

"What?"

"All of it. A sick kid and a stubborn one. You've got an answer for every situation."

"I'm used to sick kids. It's kind of my business to know what to do for them, so taking care of Ty came naturally."

"And Jazmyn? How do you know just the right buttons to push with Jazmyn? She's not the easiest child in the world."

"No," Devin said. "But I like her. She's a great kid."

"She is," he agreed. "Not everybody sees that, though."

"Once you understand her, it's easy. It's obvious she hides her uncertainties, her grief, her fear by trying to control everything around her. I get that, believe me."

He stared at her, stunned by her perceptiveness. "She does! That's exactly it! She has to be the one in charge every frigging minute and has an opinion on *everything*. It drives me crazy."

"Because deep down, she knows she isn't really in control of anything."

Two months of frustration and difficulty suddenly seemed to come into clear, vivid focus. A moment of insight just rocked his entire relationship with his daughter and gave him a completely new perspective.

"I can't believe I never realized that before. You're exactly right! Damn, you're good."

She gave a little laugh. "No. I just know what it's like to feel scared and out of control."

As soon as she said the words, she immediately looked as if she wished she could call them back.

When had she felt out of control? What were those secrets he sensed in her eyes?

He was intensely curious about this woman and her compassion and understanding. He opened his mouth to probe a little but she cut him off with questions of her own. He had a feeling she was turning the tables so he couldn't look too closely into her psyche.

"So your father," she began. "What's the story there? Why is he barred from talking to your kids?"

He tensed, as he always did when the topic of conversation involved Stan.

"It's a long and ugly story. Why ruin a lovely dinner? Even one that ended up with a six-year-old yakking up?"

She smiled a little, though she gave him a probing look.

"Why indeed," she murmured.

He suddenly wanted to tell her, with a contrariness that was more like Jazmyn than him. Stan could be charming and persuasive—he'd been a corporate attorney, after all. Devin probably thought he, Cole, was being completely unreasonable about the situation, keeping his children from a man who only wanted to forge a relationship with them.

He didn't want her thinking poorly of him—well, more poorly than she probably already did, considering he was obviously way, way out of his depth with his own family.

"My mom died of a rare and aggressive cancer when I was eleven. Tricia was only seven."

Her mouth flattened into a thin line and her shoulders seemed to tighten. "I'm so sorry."

"Mom was…pretty wonderful. I guess all kids think their mothers are awesome, but ours really was. The kind of mom all the other kids wanted, who played out in the yard with us and made blanket tents in front of the fire on rainy days and taught us how to love books and music and art. Losing her was devastating."

"I'm sorry," she said again.

"It was a tough time," he said. "Instead of reaching out to comfort his grieving children at the loss of their mother, as most fathers might do—as I'm trying to do—Stan focused only on himself, as usual. He'd just taken a high-powered new job overseas and decided two grieving kids would only get in the way. So the day after her funeral—Christmas Eve, actually—he dropped us off here with his parents at Evergreen Springs and then proceeded to completely forget about us."

"I had wondered how you came to live with your grandparents."

"Yeah. Great story, isn't it? The challenges of single fatherhood were apparently more than Stan wanted to take on. It was easier to simply dump his responsibilities on someone else and be done with it. We barely knew our grandparents. Before that, I'd been to the ranch no more than a handful of times my entire life. Now suddenly we were living with them. After he left us here, we heard from Stan maybe once or twice a year—if that."

"It must have seemed as if you lost two parents the day your mother died."

"Exactly. That's just how it felt."

He hadn't shared this with his sister and didn't want to admit it, even to himself, but the past two months had actually given him a shade more compassion for his father—at least a little more than he had before he claimed full responsibility for his children.

This parenting gig was hard. Being a single father was even harder, having no one else to share the load and feeling overwhelmed every damn minute.

Cole still didn't see that as reason enough for Stan to abandon his responsibilities.

"Has he reached out to you over the years?"

"A few times. Obviously nothing with any meat behind it."

His father had tried to get Cole an attorney from his own firm to represent him in the criminal trial. He had refused on principle, not willing to take anything from the bastard, even a referral.

Maybe if he had swallowed his pride a little, he might have been able to beat the charges against him, or at least received a reduced sentence. Self-defense would have been a viable argument, since he hadn't been the one to start the altercation.

He wasn't going to second-guess himself at this late date, though.

"Why has he come to Evergreen Springs?" Devin asked.

"Who knows? If I had to guess, I would say that he's suddenly hitting an age when he realizes he's alone in the world and he apparently thinks he can come back in and make everything right again. He thinks if he sticks around and keeps hammering and hammering at me, I'll just let him into my children's lives for some kind of do-over. Screw that. I don't care what it takes—I won't let him hurt them, too."

UNDERNEATH THE IMPLACABLE TONE, Devin heard something else in Cole's voice—a thin, barely detectable strain of old pain.

Her heart ached as she pictured him as a grieving boy being abandoned by his father, dropped off with people he barely knew. No matter how loving his grandparents might have been, any child must have wondered why he couldn't live with his father.

She had known Tricia was raised by her grandparents but for some reason, it never occurred to her to ask why. The selfishness of that omission was beyond mortifying.

She wanted to hug both Cole and Tricia now. In some ways, the situation wasn't unlike what Devin's sister, McKenzie, had faced when she came to Haven

Point at around that same age to live with the father she had never met.

It had been quite the scandal in Haven Point at the time. Devin's father had also been an attorney—she and Cole shared that. Richard Shaw had been well respected and well liked. When his half-Latina love child showed up out of the blue, tongues had certainly wagged all over town.

Devin had been twelve, old enough to understand that her father had done something very wrong. Xochitl Vargas—McKenzie's name before it had been legally changed after she came to live with them—was younger than Devin. Even she had understood her father had cheated on her mother and none of them could escape the whispers around Haven Point.

Her mother had agreed to let the young girl live with them after her mother's death but she hadn't been happy about it. The coldness in her house for those first few months had been devastating.

But Devin had also understood, even at twelve, that none of it was Xochitl's fault. Her half sister was an innocent, frightened girl who had just lost her mother. Devin had loved Xochitl/McKenzie from the beginning for her courage and strength and loved her even more now. She deeply admired how hard her sister had struggled to carve a place for herself in Haven Point.

Because of that, Devin had an added measure of compassion for the tumult Cole and his sister must have gone through when their world suddenly upended—and the scars that could leave behind.

She was a healer by nature, though, and that strain of hurt haunted her. If his father wanted to try making amends now, didn't that show he regretted what he had done? If Cole could find it in his heart to let his father inside his life a little, perhaps both of them could manage to find some sort of peace.

"You're in a tough situation now, with Tricia in the hospital," she said, choosing her words with care. "Couldn't you use his help with the children, if he's willing to give it? Even after you hire a permanent housekeeper and Tricia comes back from the hospital, it never hurts to have a little wider support network."

A muscle flexed in his jaw and he looked as tough and dangerous as an Old West outlaw. "It wouldn't matter if I were caught in an avalanche up in the Redemptions. I still wouldn't want his help."

"Does a suffocating man really care who's digging him out?"

"He does, if he knows the guy on the other side of the shovel tossed him over the cliff a long time ago and walked away without looking back."

She saw his point. She also saw a man who seemed very alone in the world right now and in need of assistance wherever he could find it. If his father was here wanting to extend a hand to his son and grandchildren, it made perfect sense to her that Cole should take advantage of that.

That echo of old sadness she had heard in his voice haunted her. She wanted so much to make it better, though she knew she didn't possess that power.

Medical school had taught her early the grim realization that she simply couldn't fix everything. Sometimes the best she could do was hold someone's hand and offer what small comfort she had.

Before she could do anything, Jazmyn hurried down the stairs wearing a flowered flannel nightgown and fuzzy blue slippers. Her hair hung in wet strands around her face and she looked as if she'd barely dried off before dressing.

"Okay," she chirped. "I had my shower. Can you read to me now?"

"How about we get those tangles out of your hair first?" Devin suggested. "You can read to me while I do it, from whatever book you want. Go find a book and a comb and I'll meet you in your lovely room."

"Do we have to comb my hair? It hurts."

"Yes," her father said firmly.

She sighed but rushed back upstairs to find the items.

"You don't have to stick around," Cole said as soon as she left. "Believe it or not, I can comb hair *and* read books."

"I don't mind. I'm looking forward to it, if you want the truth. I don't get the chance to read too many bedtime stories. Or comb hair, for that matter. I'll read to her and then check on Ty one more time before I take off."

She followed Jazmyn up the stairs to her room and spent a very enjoyable half hour with her. Jazmyn was sweet and uncharacteristically docile, obviously tired after a busy day at school and all the activities they had done together afterward. She seemed even more relaxed after Devin finished combing through her wet hair and reading the truly delightful holiday story that had captured everyone's imaginations the previous Christmas.

"I love that story," Jazmyn said with a happy sigh after she finished reading. "Did you know there's going to be more Sparkle stories? That's what my teacher said, anyway."

"I'd heard. I can't wait."

Jazmyn, tucked into her cute bed, smiled a little, then grew silent for a long moment, her fingers clutching and unclutching the quilt.

"Is Ty going to die?"

The fearfulness in her voice wrenched at Devin's heart. Poor thing—still traumatized from her mother's death. She must see every sneeze, every cough as reason to fret in a suddenly uncertain world. "Oh, honey. No. I think he's just got a stomach bug. Or maybe he ate too many of the treats while we were at my sister's store. With any luck, he'll be just fine in the morning."

"Are you sure?"

"Yes. Positive."

Relief flickered in blue eyes very much like her father's. "Whew. I don't want him to die. He can be a pain and everything but I love him and I would really miss him."

"Have you told him that?" she asked, thinking of the girl's sometimes negative behavior to her brother.

"What? That I love him? Sure."

She thought again that this wasn't her business but

a few well-chosen words surely couldn't hurt. "Sometimes people say one thing but act another way. Have you noticed that?"

"All the time," Jazmyn said. "Like my dad saying we should be nice to people but not letting us talk to our grandpa and I don't even know why."

She wasn't even going to dip a toe into those deep waters. That was for Cole to explain.

"Sometimes we say hurtful things to the people we love most. Do you think it makes Ty feel good when you're always telling him he can't do things as well as you do? Like coloring pictures or cutting out paper strips or building snowmen?"

"He can't. He's just six and I'm eight. I've had way more chances to do those things than he has."

"Maybe so, but I believe it hurts his feelings when you remind him all the time that you're better at everything than he is. Maybe you could try pointing out how much progress he has made at something or offer to show him how you do it. Could you do that?"

"I guess," she said doubtfully.

Devin smiled and squeezed the girl's hands on top of the quilt. "You're a good girl, Jazmyn. Sleep well, sweetheart."

Once Jazmyn was settled, Devin turned her light off and left the door ajar on the girl's orders, then walked down the hall to Ty's room.

The glow from his Buzz Lightyear night-light illuminated his face, which looked much more relaxed and peaceful. He didn't look nearly as pale and seemed to be sleeping peacefully.

She gently tucked back a strand of hair that had slipped into his eyes, subtly checking his temperature at the same time. No fever, she was happy to see. By all indications, he appeared to be feeling better. For Cole's sake, she hoped they would all sleep soundly and comfortably through the night.

Devin let out a sigh. How had these two children become so dear to her in such a short time—funny, strong-willed Jazmyn with her bold opinions and her deep streak of creativity and Ty with his sweet, loving nature and curiosity about the world around him? She adored them both.

She would miss them when these few days were over and Cole no longer needed her help. Perhaps she would have been smarter to guard her heart a little better so she wouldn't feel the sting of loss or the long-familiar emptiness of wondering what might have been.

Her life wasn't empty, she reminded herself sternly. She was doing exactly what she'd dreamed of since she was a little girl bandaging all her dolls' injuries. She loved helping people in her hometown, bandaging them up when they needed it, holding their hands when they didn't, dispensing advice and antibiotics and her concern.

She loved her beautiful house on the shoreline, waking up to the loons and the Canada geese and the reflection of the stunning Redemption Mountain Range on the turquoise-blue waters.

She had dear friends in town, her sister, McKenzie, and their wider circle of friends and knew she could count on each one to jump off a raft into the frigid lake to save her.

What more could she want?

Maybe she had moments of loneliness, times when she yearned to be part of something *more*, but she couldn't fill that loneliness by pretending she had a role in these children's world. She was only helping out their father while he was in a bind, tossing at least a small life preserver to help him stay afloat a little longer in the churning waters of his life.

Making this into anything more was dangerous to her psyche. Her presence in their lives was transitory and ephemeral. She was friends with their aunt, but beyond that, she had no real role here and needed to keep that in mind.

He was waiting for her in the entry at the bottom of the staircase, his hair oddly damp. He looked as if he'd just stepped out of the shower, an image that made her insides suddenly flutter with nerves.

"Did I hear you check on Ty?"

"I did. He seems to be doing okay. His color is better and even the low-grade fever seems to have broken. I'm going to keep my fingers crossed that you all get some sleep tonight."

"Should I make a point of checking on him during the night?"

"Good idea." Though he seemed to be a little out of his depth, Cole was a good father, trying hard to take care of his children.

"It's snowing a bit. I shoveled the walk for you

and brushed off your car. You'll have to be careful. It's slick out there."

Ah. That explained the wet hair. It must be from melting snowflakes.

He had gone outside in the cold and snow to take care of her. Warmth seeped through her at the sweetness of the unexpected gesture and she wanted to stand here for a moment and bask in it. She had been self-sufficient for a long time, through college, then medical school and her residency and internship. It felt deliciously addicting to have someone else watching out for her.

"Thank you. That was very kind."

"Compared to everything you've done for me and the kids, it's a tiny thing. But you're welcome."

She paused, feeling awkward suddenly. She was aware she owed him an apology but the words were harder than she might have expected, clogging in her throat like spring runoff through a logjam.

"I'm sorry about pushing you earlier, about your dad," she finally said. "It was rude and intrusive of me and I should never have been so quick to offer an unsolicited opinion. In case you haven't noticed, I like to fix broken things."

To her shock, he laughed, the sound low and rough and unbelievably sexy in the quiet house.

"Good thing you went to medical school, then."

"Yes. Isn't it?"

She smiled back and they shared a comfortable, amused moment. He looked big and dark and gorgeous there in the glow from the small lamp in the foyer and the glistening lights from the Christmas tree and the trailing fairy lights she and his children had wrapped around the banister the other day.

The moment stretched out and shifted to something else, alive with sudden awareness that seemed to sizzle in the air between them.

His smile slid away, leaving his features stark and hungry.

He wanted to kiss her. Cole Barrett, this rough and tumble, ruggedly, overwhelmingly sexy man wanted to kiss *her*.

Devin swallowed, aware of the thud of her pulse, the jittery dance of butterflies in her stomach. Desire was a heavy ache inside her.

She made some sort of sound—a sigh, a breath, his name, she wasn't sure. The next moment, he uttered a curse, stepped forward and lowered his mouth to hers.

CHAPTER ELEVEN

OH, THE MAN knew how to kiss.

His mouth was firm, focused, determined, as if he had a goal to kiss her senseless and wouldn't stop until he reached it.

She wrapped her hands around his neck, savoring the hard muscles against her soft curves, the steady solid strength of him. She never thought she was all that interested in big men. They seemed too *physical* somehow. Intimidating.

Cole, however, seemed to be just right. She felt slight in comparison but not overwhelmed.

He smelled delicious, leather and cedar and pine, and he tasted even better. She wanted more. Either he was amazingly prescient or he wanted the same thing. He made a low, sexy noise in his throat and deepened the kiss, snugging her tightly against him. His body was rock hard against her and her whole body responded accordingly. Everything inside her seemed to melt like gourmet chocolate bits, soft and gooey and warm.

Yes. This was the best idea *ever.*

She wanted it to go on forever, to just forget about everything else she had to do and stay right here in his entryway, being kissed with delicious, single-minded purpose by Cole Barrett.

She might have, if his dog Coco hadn't wandered in to investigate the strange noises they must have been making. The dog brushed against the back of her leg and Devin, not aware she was even there, gave a little gasp.

Cole froze and his eyes popped open. His irises were huge, dilated with heat and passion, and he looked dazed. He blinked as if to clear his mind and she watched reality crash back like that avalanche he'd been talking about earlier.

He pulled away, eyes still drenched with desire. A moment later, that expression was replaced by one of dismay.

"Sorry. I'm sorry. That was out of line."

"It was?" She couldn't seem to catch her breath and she felt stupid, suddenly, her brain numb and her thoughts a wild scramble.

He drew in a ragged breath. "It's been a long while since I've spent this much time in the company of a soft, pretty woman. A *very* long time. I'm afraid I may have…lost my head."

His words seemed to slip through the haze around her, more seductive, even, than his kiss.

She hadn't felt like a soft and pretty woman in forever, maybe not since finishing medical school and starting her residency. Her studies had been everything. All she wanted was to become a doctor, to help others heal as she had been helped.

It wasn't that she never dated. She had even had

one serious boyfriend in college, a fellow premed student she met her sophomore year. They had dated all through her undergraduate studies and had even applied to the same med schools.

He had been brilliant, just as driven as she was. In some small corner of her mind, she thought perhaps the relationship had the potential to get serious eventually, until they were accepted to med schools on opposite sides of the country.

Kyle ended up marrying another woman just six months after they met, while he was still in med school, and they quickly started a family. Some part of her still wondered if that was why they'd drifted apart with distance, because he wanted what he knew she could never give him.

Regardless, somewhere along the way, she had become so focused on her calling as a physician that she had forgotten she was also a woman who sometimes needed quite desperately to feel sweetly feminine.

For that brief, glorious time in Cole's arms, she had been reminded of the heady power in knowing that a man wanted her in the most basic of ways.

She drew in a shaky breath, wanting more than anything to rewind the clock a few moments to relive that magic.

Not a good idea, when one of his children was sick upstairs and the other was still probably awake and could come sneaking down the stairs at any moment.

"Apparently we *both* lost our heads," she finally answered, declining to mention that some giddy, previously unknown part of her didn't mind one bit.

"It won't happen again," he said sternly, almost as if he could read her mind.

That little part of her seemed to sigh with disappointment. "Sure. Of course. It was a mistake, all the way around."

It hadn't *seemed* like a mistake, though. It had seemed bright and wonderful, every Christmas wish she had ever whispered to herself all rolled up in one big, gorgeous package.

"I should probably go." She pointed vaguely toward the door. "I've got to stop by the hospital and check on some patients."

"Right. I'll grab your coat."

She didn't want to think about how relieved he sounded.

"Thank you. I hung it in the hall closet. It's navy blue wool with a knitted scarf."

"I'll find it."

She could find it herself but it seemed pointless to argue. And how stupid of her to describe the coat, as if he wouldn't recognize a coat that didn't usually hang in his closet.

In a moment, he returned with her coat in his hand, the draping, multicolor scarf trailing along. The contrast of such a frilly item in his masculine hands was oddly arousing. She swallowed again and forced herself to focus on the evergreen garland climbing the stairs.

"Thanks," she managed to murmur when he handed over her things.

"You're welcome." He gave a strained sort of smile

and held out the coat to help her into it. Again, she had to hide her shiver at the sensation as the heat of him standing just inches behind her seeped through her. She quickly slipped her arms through the sleeves and tied a knot in the scarf.

He stepped away, shoving his hands into his back pockets. "I hate to sound like a broken record but thank you for all your help, especially with Ty. You probably figured out that I don't have a lot of experience with sick kids."

With his casual stance and tone, she might have thought him completely unaffected by their kiss if not for the little twitch she could see in the muscle along his jaw.

She could pretend, too. She forced a smile as nonchalant as his, even as awareness seemed to writhe and curl around them like smoke. "Good thing I was here, then, when he decided to lose it. I *do* have a lot of experience with sick kids."

"You were great with him. Calm and patient, even when he started to get tetchy there before he went up to bed. I'm not sure I can be that calm."

"You will, with a little more practice. You didn't panic. That's the first step when it comes to dealing with a sick kid, whether he's losing his lunch or running a fever."

"I guess. Regardless, I owe you. Again."

They were both trying very hard to pretend that kiss had never happened, she realized.

She, at least, wasn't succeeding.

"I'm planning to help you tomorrow, right? That

was our agreement. My office schedule got changed around a little but I'm sure my sister could pick the children up after school. They had a good time hanging out at her store and I know she wouldn't mind their company again."

"I don't think I'll need your help tomorrow."

"Are you sure?" she asked, surprised at how disappointed she felt.

"Don't worry. Our agreement will still hold, especially after all your help with Ty tonight. My own schedule is pretty light tomorrow. I don't have any trips out of town, so I'll be here when they return from school—providing Ty is up to going to school, that is."

"I'm not infallible by any means but I think he'll be fine." She paused. "He would hate missing school right now, since he told me earlier today his class is working on a few top secret projects of the Christmas gift variety. Don't tell him I told you, though."

He smiled a little and some of the tension still humming around them started to ease. "That seems to be the order of the week. This morning at breakfast, Jazmyn mentioned something about her class being up to the same thing."

"How fun. I miss those days of being a kid, just about out of my head with excitement for weeks before Christmas. That must be the best part about being a parent, being able to relive that feeling through your kids."

"I hadn't thought about it. This is the first Christmas I've spent with them, ever."

She stared. "Seriously? Didn't you, like, trade off or something with their mother?"

He laughed roughly, without humor. "We weren't quite that civilized."

"You didn't have a divorce decree?"

His features hardened. "Yeah. Which was basically worthless. Sharla ignored the decree and did her own thing. She knew I couldn't win against her in court. She did what she wanted most of the time, letting me have visitation only when it was convenient for her. Turns out, Christmas never was."

Because of his troubles with the law that she still hadn't found the nerve to ask him about? "All the more reason you have to give your kids an amazing holiday, Cole, whatever it takes."

"I'm working on it."

"If you need help—"

"I've got it," he said curtly.

She stiffened, then reminded herself she had no right to feel hurt.

"I'm sure it will be amazing." She gave him another fake-casual smile. "I really do have to go. Unless I bump into you at the rehab center at the hospital while you're visiting with your sister, I suppose I won't see you again until Wednesday."

He gave her a blank look. "Wednesday?"

"That's the day I'm planning to bring my yoga class to soak in your hot spring."

"Oh, right. How could I forget?"

She had to smile at his mock-gloomy look. Or

maybe it was a genuinely gloomy look. Cole was a hard man to read.

"Yes. We'll be here about five. They're all very excited. This morning, Archie Peralta said he was looking for his favorite red Speedo. So that should be fun."

His mouth twitched and she thought for a moment he would smile once more. She found herself waiting for it rather breathlessly but he only tilted his head, an amused light in his eyes that still made her want to sink into his arms again.

"I believe I will find something else to do on the other side of the ranch right around that time."

"Chicken."

"Damn straight. Old guys in Speedos scare the living daylights out of me."

"I'm sure you'll survive," she said, managing a laugh, even though some part of her wanted to be back in his arms. "I really do need to go. I'll see you then."

Despite the kiss and the subsequent awkwardness of it, she was still smiling as she walked down the shoveled sidewalk and climbed into her car, the windshields clear of snow.

The steering wheel was freezing against her bare hands and the car's heater blew out only cold air from the engine that hadn't warmed up as she pulled away from the ranch house and set off down the long, curving drive toward the main road.

She didn't care about the cold slapping at her. She was almost grateful for it. She needed something to jerk her back to the harsh reality that she had made a huge mistake. She shouldn't have kissed him.

Now she would only be left wanting more.

COLE WATCHED DEVIN'S taillights move down the driveway and then disappear as she rounded a curve on her way back to town and her real life.

What the hell had he just done?

That kiss. He closed his eyes, still tasting the sweetness of her on his lips, strawberries and clotted cream and delicious woman.

He had just about lost it back there, had come within a heartbeat of abandoning four years' worth of hard-fought control. Another moment or two and he would have forgotten the kids, the ranch, the vast gulf between him and the lovely doctor. He had wanted her as he had wanted nothing else, ever.

Those first hellish days of detox in jail, he remembered shaking with the hunger for another drink.

This ache inside him for the lovely doctor beat that hunger all to hell.

It would be worse now. So much worse. He couldn't unkiss her now, untouch her. The memory of her trembling mouth, her instant response, was bound to drive him crazy.

More enticing even than her kiss had been the sweetness of having someone to lean on. Knowing that she was here with his kids had completely set his mind at ease as he had run errands in Boise.

They were safe with her, his two precious kiddos—maybe even more safe than with him alone. She, at least, knew what to do about a puking kid, while Cole had been frozen, standing by like an idiot as she dealt with the situation.

At the reminder of Ty, he climbed the stairs and cracked open his son's door. A shaft of moonlight broke through the clouds and burst through the blinds, resting on the boy's face.

Devin was right. His color was better and he seemed to be sleeping calmly. Cole hoped he would be okay in the morning, able to attend school. Seeing either of his kids suffer for any reason hurt his heart.

Ty made a sound and rolled over in his sleep, a lock of hair falling over his forehead.

What a great kid he was. Cole had loved him from the very beginning, this little creature with the big eyes and the huge heart. Sure, he had his suspicions— by then he knew very well about Sharla's frequent infidelities—but he would never let those suspicions grow into anything else. They were only pernicious little gnats of thought that buzzed in his ear once in a while, before he could swat them away.

Ty was his. Cole didn't give a damn about DNA. They had still been married when he was born and Sharla had put his name on the boy's birth certificate. As far as Cole was concerned, that was the only thing that mattered.

His kids were the best thing he had going. His entire purpose revolved around them. They were the reason he was working so hard to bring the ranch back from near bankruptcy, to give them a legacy they could be proud to claim.

He needed to keep that thought in mind and not lose focus—even if that meant subverting this wildly inconvenient attraction to a woman he could never have.

CHAPTER TWELVE

Soaking in Evergreen Springs on a December afternoon was even more amazing than Devin had hoped.

The water was the perfect temperature for it and even after just a few moments, she could feel the tension of her crazy workweek slipping away.

"This is the life, eh?" Archie Peralta beamed at her, just his head and shoulders visible above the water's surface. His thick graying mustache had little crystals of frost in it. Fortunately, he hadn't worn his Speedo but a pair of board shorts with palm trees on them that had looked almost fashionable before he slipped into the water.

"It is, indeed," she answered.

She looked around at her yoga class enjoying the water, each looking at least a decade younger as they soaked. They had all needed this, just a brief respite from their worries and burdens. Archie had been devoted to the care of his wife, stricken with Alzheimer's, until she died a short time ago. Paul Weaver, a retired dairy farmer, had the beginning stages of Parkinson's. Eppie and Hazel Brewer, sisters a year apart who had married twin brothers, both had arthritis.

Each of the other senior citizens in the water coped with similar age-related ailments.

If she didn't know them already and hadn't treated many of them, she never would have guessed. Right now, they were all laughing together, relaxed, happily splashing each other like children on a hot summer day.

Tendrils of mineral-scented steam rose up all around them in wispy columns as they soaked. From what Cole had told her about Evergreen Springs and her study of the history of the local mineral springs, she knew the local waters contained sulfur for skin health, boron for building muscle mass and strengthening bones, magnesium for energy, and potassium, which helped reduce high blood pressure. The sodium level was high in the local waters, which some claimed eased the pain of arthritic symptoms.

In addition to the soothing waters, this particular hot spring was perfectly situated, with a lovely vantage point of Lake Haven and Haven Point. The relaxing view was a form of therapy all its own.

If Cole ever opened it up to the public and charged admission, he could make a mint. She completely understood why he protected it so assiduously, though. Too many people would ruin the secret magic of the place.

She looked over at the smoke coming from the chimney of the humble little hut beside the water and felt a funny ache in her chest again. She had arrived at the ranch not knowing quite what she would find and discovered that not only had Cole plowed the road to the spring but he had also set a fire in the changing hut to warm it for them.

"Iris used to tell me about this place." Sharon Bybee wore a flowered bathing cap as cheerful as her smile on her steel-gray curls. "She was always inviting me to come and have a soak. I can't believe I never took her up on the offer. I could have been enjoying this for years."

"How long can we stay?" Paul asked.

"And when can we come again?" Ronald Brewer, her friend Eppie's usually quiet husband, asked with more enthusiasm than she'd ever heard.

"It's probably not safe to soak too long. I'll have to do a little more research about it but I would say no more than an hour. We'll start climbing out in a few moments. As to when we can come again, Cole has agreed to let us use the springs twice. I'm thinking perhaps next week. Perhaps Monday or Tuesday."

"What about after that?" Hazel asked. "I know *I'm* going to want to come up here again. I haven't felt this relaxed in years. My knee isn't hurting one darn bit. I feel like I could hike to the top of that hill over there."

She had been afraid of this, that giving them all a taste of how good the waters could make them feel might lead them to want things she couldn't promise.

"I'm sorry. Our deal was only for a few visits. I'll see what I can do, but I can't make any other promises."

"Ah, well. At least we got to enjoy it today," Archie said. "You know what they say. Don't be sorry that it ended. Be glad that it happened."

"I bet you have that pinned on a Pinterest board somewhere, don't you?" Edwin Bybee, Sharon's husband, teased.

Archie didn't look at all fazed. "Hey, don't knock it. I get the best recipes there."

"That quinoa you brought to the last social was delicious," Barbara Serrano assured him. "Even if it was quinoa."

Devin listened to their chatter with a smile as she moved her arms back and forth in the water that felt like a warm embrace.

After a few more moments, she gauged it was probably time to start herding them out.

"Looks like the sun is starting to go down. We should probably start working our way out. Ladies first in the dressing hut. You men can soak a few more minutes."

She helped them all out of the water using the stone steps some previous Barrett had created in the water, then along the short path Cole must have shoveled. The cold air was invigorating after the long soak and she had some idea why people in the northern climates loved their saunas and snow-rolling afterward.

When everyone had changed out of their swimming suits and into dry clothes, they headed toward Archie's and Ronald's SUVs.

"Thank you all for coming. I'll see you tomorrow morning for class and let you know about the next time we can soak."

"Yes," Hazel said. "You tell that handsome Cole Barrett when you see him that I'll gladly make him a Dutch apple pie every time he lets us soak. Make sure he knows my pies are famous from here to the Oregon state line."

She smiled. "I'll do that, sweetie. Thanks."

She waited until they started to drive away before she climbed into the big old pickup truck with the plow she had traded in return for medical care with a patient who had six accident-prone children. It had proved a wise decision. Usually she drove her SUV but on snowy mornings, the plow was invaluable for scraping out her own driveway and a few of her neighbors.

Every muscle and joint felt deliciously loose and relaxed as she started up the rumbling engine and headed down the hill toward the ranch house behind the other SUVs.

She needed to talk to Cole about which day would work for their next visit. While she knew it made all the sense in the world to stop now while she was here, she wasn't sure she was ready to see him again. That earthshaking kiss seemed to have been seared into her memory and she couldn't stop thinking about it.

Maybe once she saw him again, she would be able to push it away once and for all. She pulled up in front of the house, anticipation zinging through her, both to see the children again and to see Cole.

To her surprise, Leticia Robles answered the doorbell. As always, she looked graceful and lovely, with her high cheekbones and her salt-and-pepper hair coiled into a roll at the back of her neck.

Every time Devin saw her, she felt an echo of old pain. Letty's husband had been one of her first patients when she finished her internship and returned to the Lake Haven Hospital. She had been working in the emergency department when the ambulance had brought in Mike Robles in full cardiac arrest, with no pulse and no heartbeat. The paramedics had been working without success to resuscitate. She had tried for an hour longer, with every tool at her disposal, until she had finally had to admit defeat and declare him dead.

The professional failure had been devastating, a brutal introduction to small-town medicine, losing the husband of a friend.

Letty had always been kind to her, though, and had never once questioned whether Devin could have done anything differently.

"Letty! Hello."

"Hello, my dear. Come in where it's warm. You look like you just stepped out of the shower."

She gave a wry smile. "We've been up at the hot spring. I did my best to keep my hair dry but the ends got a little damp, anyway. I've been meaning to call you. When did you start?"

"Today, actually."

"And how is it going?"

"It's early days yet, but I know I'm going to like it. It couldn't be more perfect, actually. I'm free most of the day to be with my mom in the nursing home while the children are in school, then I can come here during the afternoon and evenings to help out with a little cleaning and cooking."

Oh, what a relief. The minute McKenzie had

suggested Letty, Devin had thought she would be ideal for Cole and his children.

"And how are you getting along with everybody?"

"Again, early days, but so far so good. They're dears, all of them. Ty is so sweet and kind. Jazmyn is a bit of a character but I love her spunk. And though I would never tell him this, Cole needs as much care as the children."

He would *hate* hearing her say that, but Devin had to agree.

"I think you're all perfect for each other."

"It's been less than a day, but I'm inclined to agree." Letty smiled, looking worlds happier than the last time Devin had seen her. Not only had she lost Mike just a few years earlier but at the end of the summer, her daughter's husband received a job offer in a distant state and they had moved with Letty's only two grandchildren.

Devin suspected her friend would have moved with them despite the extended family she had living in the Lake Haven area if not for her devotion to her mother.

"I need to speak with Cole. Is he around?"

"He's down at the barn. I told him I had to leave at six for my library board meeting, so I'm sure he'll be up by then, if you'd care to wait around."

"I'll just go find him down at the barn," she said, just as a little figure in a Superman cape bounded into the room.

Ty barreled to a stop at the sight of her. "Hi, Dr.

Devin!" He beamed that joyful smile that made her heart feel as if it was going to burst with happiness.

"Hey, buddy." She knelt down and he immediately swooped in and threw his arms around her neck.

"I missed you," he said.

Her heart cracked open a little more. "I missed you, too."

He drew away, crinkling up his nose. "You smell funny."

She laughed and stood up. "I've been soaking in the hot spring. I need to go home and have a good shower now to wash the minerals off."

"We have three showers. You could do it here."

"Thanks for the offer, kiddo. Maybe next time."

"Are you coming back to the hot spring? If you do, can I go with you? I love to swim and I can even hold my breath under the water."

"We'll have to ask your dad. If he doesn't mind, I would love to have you and I know my friends would, too. I'm on my way to talk to him right now and I'll be sure to bring it up."

He beamed with anticipatory delight, then apparently moved on to another subject.

"Mrs. Robles, may I have another cookie? They are *so good*."

Letty smiled, running a hand over the boy's hair. "You may. Just one, though. Otherwise you won't want to eat my delicious chicken curry."

"Ooh. Chicken curry. Yum."

Letty chuckled after the boy as he raced off, then

she turned to Devin. "Would you like me to put some in a container for you to take home? There's plenty."

"Ooh. Chicken curry. Yum," she echoed Ty. "But as delicious as that sounds, I'd better pass. I'm having dinner at Kenzie's place tonight. Ben comes into town again tomorrow to stay through the holidays, which means she'll be a little distracted from now until after Christmas."

Letty smiled. "It warms my heart to see her so happy."

"I know. I never would have thought Ben Kilpatrick would turn out to be the perfect man for her. I guess I'm not as smart as I like to think."

"You were smart enough to know how perfect this setup would be for me." Letty hugged her just as Ty had done. "I'm not stupid, you know. I know you did this as much for me as for them."

"I was hoping everyone would benefit. It's wonderful to know I was right."

She only hoped Letty could stay on for a while, she thought after she said her goodbyes. Tricia would need plenty of help with her babies when she brought them back to the ranch, which might keep the older woman from missing her grandchildren so much.

She decided to drive her pickup truck down to the barn so she could leave more quickly from there to head home and shower before dinner. It was an old, graceful building, steeply gambrel roofed with lean-tos along both sides and painted bright red. Cole obviously took great care of the building. The white trim around the doors sparkled in the fading sunlight.

As she parked the truck and headed for the door, her stomach fluttered with nervous anticipation. This was ridiculous, she told herself sternly. So she had kissed the man. What was the big deal? Just because she hadn't been able to sleep for days without crazy, lust-fueled dreams didn't mean she couldn't have a normal, civilized conversation with the man.

What was the etiquette at a barn? she wondered. Should she knock? That seemed silly, for some reason. After dithering for a moment, she finally simply pulled open a small side door. The place was huge inside and smelled of fresh hay, leather and horses.

She opened her mouth to call out a greeting but heard someone singing along in a surprisingly good baritone at the far end of the barn to a country music version of Nat King Cole's song about chestnuts and open fires playing on a radio.

Who would have guessed the man had such a good voice? And that he sang to himself when he thought he was alone? She found it unexpected and charming and couldn't do anything but follow the sound.

When she reached the stall where he was working, she found him brushing down a beautiful roan mare, who seemed to be enjoying his impromptu concert along with the attention.

Devin wanted to lean over the railing of the stall and just listen to him—okay, and watch, too, if she were honest—but that would be rude and voyeuristic of her. Right?

She cleared her throat and he immediately dropped

the brush he was using on the horse and whirled around.

"Sorry!" she said. "I should have knocked or something."

Color rose over his cheeks. "You just startled me, that's all."

"Didn't you think there might be a chance I would want to stop by to say thanks?"

"I didn't expect you to spy on me serenading my horse."

"I only heard the part about children finding it hard to sleep tonight." She smiled. "You have a great voice, Cole. You could have been a country music star yourself."

She didn't add that he had the hot, dangerous cowboy thing down without even trying. The women would have gone crazy over him.

He snorted. "Think I'll stick to training horses, thanks. Anyway, you didn't have to thank me for anything. We had a bargain."

"You agreed to let my yoga class use your hot spring a few times. I never expected you to plow the road up to the hot spring or clear a path to the water or warm the changing hut with a cheerful fire."

"It was no big deal." He pulled his phone out of his pocket and tapped the screen a few times. He must have been streaming to a speaker as the music turned off instantly.

"It was a very big deal to me," she said softly. He looked up and for a moment, their gazes met.

The memory of that kiss suddenly seemed to

spring to life between them. She caught her breath, remembering the taste of him, his silky hair beneath her fingers, the intoxicating feeling of being protected and safe in his arms.

In an instant, the barn seemed to become a secret, intimate place, alive with the rustle of hay, the creak of the old building shifting, a horse stamping somewhere down the line of stalls.

What would he do if she found an empty stall, dragged him to it and tugged him down into the hay?

She pushed away the crazy impulse. She hadn't come down here to relive a few moments between them that never should have happened. She was here only to thank him for his kind gestures and to talk to him about the next time her yoga class would use his hot spring again.

"I mean it, Cole. Thank you for everything. When I saw the smoke coming out of the chimney of the warming hut, I was so touched, I almost burst into tears right there at the hot spring in front of everyone."

AS LONG AS she stayed on that side of the wall around the stall, Cole figured he was safe.

He could do his best to ignore the damp hair curling in tendrils around her face and her soft skin, rosy from the cool air. "It was no big deal," he said, "especially compared with everything you've done to help my kids. All that food, decorating the tree, helping with the kids when I had to run to Boise. I only wanted to repay my huge debt a little."

"You made a good start today, cowboy." A shaft

of sunlight burst through the dusty row of windows high above them, slanting down to turn her hair copper and gold.

He wasn't safe, no matter how many walls he kept between them. He hadn't been safe since he walked into that emergency department with his baby sister and saw her walking toward them looking calm and competent and beautiful.

"I still have a ways to go."

"Then you won't mind if we come back, will you? I was thinking Monday afternoon. Would that work?"

He scanned through his mental calendar. He had a new horse coming in that morning but he should still have time to clear the road up to the hot spring for her. "That should work."

"Thanks."

That shaft of sunlight reflected gold against the back wall of the barn and caught her attention. She turned and looked at what he considered his wall of shame and he watched her eyes go wide.

"Wow. That's some fancy rodeo bling you've got there."

Every belt buckle, trophy or saddle he'd ever won hung on the back wall. She moved toward it for a closer look and spent several moments gazing at the display.

More embarrassed than he'd been even when she caught him singing, he left the stall and walked toward her, compelled to explain himself. "You're probably thinking, what sort of arrogant SOB hangs up all his own awards so he can look at them every day."

She sent him a sideways look. "Oh, is that what I was thinking? Funny, I thought I was being quite impressed at the skill and effort that must have gone into earning all this."

He sighed. "If I had my way, I would have hauled them out to the landfill a long time ago, but they make a good conversation starter with clients."

"Do they?"

"They seem to think this all means the person they're trusting their horse to knows a thing or two. It's only for business. Like I said, I'd like to toss it all in the trash."

She frowned. "You're not a little proud of what must have been years' worth of accomplishments? I would think you'd get the same charge from looking at your trophies and things as I do whenever I catch sight of my medical school diploma—which, for the record, I hang proudly on the wall of my office for all to see. I don't think that makes me an arrogant SOB, either."

It was another reminder of the glaring chasm between them. She had graduated medical school, while he barely made it through two years of college on a college rodeo scholarship before he quit to compete on the professional circuit.

What the hell had he been thinking to kiss her the other night? She saved lives, while he could barely manage to keep his own together.

She was looking at him with far more admiration than he deserved. While some part of him wanted to bask in it, he knew that wouldn't be fair, not when the reality was stark and ugly.

He gazed at a saddle he'd won for the all-around at some Montana event he guessed he must have competed in nine years ago. Case in point, right there. He had no clear memory of the competition, the horses he rode or why he'd placed so high in those particular events.

"I might have been more proud of what I accomplished on the circuit," he said gruffly, not looking at her, "if I remembered half of it. Truth is, I was a drunk ass most of the time."

The words seemed to seethe between them, harsh and ugly. She said nothing for a long moment, the silence broken only by the new green broke quarter horse he was set to start working with.

Finally he had to look at her, expecting revulsion. Instead, she was gazing at him with soft, steady compassion.

He wanted to lean into it, into her, and let her calm comfort wash over him. No. It didn't belong there. Why would she be compassionate for someone who had made his own choices and suffered the consequences for it?

He hadn't been making a joke. He had been the worst kind of selfish bastard, and it suddenly seemed fiercely important that she realize that.

"I shouldn't be here at all," he answered. "It's some kind of damn miracle that I wasn't killed somewhere along the line, either from some jealous boyfriend out for revenge or from breaking my neck falling off a horse because I had no business being up there while I was drunk off my ass. I was reckless and unbelievably stupid in my twenties. While you were throwing yourself into medical school, preparing yourself for a life of taking care of other people, I was playing hard and beating my body and my soul into the ground, without a single thought to who I might hurt along the way. I don't deserve any of this."

She was silent again, and then she nudged her shoulder against his, just for a moment, a gesture of such support and compassion that he felt emotions choke his throat.

Too soon, she eased away. "You could look at it that way," she said softly, "or you could hang your awards with honor and be proud that you've moved past that man you were and the mistakes he made and are now trying to make something different out of your life. You're working hard to make this ranch a success, you're helping your sister and her twins, you're trying to do your best for your children. That speaks to me of courage and strength and character."

Oh, it would be tempting to let himself believe the nice little picture she painted of him. He wanted to be that man, someone good and decent, but his gnarled past still wrapped around him like some kind of parasitic vine, choking the life out of him.

He couldn't let her go on having this rosy image. He had to tell her the truth, even though the words tasted as sour as turned milk.

"I told you I had to go to Boise the other day to pick up some parts. That was partially true, but I had

another appointment there, too. With my parole officer, which I have to do on a regular basis. I'm an ex-
con, Doc. I served almost two years in prison, hard
time, for assault with intent."

He gazed at her, waiting for the shock and disgust
he fully deserved. This was where she would run
screaming out of the barn and stay far away from
him and his kids.

Instead, he was the one shocked when she only
gave a calm nod.

"I know," she said.

He stared. "That's bull! You didn't know."

She made a rueful face. "Okay, technically you're
right. I didn't *know*-know. Not details, anyway. I'd
heard the rumors only—that you'd had trouble with
the law—but they came from a pretty reliable source.
McKenzie heard it from one of our friends who is on
the Haven Point police department. McKenzie didn't
know any specifics—she was just trying to warn me
off."

The idea of her sister and her friends talking about
him to her was more than a little unsettling. "Why
would your sister think you needed warning off?"

Her cheeks looked suddenly pink in the dim
patches of sunlight coming in through the high windows. "She, um, knew I had been spending a little
time here at Evergreen Springs helping out. The day
I brought the kids to her store, she took me aside and
told me you had a mysterious past. She wasn't gos-
siping. She was just being her overprotective self."

As she should be. He wasn't the sort of man he would want *his* sister hanging around, even when she was only helping him out of a tight spot.

"Isn't she your younger sister, though?" he asked. "I thought that ball usually rolled downhill."

Her color rose a little higher. "Usually. Kenz worries about me far more than she should. But we were discussing your prison time. Assault with intent. It must have been serious if you served time for it. What happened?"

He might be a dumb cowboy but he didn't miss the way she quickly changed the subject away from her sister. Something was up there, some mystery he had yet to figure out about Dr. Devin Shaw.

As much as he would have liked to turn the attention back to her and ask what she was hiding, he knew that would be the coward's way out. She wanted to know what he had done and he couldn't see any way to avoid telling her, straight up.

What a damn mess he had made of his life. Regret made a pretty miserable companion, especially when it followed him everywhere.

"It was a bar fight with another rodeo cowboy, somebody who outrode me in the arena earlier in the evening and took the purse. It was a big one, with a lot of qualifying points for the big dance in Las Vegas. The NFR, the pro-rodeo finals. We happened to hit the same shit-hole bar afterward and had words over a couple of drinks. The words turned into fists and the altercation spilled out into the parking lot. The prosecution said the whole thing was premeditated, said I purposely led him to my pickup truck, where I had a tire iron ready in the bed. Didn't matter that he started the fight or used a broken bottle to give me this."

He pointed to the jagged two-inch scar on the side of his head where the cut had nearly sliced off his ear.

"Because of those fifteen minutes out of my life, Rowdy Barnes had to quit the circuit. He had a broken arm, broken jaw and permanently lost sight out of his right eye."

"Was it premeditated?" she asked in a level voice.

He shrugged. As far as he was concerned, this was the worst part. "I don't know. Maybe. I was drunk off my ass. I don't remember anything past the fifth whiskey that night. All the jury cared about was that he outrode me earlier in the arena and that he'd slept with my wife, which gave me ample motive, apparently, to take him out."

Not that Rowdy Barnes had been the only one to sleep with Sharla. By the time Rowdy and Sharla hooked up, Cole had been past caring about anything his wife did. Their marriage had been over, but even then, he hadn't been man enough to stop drinking so he could take care of his kids.

His arrest had done more to sober him up and drive home what he was doing to his life and the people left in it who somehow still loved him than a year in rehab ever could have done.

He had tried to make things right. He paid restitution, he had gone to rehab in jail awaiting his trial and sentencing, and then served his time and returned to Evergreen Springs a changed man.

No matter how hard he tried, though, he couldn't change his past. It was like a huge, disgusting stain on a favorite shirt. He could wash it and wash it but some shadow still remained to remind him of all he had done.

"I'm an ex-con, alcoholic, washed-up rodeo cowboy and failure of a father. Your sister was right to warn you off, Doc."

She studied him, her green eyes unreadable in the patchy, dusty sunbeams. "That's a very impressive résumé. One that paints a grim picture of the man you *used* to be. But isn't what really matters who you are now?"

"What if I can't answer that yet? What if I'm still trying to figure it out?"

"I guess that makes you no different from the rest of us, then."

She had a way about her, a calm comforting sense of peace he found even more appealing than that sexy mouth and the green eyes that reminded him of brand-new aspen leaves.

The kiss they had shared hadn't been far from his thoughts since the other day. Now it seemed to blow up in his memory as if it had only just happened. He remembered each sigh, each whisper of breath, each taste and sensation.

He wanted to reach for her again, so badly he had

to shove suddenly trembling hands into the pockets of his jeans.

He meant what he said. He didn't know who he was yet. He was trying to be a good father, a caring brother, an honest, hardworking rancher. Did he have moments when he wanted a drink so badly he shook with it? Hell, yeah. But he wanted to be a decent man more—the kind of man who might one day be worthy of someone like Devin Shaw.

Because he couldn't have *her*—and because he was starting to realize every moment he spent with her that he wanted her desperately—he spoke with a little more bite than he would have otherwise.

"What do you have to figure out? Seems to me you're living the life, aren't you? A young, beautiful, well-respected doctor with a busy practice. You've got it together."

"I wish that were true, but everybody's got stuff, Cole. Some of it might not be as obvious as a prison stint on your permanent record but nobody gets to walk through this world on a trail littered with rose petals. Thorny bushes, deep ravines, jagged glass. Everybody faces something."

"What about you?" he was compelled to ask. "What have you faced?"

She was quiet for a long moment, and he saw something flicker there, something dark and sad that made his chest ache.

"Medical school," she finally answered. "It just about killed me."

She said the words with a casualness that told him instantly she was covering up for something else. What had happened in her past to put those shadows there? Why was her sister so protective of her?

He had spilled his dark secret and had to admit it was like a little sharp spur rowel spinning in his chest to realize she wasn't willing to do the same.

She suddenly looked at her watch. "It's later than I thought. I need to go. I'm meeting my sister for dinner. Oh, and Letty mentioned she'll be leaving at six."

"Right. I should head up to the house."

"How is she working out, by the way?"

"Great. She seems ideal. I just hope Jazmyn and Ty don't scare her away."

"She's a tough cookie. Don't worry. I think she's more than a match for the two of them."

"Well, thanks for facilitating it."

"You're welcome. And thanks again for making it easy for me to take my group to the hot spring. Everyone was so impressed. I think Eppie and Hazel Brewer would like to move in. What an amazing place, a mineral spring that not only is the perfect temperature but also comes along with a stunning view."

"It's really magical at night. You ought to come out sometime after dark."

He regretted the offer as soon as he made it. Suddenly he could picture her sliding into the water, all lithe and curvy and sensuous. His body stirred even more, especially as he imagined being wrapped around her there, the stars thick and bright above them, the warm water and steam swirling and writhing around them as he lowered his mouth to hers, as he surged inside her.

"Oh," she breathed. "That would be amazing."

He almost groaned aloud but managed to focus on opening the door for her.

"I guess I'll have to be content for now to come back on Monday afternoon. That's the day that works best for my yoga group. Is that okay with you?"

After what he told her, it would be better for both of them if she just climbed into that pickup and kept on driving but he had made a deal with her and hadn't yet paid his side of the ledger.

"Yeah. That should be fine. I'll have the warming hut ready."

She smiled and out in the fading sunlight, she was breathtaking. "Thank you. Oh, by the way, Ty wants to come and soak with us next time. Would you mind if I pick up him and Jaz on our way up? I'll keep a close eye on them, don't worry."

"You don't need a couple of kids underfoot. Sounds like you have your hands full with the older set."

"They would love having Ty and Jaz come, I promise. It would be like having a dozen grandparents, all watching out for them."

He supposed it wouldn't hurt his kids to spend a little time with some friendly senior citizens, especially since his kids had been screwed in the grandparent department. The only two they had were Sharla's piece-of-work mother and Stan.

"I suppose it would be okay."

"Perfect. I'll talk to Letty and make the arrangements."

She smiled and with a wave, she climbed into her pickup truck. He watched her drive away for only a moment before he forced himself to turn and walk up to the house.

CHAPTER THIRTEEN

"I KNOW YOU'RE going crazy in here," Devin said to Tricia Hollister a few days later, "but it would be optimal for the twins if you can hold on another week."

Tricia groaned. "I'm doing all I can in that department. I'm only getting up to go to the bathroom, even when I'm going out of my head with boredom. The problem is, I don't think it's necessarily up to me."

"Not completely." Devin squeezed Tricia's fingers. "Those twins have minds of their own and will come when they decide to come. You're doing great, though. Dr. Randall was just talking to me about how pleased he is with the progress. The twins have grown so much this week, though they're still a little on the small side. You must not be eating enough ice cream to fatten them up," she teased.

Tricia gestured to a clear box on a nearby shelf. "I feel like I'm doing nothing but eat. I can't believe all the goodies McKenzie and the rest of your friends have been bringing by. And not just cookies and granola bars."

She pointed to a little Christmas tree on a table by the window decorated with hand-knitted striped baby booties and little knitted caps in blue and pink.

"Oh, that's darling. Who brought that?"

"Barbara Serrano, of all people. I think I've met her only three or four times in my life. She said a whole group of people pitched in to make all the decorations."

"Nice. And it looks like you have some of Anna-lise Larsen's famous sponge cake. Lucky."

Tricia smiled, then with the rapid-fire emotions pregnancy could bring, her mood shifted and she looked as if she were on the verge of tears. "Why is everyone here being so kind to me? I don't even know these people anymore."

She smiled and squeezed Tricia's hand. "You still have friends here. You always will. Anyway, Haven Point is a nice place. People here want to help when they see someone in need."

"Am I in need?"

"You're pregnant with twins and here by your-self, except for Cole and the children—and you're stuck in this hospital, day after day. I would say that qualifies you."

"I don't know what to think," Tricia said. "I have at least two or three visitors every day, people I barely knew even when I lived here, whom I haven't spoken with in years. I know you're sending them to keep me company so I won't feel so alone, Devin. Don't try to pretend you're not."

"I wish I could take credit but that was McKenzie's idea. I'm good at recognizing problems—she's better at solving them. I mentioned you were stranded in a hospital in a town that hasn't been your home in many

years, away from any support network you might have
had in California. I thought you might be bored."

Tricia pointed to a stack of colorful material folded
up in the corner. "McKenzie apparently agreed. She
brought all these pieces of fleece for me to edge and
tie. Apparently they are blankets to be sold at a booth
at tonight's Lights on the Lake Festival. I must have
made a dozen of them over the last few days."

Devin marveled all over again at her sister's wisdom. The core human emotional needs were basic:
to feel loved and to feel needed. By sending visitors
to Tricia's bedside and giving her projects to help her
keep her hands and mind occupied, McKenzie was
filling both those needs.

She had often thought that McKenzie's difficult
childhood—losing her beloved mother to illness and
then being thrust into the lives of a father who hadn't
known she existed *and* his less-than-welcoming
wife—had turned her sister into a woman of extra-
ordinary compassion.

It was one of the many reasons she adored her sister and, more, was infinitely proud and honored to
have her as her friend.

"Those look fantastic. I especially love the one
with the *Frozen* characters. Is somebody coming to
pick them up for the sale tonight?"

"Yes. Eliza Caine." Tricia seemed guarded suddenly. "She called just before you showed up and said
she would be here within the hour."

"Oh, have you met her? Eliza's a sweetheart. And
her little girl, Maddie—totally adorable. You'll love

both of them, I promise. You won't meet anyone kinder."

Tricia shifted on the bed, looking suddenly uncomfortable. "I have met her, actually, this summer at a Caine Tech function, just prior to her marriage to Aidan. She seemed very nice."

Devin frowned, trying to make sense of that. After a moment, Tricia sighed. "Sean works for Aidan Caine in California. He's a vice president over project management."

Devin stared. "Seriously? I had no idea your husband worked for Aidan."

"Yes. He's been at Caine Tech for years. I know Ben and Aidan well."

"What a small world," Devin exclaimed.

"Not really. I knew Ben from high school and he hired me after college to work in the Caine Tech human resources department. That's where I first met S-Sean."

Her voice broke on the name and Tricia suddenly burst into noisy tears. Those darn pregnancy hormones left every emotion close to the surface—or at least that's what Devin had heard. She had no first-hand experience and never would.

"I miss him so much. I want to call him a hundred times but I just... I can't."

Devin handed her a tissue from the box by her bed. "Would you like me to call him? I'm asking as your friend, not as one of your physicians. You need all the support you can find right now."

"N-no," Tricia answered. She sniffled a few more

times, then seemed to regain control over her errant emotions. "He doesn't want the children. He made that plain. He doesn't want them and because I do, he doesn't want me. It's as simple as that, even though it breaks my heart. You and Dr. Randall said I should avoid stress as much as possible. Having Sean here, knowing he doesn't want to be here, would be the biggest stressor I can imagine. I don't want him to know."

Devin frowned, struck by a sudden realization. "He works for Caine Tech. Eliza is coming here within the hour. Aren't you afraid word that you're in the hospital might trickle down to him through Aidan and Eliza?"

"I thought of that. I had to tell Eliza the situation between Sean and me is complicated right now. I asked her not to say anything. She doesn't like it but she agreed. I'm not sure she's even told Aidan she's coming here."

Devin didn't necessarily agree with all the secrecy, but she had to remind herself it wasn't her business. In one thing, Tricia was right. Emotional upheaval wouldn't be good for her *or* her children. If she thought keeping the baby's father away was in their best interest, Devin couldn't argue with her.

"Enough about Sean. I don't want to talk about him anymore," Tricia said firmly, wiping at her eyes with the tissue as if she could blot away the tangled stress of her marriage. "I understand from Ty and Jazmyn that you brought some friends out to soak in the mineral spring the other day."

"Oh. My. Word. It's amazing." All of Devin's muscles seemed to relax simply remembering the healing waters.

"I know, right? Going up there to soak was always my favorite part about coming back to the ranch to see my grandmother after I moved out. I wasn't sure how safe it was with the pregnancy so I haven't gone to soak since I've been home. My aching back could really use it right now. You should go there sometime at night, when the stars are thick overhead and you feel like you're the only person in the world. It's like nowhere else on earth."

"Cole said almost the exact same thing!"

Tricia raised an eyebrow. "Did he? I'm shocked he told you about the hot spring. He's not the most talkative cowboy, in case you didn't notice."

To her dismay, she felt herself blush for reasons she couldn't have begun to explain—though if she had to guess, it probably had something to do with that stunning kiss she couldn't get out of her head.

Or perhaps because Cole *had* talked to her, about his past and his regrets, other things she couldn't seem to stop thinking about.

"He didn't really tell me about the hot spring. I sort of stumbled onto it when we were looking for a Christmas tree, and then I bribed him into letting me bring a few friends up there."

"Bribed him, how?" Tricia asked with interest. "My brother rarely does anything he doesn't want to do."

Devin started to answer but the door to Tricia's

hospital room burst open before she could and a familiar young man galloped inside.

"Hi, Aunt Tricia," Ty said with his cheerful little smile. "Jaz and me were having a race and I won."

Jaz rushed inside breathing hard, in time to hear those words. "Because you cheated! I didn't say *go* yet and you went, anyway. It doesn't count. You didn't win. Hi, Aunt Tricia. Hi, Devin."

"Hello to both of you," her aunt said while Devin's heartbeat kicked up a notch. If the children were here, their father couldn't be far behind. She hadn't seen him since that day in the warm, hay-scented barn, and her insides suddenly shivered with mingled anticipation and nerves.

"I'm so happy to see you!" Tricia said to the children. "How on earth did you both know I needed a hug today?"

Ty giggled and immediately complied, leaning over the side of the bed to wrap his arms around his very pregnant aunt. Jazmyn was a little slower to comply but hugged her, too, before stepping away.

"Did you have your babies yet?" Ty asked, apparently oblivious to the huge belly he had just hugged.

"Not yet," Tricia answered ruefully. "Still waiting."

"I hope it's soon. I want to play with them."

"You can't play with brand-new babies," Jaz informed him in her know-it-all tone. "All they do is cry for a long time. That's all *you* did, anyway."

Again, since they were only a few years apart, Devin highly doubted Jazmyn had any memory of her brother's early days but she decided not to bring up that little detail, especially when Cole came through the doors an instant later. He wore jeans and a suede jacket as well as boots and a cowboy hat.

The nerves in her stomach suddenly seemed to cartwheel around like children on a grassy slope on a summer day.

She didn't miss the almost comical double take he did when he spotted Devin beside his sister's bed. "Oh. You have company."

"I'm not sure I qualify as *company*, exactly." Devin was quick to hold up her stethoscope. "I've been poking and prodding."

"And?"

"Everybody's doing fine," Tricia answered. "Devin wants me to cook the babies in here for another week or so if I can manage it."

Ty's eyes widened into an expression of alarm. "Cook them? Won't they get hot?"

"Figure of speech, kiddo," Devin assured him. "The babies are still a little on the small side, especially because there are two of them in there. They will be much more healthy if they stay where they are for now, to give them a little more time to get bigger."

He seemed satisfied with that answer and quickly moved on to another subject.

"Guess what, Aunt Tricia? When we were driving here, we saw a big sign for a boat parade tonight. On the lake! Dad says maybe we can go."

"Did I?" Cole drawled.

"You didn't say we *couldn't* go," Jazmyn pointed out with an unerring logic that made Devin laugh.

Cole's gaze momentarily landed on her and something hot and hungry flared there for a moment before he quickly looked away—not before her pulse jumped as if she had tachycardia.

"As I recall, I didn't say a word when you badgered me about it all the way here."

"Well, can we go? It's a parade! On the lake!" Jazmyn exclaimed.

"With boats," Ty added, just in case his father had missed that salient point.

"You really should take them." Devin obligingly added her voice to the chorus. "The Lights on the Lake Festival is one of the highlights of the year around here. You've been before, haven't you?"

He shook his head. "No. I'm afraid not."

"It's really fun. After the boat procession on the water, there's a wonderful fair along the lakeshore with food and shopping and music. The proceeds from everything go to benefit either the local food bank or the literacy program at the library."

"It's December in Idaho," Tricia exclaimed. "Whose crazy idea was it to have a boat festival in Haven Point in December? I'm amazed the lake isn't frozen."

"It never freezes all the way across, only along the shoreline, and that's usually not for another two or three weeks. The festival never feels cold, anyway. Everyone bundles up and we have barrel drum fires and outdoor propane heaters set around for warmth. It's a fun party."

"Are you going?" Jazmyn asked.

"Absolutely." She smiled at the girl. "I love the

Lights on the Lake Festival. It's one of my favorite things about the whole holiday season."

"You should all go together," Tricia suggested.

Devin almost fell over. Where had *that* come from? She sent Tricia a startled look. She wasn't sure she liked that mischievous glint in her friend's eyes as she gazed between Devin and Cole. Could she sense the tension simmering between the two of them? No. That was ridiculous.

But why else would she have made the suggestion that Devin spend more time with her brother and his children?

"Yay! I want to see the parade with you, Devin!" Ty said, slipping his little hand into hers and gazing up at her with those big, long-lashed dark eyes that slayed her every time.

"That would be *so fun*!" Jazmyn added her voice to the chorus. "You can come with us to the parade!"

"I'm sure Dr. Shaw already has plans for the evening," Cole said firmly.

"I am supposed to meet up with my sister and her fiancé," she admitted. "But to be honest, as much as I love them both, I wouldn't mind not having to be the third wheel there."

"There. That settles it," Tricia said. She shifted her bulk on the bed to a more comfortable position. "You can all go to the festival together and then come back tomorrow and tell me all about it.

"Yay!" Ty and Jazmyn both exclaimed at the same time. Their father, Devin noted, didn't look nearly as enthusiastic, but she had to give him credit for not trying to wriggle out of the plans his sister was making for him.

"What time does it start?" he asked.

"The parade usually begins at twilight, about six-thirty. I'll see if McKenzie can score us some good seats. The mayor usually has a few extra spots in the VIP section."

"This is the sister you didn't want to sit with so you wouldn't be stuck as a third wheel," Cole said drily.

"That's the one. I won't be the third wheel if I'm with all of you," she pointed out.

He gave a rough laugh, which had his sister's eyes widening with surprise and renewed speculation.

"We can pick you up," Cole said. "Should we say six?"

"Perfect. That will give me time to go home and grab my wool socks and coziest boots. The only part of me that ever gets cold at the Lights on the Lake Festival are my toes."

"Got it," he answered. "Warm boots all around."

She smiled when the voice communication badge she wore around her neck alerted her to an incoming message.

"Dr. Devin Shaw. Can you take a call from...Dr. Russell Warrick."

"Yes. In one minute," she answered the automated voice, then turned to Tricia and her family.

"I'm sorry. I need to take this. It's my partner." He was also her sister's future father-in-law, but that was a complicated situation she didn't need to explain right now.

"Of course," Cole said.

To her delight, the adorable Ty hugged her around the waist, which was as high as he could reach. "Bye, Dr. Devin."

She hugged him back as sneaky little tendrils of emotion seemed to curl around her heart and tug hard. "Bye, honey. I'll see you again in a few hours."

Not to be outdone by her brother, of course, Jazmyn swooped in for a hug, too.

She smiled and returned the embrace before stepping away and squeezing Tricia's arm. "Hang in there, okay? I'll check back with you tomorrow."

"You do that. I want to hear all about the parade."

"You got it. I'll see the rest of you tonight," she said, waving to the room in general.

As she left to take her call from Russ, she was aware of a heady excitement zinging through her veins and realized she was looking forward to the Haven Point Lights on the Lake Festival more than she had anything else in a very long time.

CHAPTER FOURTEEN

THIS WASN'T A DATE and everybody had damn well better remember that.

Especially him.

Cole glowered as he pulled his pickup into Devin Shaw's tidy driveway. She lived in a much bigger home than he would have expected for one person, a two-story cedar and rock house that seemed to fit in nicely with the surrounding pine and fir around the lakeshore.

"Wow. Devin lives right on the lake," Jazmyn said from the back row of the crew cab, gazing at the house with admiration.

"She could go fishing right from her backyard!" Ty exclaimed.

"Probably," Cole answered with a little smile. He and Ty had been talking about going fishing in the spring and it had become a bit of an obsession for the boy.

"Why don't *we* live on the lake?" Jazmyn asked.

He sighed, wondering if she would ever be happy with her lot in life and how he could help her see she had it pretty good right now, despite the fumbling efforts of her father.

A few months ago, she was traipsing from crappy apartment to dingy trailer home with her mother and whatever dude Sharla was currently hooking up with. Now Jaz had a safe, secure home with her own bedroom in a lovely Rocky Mountains setting—yet she still wanted something different.

"We live on a ranch with horses and cows," he explained. "They take up a lot of room, which I'm afraid you can't find down here by the lake."

Seeing this elegant house, with its gleaming windows and the sunroom on the lake side, seemed another glaring reminder that he and Dr. Devin Shaw were total opposites. They lived in different worlds. He was a rancher with manure on his boots more often than not; she was a physician who lived in a beautiful sprawling home on the lake.

The differences ran much deeper than that, of course. Her life was one of purpose and meaning, of helping to save lives. She had things figured out, while he was barely hanging on.

She wasn't for him. Somehow they seemed to have developed a friendship of sorts, but that's all it would ever be. He needed to keep that thought firmly in mind throughout this evening—that wasn't a damn date!—and keep his hands to himself.

"Do you think she can go swimming, too, right from her backyard?" Ty asked in a breathless sort of voice.

"Don't know why not."

"Wow! She's lucky!" He sounded as if that concept was the most amazing thing he could imagine.

"It would be too cold now, though, right, Dad?" Jazmyn said. "The lake would be *freezing*. Not like our hot spring."

Our hot spring. It was the first time his daughter had ever claimed ownership of anything to do with the ranch. She had always acted as if her stay was completely temporary, as if her grandmother Trixie was going to swoop in any moment and take her away from the misery of living with him.

His heart gave a little tug and he decided to take that as an encouraging sign.

He cleared his throat. "Right. Our hot spring is a much more comfortable temperature. Even in July, that lake is *cold*, but it's still fun. We'll have to go this summer."

"Okay," Jazmyn said. "Maybe we can come swimming at Devin's house."

"You and Devin can go swimming and Dad and me will go fishing," Ty suggested.

He didn't have the heart to tell either of his children that by the time summer rolled around, Devin might have forgotten all about the rancher and his children she had taken pity on and helped out during the holidays.

This wasn't a date, he reminded himself yet again, even though it felt suspiciously like one as he climbed out of his pickup truck and headed up the walk.

She opened the door before he reached it. "I saw your headlights. Yes, I've been anxiously waiting by the door for you. I told you, I adore the Lights on the Lake Festival."

She was all bundled up, he saw, in a baby blue parka, a wool hat with a pom-pom on top and matching gloves and scarf, and she had several blankets over her arm as well as a backpack.

"What can I carry?" he asked. She handed over the blankets, which were still warm from her body heat.

"Isn't it a glorious night?" she asked as they walked to the pickup truck. "We couldn't have asked for better weather. Not too cold, not too snowy. Ideal boat parade weather."

"Seems to me, ideal boat parade weather would be in the middle of July."

She laughed. "Good point. You're right. I guess we're all a little crazy to find this so fun."

He opened the door of the pickup and set the blankets in back by the kids, then gripped her elbow to help her up. She smelled delicious, he couldn't help noticing, of flowers and strawberries and vanilla ice cream.

"Hi, guys," she said to the kids in the backseat.

He heard them greet her with enthusiasm before he closed her door and walked around to the other side, reminding himself firmly one last time that this wasn't a date. They were friends. That's all.

"I like your house," Jazmyn announced from the backseat as he climbed in.

"Thanks," Devin said. "I like it, too. I should, I guess. I've lived in it most of my life, except when I was away at school."

Cole glanced over. "Really? That's your childhood home?"

She looked a little embarrassed in the stretched-out late-afternoon light. "Yes. I bought out my mother's and McKenzie's shares after my father died a few years ago. It was a good investment. Real estate around the lakeshore continues to climb in value as more people discover the area. Besides that, I like the style of the house. Yeah, it's more than one person needs, but it works for me."

"Do you have a dog?" Ty asked.

"No. I'm afraid not. I'm pretty busy. It wouldn't be very fair to leave a dog alone all the time. Instead, I've got a couple of cats who do a very good job of keeping each other company."

"I like cats, too," Jazmyn said. "I've always wanted to have one of my very own."

Something else he didn't know about his daughter. Apparently she still had untapped dimensions she hadn't shared with him. He knew she liked playing with the barn cats but she'd never said a word about wishing she had one of her own.

"I like cats, I guess," Ty said. "But I like dogs better. They play more and they're funny. Grandpa's dog, Buster, is *so* cute. When we throw a ball for him, he catches it and brings it right back and he's just a puppy!"

"Ty!" Jazmyn said the name as a warning. When he glanced in the rearview mirror, Cole saw she looked panic-stricken.

"What?" her brother asked.

"You're not supposed to say that, remember?"

"Say what?"

As they were stopped at a stop sign, Cole continued gazing in the rearview mirror. He saw confusion and then nervous guilt cross his son's features as he looked at the back of his father's head. "Oh."

Fury growled through him, the impotent anger he always experienced when his father's name came up. Damn Stan anyway for coming back and making everything that much harder.

"When did you play with your grandfather and his dog?" Cole was pleased to hear his voice sounded calm and reasonable. He might be livid at his father but the children didn't need the trickle-down from that.

Jazmyn waited a beat before answering. "Yesterday," she said, her voice small. "When we walked up to the house from the bus stop, Buster was playing outside in the snow and he—Grandpa—was watching. Buster came right over to us and he was so cute and we played fetch for just a minute, then I remembered we weren't supposed to talk to our grandpa," she finished in a rush.

"Only, I don't know why," Ty said. "He's nice. And so is Buster."

The puppy might be nice but his father certainly wasn't—or at least the version of him Cole had known. Maybe Stanford was trying to reinvent himself as some kindly old man who had a puppy and wanted a relationship with his grandchildren, but Cole wasn't buying it. His father was self-absorbed and egotistical and only cared about his own momentary pleasures.

"Why are you so mad at him?" Jaz pressed when he said nothing.

"Did you have a big fight?" Ty asked.

Cole glanced across the truck cab at Devin and saw her watching him with curiosity on her lovely, serene features. He didn't know what to say, to any of them. He hated when adults flaked off kids' questions by telling them a situation was complex and difficult, but what else was a guy supposed to do when that was the damn truth?

"We didn't really have a fight," he finally said. "It's a long story but…he wasn't the best dad around. He made me and Aunt Tricia feel like we didn't matter to him, like he didn't love us as much as a dad should love his kids."

His children fell silent, absorbing that. He didn't dare look at Devin, though he could feel the weight of her watchful gaze.

"Grandma Trixie said you must not love us very much," Jazmyn announced, "because you didn't want us to live with you and you didn't pay my mom enough to take care of us."

He tightened his hands on the steering wheel at the devastating words from his eight-year-old daughter. Did Jaz believe the vitriol her grandmother loved to dish up about him? He had a feeling that probably wasn't the worst of the things Sharla and her mother said about him.

He chose his words carefully, driven to defend himself without openly criticizing their grandmother.

"Maybe your grandma Trixie didn't have the whole

story, either. That happens sometimes. But you know I love you both more than anything, right?"

"You said you love us bigger than the mountains and the lake and the big blue sky," Ty said with his sweet, open grin. Cole gazed at him in the mirror, awash with love for this kid he loved so much, who probably wasn't even his.

"You know it, partner."

Jaz didn't say anything, deliberately turning to look out the window at the snow-covered scenery passing by. He sighed. He had no idea how to reach this difficult, contrary little girl. Sometimes he thought he was making progress with her, proving that he loved her and she was safe with him here at the ranch. Other times, he felt as if he was pounding his head against that windshield in front of him.

He couldn't really blame her, either. She had spent eight years being poisoned against him by all the important people in her life. How was she supposed to trust him when her mother and grandmother had done their best to convince her he was a bastard?

Lost in his bleak thoughts, he felt a whisper of physical contact and glanced down to see Devin's hand on his arm. She gave a comforting squeeze, which seemed to seep through all the warm layers of clothing he wore.

She couldn't know what a disaster his marriage had turned into or the bigger mess that came out of his fiery divorce and subsequent custody battles. She only knew he needed solace. The simple gesture left a curious ache lodged right under his rib cage.

For the rest of the short drive to the long park that ran along the lakeshore in town, he didn't want to move his arm, afraid to lose that tantalizing, comforting contact with her.

"Is this it? Are we there?" Ty asked.

"This is it," Devin said cheerfully.

The park was crowded all along its length. He was lucky enough to find a parking space not too far away, and as they walked through the cold December night toward the festivities, he could see little glowing fires in barrels and families on lawn chairs and a busy section where vendor tents had been erected—exactly the sort of scene he had studiously avoided since he came to Haven Point.

He had kept to himself, for the most part, since his return. But while he might prefer cloistering himself away at the ranch with his horses and the dogs, that self-imposed isolation was no longer possible. His children needed this: the lights, the noise, the crowd, the *fun*.

He wanted them to build a home here, a life with him. In order to do that successfully, they needed community, connections. This sort of event was ideal for creating ties that would make them feel they belonged here.

"They have peppermint cotton candy!" Ty exclaimed. "Can I have some, Dad? Can I?"

That sounded like the most disgusting thing he could imagine but then he wasn't a six-year-old boy.

"You can't have one of everything that catches your eye. After we've been here awhile and you have the chance to see all the available treats, you can pick one thing, deal?"

"Aww," he said, so dejectedly that Cole had to smile. Devin smiled as well and the two of them shared a quiet, amused moment over the boy's dramatics. Despite the crowd and the noise, a subtle dangerous intimacy seemed to swirl and eddy around them.

"I know what I want already and I don't need to see anything else," Jazmyn announced, and they both jerked their gazes away.

"What's that?" Devin asked.

"Hot kettle corn. It's my favorite."

"That does sound good," Cole answered.

"No, it *smells* good," Jaz said.

"And *tastes* even better," her brother said with a giggle. "I want kettle corn, too."

"Can anybody see the booth? We can grab some for the parade."

"Great idea," Devin said. She craned her neck to look. Cole found it first, at the far end of the concessions row.

As they walked toward it, Devin waved to just about everybody they passed and exchanged greetings with most of them. She seemed to know everyone and it became even more obvious that she was well liked in town.

He felt more than a few curious looks in his direction, people probably wondering either who he was or what the hell she was doing with a man like him.

As much as the kids needed this sort of thing, he *didn't*.

The line for kettle corn was fairly long. The woman in front of them beamed when she spotted Devin and immediately launched into a soliloquy about some new medication Devin had prescribed and how much it had helped.

Devin listened with a patient smile as the woman went on and on. Just before they reached their turn to order, an elderly man approached them and started asking about a crick in his neck and a young mother with a baby in a sling interjected with a question about colic.

"Sorry," Devin said after she finally extricated herself from the crowd and they grabbed their kettle corn bag.

"Does that happen everywhere you go?" he asked as they walked away from the booth.

She made a face. "It's part of being a physician in a small town. I'm friends with many of my patients, which means they feel like they can talk to me wherever we happen to meet, not just in an exam room. Even at the grocery store, people still want to ask me questions about their arthritis or their backache. Usually I don't mind, unless they come up to me in a restaurant and start talking about changes in their stool."

He had to laugh. "I guess you have to draw a line somewhere."

"Yes. That's mine." Her phone chimed and she pulled it out of her pocket, gazed at the text message, then thumbed a quick answer.

"My sister," she said to him. "She's saving spots for us near the bowery. The parade's going to start in a few moments. Shall we start making our way over there?"

"Good idea. Kids, come on."

They headed in that direction, stopping only long enough to buy a colorful light-up magic wand for Jazmyn, who insisted she would *die* if she didn't have it, and a similarly outfitted plastic sword for Ty. He figured both of them would probably be broken by morning but they would be fun for a moonlit parade.

"There's McKenzie," Devin said when they reached the covered structure used for picnics and family reunions and the like.

She pointed to a slim, very pretty woman who looked vastly different from Devin. The young mayor of Haven Point had dark hair and eyes and a dusky complexion, very different from Devin's creamy skin and auburn hair.

Cole recognized the man next to him. He and Ben Kilpatrick had gone to school together, back in the day, and had been friends of a sort.

"There you are!" McKenzie exclaimed, hugging her sister. "I was hoping you weren't being called out to some kind of emergency."

"It was a culinary emergency. A long line at the kettle corn booth."

Jazmyn giggled and McKenzie smiled down at her. To Cole's surprise, she hugged Jazmyn, then turned to hug Ty, too.

"Hey, kids! It's great to see you again."

When had she seen them? he wondered, then remembered Devin said the kids had gone to McKenzie's store with her the day he had driven to Boise.

"Guess what's selling like hotcakes over at the Haven Point Helping Hands booth?" McKenzie asked them.

"What?" Ty asked, with a wide-eyed look.

"The ornaments with the ribbons you tied, Jazmyn, and the scented rice bags you helped us make, Mr. Ty. They are both very popular items. We're making a *ton* of money for the library and we never would have been able to do it without your help."

Both of his children beamed with pride. This. He wanted his kids to feel as if they were part of something bigger than themselves, and this was exactly the sort of thing he had in mind.

If he wanted his kids to feel as if they belonged, he had to make an effort to go outside his comfort zone and be more social than he'd been in the years since he returned to Haven Point. Whether he liked it or not.

McKenzie Shaw finally turned her attention to him. "You must be Cole."

"Yes. Nice to meet you, Mayor." He extended a hand and after a few beats, she shook it, though he didn't miss the hard glint in her eyes.

McKenzie had been the one to tell Devin he had been in trouble with the law, he remembered. She was suspicious of him—as she should be—and protective of her sister. That part still didn't make sense to him, given that Devin was the older sister.

He didn't have time to puzzle it out as she hooked

an arm through Ben's and pulled him forward. "Cole Barrett, this is my fiancé, Ben Kilpatrick."

"We knew each other in school," Cole said. "Hey, Ben. Long time."

"Hello." Ben shook his hand firmly, though he seemed to be sizing him up in much the same way McKenzie had.

In high school, he and Ben had been friendly, though not really friends. They had played baseball together and had a few classes together over the years, but Ben had kept to himself in those days, sticking with books and his studies, while Cole even then had hung with a much wilder crowd.

Ben, he knew, was now one of the top honchos for Caine Tech, the huge company that was building a new production facility in Haven Point.

He had also been instrumental in introducing Tricia to her husband, who also worked at Caine Tech. Right now that didn't make Cole look very favorably on the man.

"You didn't decorate the *Delphine* for the light parade?" Devin asked.

"Not this year," Ben answered. "I only flew in this morning and there wouldn't have been time. Besides, Kenz didn't want to be in the parade. She wanted to watch the whole parade from start to finish, since she missed half of the Lake Haven Days parade."

"What do you mean? You were in the very first float!" Devin exclaimed.

"I got to see the parade *route*. I didn't get to see the parade."

"We've got some chairs here for you," Ben said, pointing to a grouping of two-deep chairs bordered on both sides by propane heaters.

The kids grabbed seats in the front and Devin fussed around them for a few moments, tucking in blankets and making sure they could see. The propane heaters sent out a steady warmth. While he couldn't say it was toasty—that was impossible when the surrounding temperature was near freezing—it was at least comfortable, especially with the blankets.

There were more chairs than people and he realized why a few moments later when several newcomers arrived.

"Aidan! Eliza!" Devin exclaimed, jumping up to give hugs to the couple who arrived with a cute curly-haired girl around Ty's age. "I haven't seen you since the wedding!"

"That's because you're always too busy to get together when we're in town," the woman said.

This must be Aidan Caine and his new wife. Caine was the founder of the company that bore his name. Cole knew Aidan had purchased the largest property in town a few years back, along with half the commercial buildings in town.

"We couldn't miss the parade," Eliza said. "It's Maddie's favorite day of the year."

"I love, love, *love* the parade," the little girl exclaimed.

"So do I!" Devin hugged her, then led her over to Ty and Jazmyn.

"I have a new friend for you," Devin told them.

"This is Maddie Hayward, one of my favorite people in the whole wide world. Maddie, these are my buddies Jazmyn and Ty."

"Hi!" she chirped, and Cole saw she was missing a tooth, just like Ty. She had the same mischievous look in her eyes, too. He had a feeling the kids, at least, would get along like gangbusters.

Someone made an announcement on loudspeakers set up around the park that the parade was about to begin and then Christmas music began playing.

He eased back in his chair, enjoying the cold night and the stars and the conversation flowing around him. At one point, McKenzie started passing around mulled wine to the adults but he declined, of course. He didn't drink anymore, ever.

Instead, he took a paper mug of the hot cocoa Eliza Caine was handing out, took a sip and couldn't hold back a little sound of appreciation that earned him a grin from Devin.

"Isn't that fabulous? Eliza made that for us one time last winter. Apparently it's a recipe from Aidan's father. I've never been able to appreciate any other hot cocoa since."

"Usually it has a little drop of good Irish whiskey but this was for the kids," Eliza said with a smile.

"It's delicious. Thank you," he said.

After that, they were too busy watching the parade for much conversation. While the Christmas music continued over the loudspeakers, boat after boat passed by, each with colorful lights and decorations.

It was a unique, fun celebration and the kids seemed

to be eating it up. Ty exclaimed that every boat was his new favorite, and Jazmyn watched with her eyes big and her face cradled in both mittened hands. As he watched the changing lights play over their features, he was suddenly so very glad he had agreed to bring them. After the trauma and pain of losing their mother, they needed a little Christmas magic and joy to give them hope.

He had less than a week to throw together a bright, perfect Christmas for them. How the hell was he going to pull it off with Tricia in the hospital? Presents, stockings, Christmas dinner. It was overwhelming for a guy who hadn't had much practice.

"Are you doing okay?"

He glanced over at Devin, bundled up beside him in a thick blue blanket. Her cheeks and nose were pink from the cold, which should have clashed with her auburn hair but somehow just made her look vibrant and more lovely than ever.

"Yeah. Fine."

"You were frowning. Is it because you're not crazy about crowds?"

He raised an eyebrow. "I'm not?"

"Well, you do sort of have a reputation around town as a bit of a, well, hermit."

"I don't mind crowds." It was the individual people *in* the crowds that usually gave him trouble.

She gave him a doubtful look. "You've been back in town for several years but this is your first Lights on the Lake Festival. Now that I think about it, I've never seen you at any of the other town events. You must go out of your way to avoid them. Why?"

That was a particularly astute observation—uncomfortably astute. Since he returned to the Lake Haven area after his release from prison, he had basically stuck close to Evergreen Springs. He wasn't an agoraphobic or anything. He traveled around to cattle auctions, to horse shows, to the occasional small-town rodeo with no problem.

If he wanted to have a successful quarter horse breeding and training operation, he couldn't live like a hermit. Especially with his past—which was a matter of public record and a source of gossip in rodeo circles, no doubt—he had to mingle, to make connections and cement old relationships.

Those public appearances seemed easier away from Haven Point, though. When he went into town, he had to wonder what people might be thinking about him closer to home. People here knew his grandparents. Plenty of them probably knew his story, knew he had let his hard living destroy a promising rodeo career and that he had spent time in prison for giving a man injuries with lifelong consequences.

Early on, he had caught a few whispers and sideways glances from a couple of old ladies in the grocery store. One time, an old biddy had even clutched her purse tightly and muttered *jailbird* under her breath when he walked past.

It had left him gun-shy to put himself out there. He didn't like wondering what people might be thinking or saying about him.

Devin knew about his past and she was still here, he reminded himself. She hadn't once looked at him with scorn or disgust. She still extended the very same warmth and kindness to him and to his children.

"If you want to stay out of trouble in prison, you learn early how to keep to yourself and be content with your own company." It was part of the truth, just not all of it. "I guess I held on to some of those old habits after I came here."

She gave him a searching look. "Haven Point isn't prison," she said in a low voice. "There are good people here who are always willing to give people a chance. Look at Ben. A few months ago, most people here hated him for closing the boatworks and letting the downtown buildings fall into ruins over the last few years. A few people still hold a grudge about that period of our town's history but most have welcomed him back with open arms."

"I'm not Ben," he said gruffly.

That was the sort of man she deserved. Someone successful, accomplished, with a bright future.

He sipped at his divine cocoa, trying not to let that thought steal all the fun of watching his children enjoy the parade.

CHAPTER FIFTEEN

SHE HAD SEEN the Lights on the Lake boat parade many times over her lifetime, but she couldn't remember it being so completely magical. The colors gleaming on the water, the enthusiastic crowd, the festive mood—all of it seemed enhanced this time. The colors seemed richer, the smells more intense, the music playing in perfect synchronicity to the boats on the water.

Part of it had to do with the children's wide-eyed delight. How could anybody be cynical when Ty squealed with excitement at each new boat and even Jazmyn clapped her hands at one boat that featured illuminated animatronic penguins throwing snowballs at each other?

Devin was honest enough with herself to admit the children weren't the only reason this particular parade seemed so perfect. The man seated beside her and the energy and awareness that sizzled through her whenever she was near him might have a little something to do with it.

She was developing a serious thing for Cole Barrett.

Throughout the parade, she couldn't help sneaking little glances at him. She loved watching this big, hard rancher interact so sweetly with his children, smiling at their excitement and pointing out different features on the boats they might have missed.

He was a remarkable man. Yes, he had made mistakes. Serious mistakes. But he loved his children deeply and she sensed he would do anything for them. They were the reason he had come to the festival, even though she guessed it was the last place he wanted to be.

How could she help but be attracted to that kind of devotion?

The parade was short, less than twenty minutes. Any longer than that and the cold would probably siphon away some of the enjoyment. As things started to wrap up, McKenzie leaned forward and looked down toward the marina, the start of the parade.

"Okay, kids. Be ready. Looks like the end of the parade is coming up. I only see one boat left. Watch carefully because I've heard rumors a special visitor might be on the last boat."

McKenzie sounded every bit as excited as if she were a child herself, which was yet another reason Devin adored her sister. She found joy in the whole world around her.

"It's true," Maddie said knowledgeably, craning her neck to see the last boat. "I saw him last year."

"Who is it?" Ty asked, wide eyes reflecting the lights from the passing boat, a classic Kilpatrick wooden motorboat decorated with giant blue and silver snowflakes.

"Who do you think?" Jazmyn asked in a "duh" sort of voice. "Santa Claus!"

"Where? I can't see him!" Ty jumped up for a better look but couldn't see around the other boats, being vertically challenged as he was.

"Here, partner." Cole picked him up easily and set the boy on his broad shoulders. At the sight of the big man holding tight to his son's legs to keep him in place, Devin's heart gave a painful squeeze.

Oh. What was she doing here? She stared at the water, inky in the December night. The colors of the boats melded, blurring into muddled rainbows.

For someone who prided herself on being smart and savvy in most areas of her life, she was very afraid she might have made a monumental mistake here. She was growing entirely too entrenched in the lives of Cole and his children. They were becoming immeasurably dear to her.

It was one thing to help out the man a little here and there while his sister was in the hospital and his family was in turmoil. It was quite another to let these children, this man, sneak into her heart while she wasn't paying attention.

In a burst of color and music and shrieking children, the parade ended with Santa Claus waving as his ride sailed on toward Shelter Springs.

"That was the best parade *ever*," Ty declared, sagging back into his chair as if he'd just swum the length of the parade route.

"It was even better than *last* year," Maddie Hayward said. "They had more boats and I liked the lights even more, especially the boat that had the *Frozen* princesses on it."

"That was my favorite, too," Jazmyn said. "Either that one or the boat with the penguins throwing snowballs."

Maddie giggled. "Oh, yeah. That one was great."

Devin loved the way children could make friends so easily. Why did it seem so much harder as a person aged? Not for her sister. McKenzie was so kind and enthusiastic that people automatically responded to her. Devin had always been more subdued, a little more content to stand back and observe.

She liked watching Aidan and Eliza hold hands, for instance, and the little besotted looks Ben and McKenzie shared, even though it made her feel more alone than ever.

She wasn't envious. She would never begrudge her sister the happiness she and Ben had found, and Aidan and Eliza seemed supremely perfect for each other.

Seeing them together only reinforced the different turn her life had taken, starting when she was a teenage girl waking up from surgery to find everything had changed.

She pushed away the familiar little burst of regret. As everybody stood up, preparing to leave, she turned to her sister. "Thanks for letting us crash your party."

"You're welcome." McKenzie sent Cole a sidelong look. He was busy folding up lawn chairs and talking to Ben and Aidan.

"I'll admit, I've been a little worried about you spending so much time with Cole and his kids, but—"

"You shouldn't be," she assured McKenzie. "Nothing to worry about here."

"I'm not so sure about that," McKenzie said.

She bristled on Cole's behalf. "He told me all about his past. He made mistakes and paid for them. That's not who he is anymore. Now he's a devoted father and a hardworking rancher. The rest of it doesn't matter to me."

"That's not the part that worries me," McKenzie said quietly. "I know you and I trust your judgment. The kids are adorable and their father…yum."

"Then why the concern?"

"I've never seen you like this." McKenzie spoke quietly, her dark eyes worried. "I just don't want to see you hurt."

"I don't know what you're talking about," she lied.

"I saw the way you look at Cole and his kids. This isn't just helping someone in need. You care about them, don't you?"

Her sister was always entirely too perceptive. "Sure. Just like I care about all my friends," she answered with a casual smile. "Don't worry about me, sis. Everything is fine."

"I hope so." McKenzie frowned and would have said more but Ty came up and tugged Devin over to watch him brandish his light-up sword at an invisible opponent.

A few moments later, Cole headed their way with Jazmyn.

"I want to see some of the booths," she said. "Dad says we can at least look at the Helping Hands booth, with the things we helped make."

"Great idea," Devin said. She said her goodbyes to the others and then walked through the cold night toward the row of tents selling last-minute Christmas gifts.

At the Helping Hands booth, she realized her mistake in bringing Cole and the children with her when she found her friends Samantha Fremont and Katrina Bailey. They were among the youngest of the Helping Hands, still in their early twenties and a little man-hungry.

When they spotted Cole in all his raw gorgeousness, Katrina nudged Sam and they both just about drooled on the spot, then gave Devin envious—and speculative—looks when they realized she was with him that night.

She introduced them all a little stiffly before walking through with the children to find the things they had helped make.

Cole ended up pulling out his wallet and buying the last soothing rice bag—"horse training gives a guy sore muscles," he claimed—and also a couple of the ornaments Jazmyn had helped with.

She said goodbye to her friends, quite certain at the next Helping Hands meeting she would receive an interrogation from the girls about Cole.

They walked into a few other booths, just out of courtesy to people she knew. As they were heading for the booth where Archie and Paul from her yoga group were selling some of their beautiful folk art wood carvings, Devin spotted a familiar figure standing just inside the canvas tent with a little yellow dog on a leash.

She tensed as Ty spotted him at the same time. "Look! There's our grandpa!" he exclaimed. "And he's got Buster with him. Can we go say hi?"

"I don't—" Cole began, but his son didn't wait for his answer before racing through the crowd toward Stan and his puppy, leaving them no choice but to follow.

"Hi, Grandpa. Hi, Buster!"

"Why, hello there," Stan said. She couldn't accuse him of coming to the Lights on the Lake Festival as some circuitous way of engineering this encounter, not when he looked genuinely surprised to see them.

He gazed at all three of them—Cole, Jazmyn and Ty—with a look of such yearning, it made her chest ache.

"Hi, Grandpa," Jazmyn said, with a wary look at her father first.

"So these are the grandkids you were talking about, Stan?" Archie smiled.

"Yes. The lovely young lady is Jazmyn and the boy is Tyler."

"Did you see all the boats in the parade, Grandpa?" Ty asked.

"I did."

"Did Buster like it?"

"I think so. You should have heard him barking when the boat with the Christmas cat went by."

Both children giggled at this, though Devin was quite sure Cole's glower intensified.

"I wish I had a boat so I could put lights on it and be in the parade," Ty said.

"Me, too," Jazmyn said. "I would put a Christmas tree on it with little elves who are decorating it."

"I would put a dog like Buster on mine and have him chasing the Christmas cat around the Christmas tree," Ty said.

The kids petted the dog for another moment before Cole finally spoke, his voice hard and distant. "Come on, kids. We've got a lot of festival to cover before we head back. And didn't you want to try the cotton candy?"

Food was apparently the only thing that would distract Ty from his new best friend. He jumped up. "Yes! I love cotton candy. Bye, Buster. Bye, Grandpa."

"See you, young Tyler. Bye, Jazmyn. Bye, Dr. Shaw. Son."

She and the children waved to him but she noticed that Cole stood as if carved out of the same granite as the Redemption Mountains as the children gave the dog one last hug.

They headed for the concessions and stood in line again for cotton candy. This line wasn't as long— though long enough for Devin to field a question from Ann Mae Lewis about the recurrence of her gout and from John Hardin about whether he should come in to have his warts burned off.

For all the hype and anticipation, neither Jazmyn nor Ty was very crazy about peppermint cotton candy—something Devin could have quite accurately predicted.

"Try some," Jazmyn said. "It's *terrible.*"

Devin laughed. "Well, with that ringing endorsement, how can I refuse?"

She took a little taste and didn't quite agree. The fluffy spun sugar melted in her mouth and left behind a minty sweet taste she quite liked.

At his daughter's urging, Cole tried it, too, and he obviously didn't mind it, either.

"It must be a grown-up thing," Ty decided.

They walked for a while, enjoying the Christmas lights sparkling in the trees and listening to the cheerful music from a children's choir on the stage set up in one corner of the park while they shared a few more tastes of the peppermint cotton candy.

"Are you done with this?" Cole asked after a few moments.

"Completely."

He chucked the rest into a garbage can, just as she noticed Ty give a huge, jaw-popping yawn. He was still holding his light-up sword but had turned it off some time ago and hadn't parried against any invisible opponents in a while. Jazmyn appeared bleary-eyed, as well.

"Let's go find our car so we can warm up," he said.

"Looks like you've got a couple of tired kiddos here," Devin murmured to Cole when they didn't argue, just followed along with slightly dazed looks.

He glanced over at them, then made a face. "Yeah. I'm afraid none of us got much sleep last night. Ty had a nightmare about his mom and the accident, which woke up Jaz and me."

"Does that happen often?"

He shoved his hands into the pockets of his coat. She had the random wish that he would hold her hand but quickly dismissed the urge as completely ridiculous. "Not as often as it did at first. Seems like when they first came to live with me, they took turns. If it wasn't one having a bad dream, it was the other one."

"They've been through a traumatic experience. Their reaction sounds completely normal, but that doesn't make it any easier on any of you. What do you do when it happens?"

He shrugged, looking embarrassed. "We read stories or talk or get up and watch something on TV until they calm down enough to sleep again."

"That's perfect," she answered. "It sounds like you're doing everything right, Cole. You're a good father."

He made a disbelieving sound and she nudged him with her shoulder. "I'm serious. You're doing a great job under difficult circumstances."

He gazed at her and she saw self-doubt mingled with gratitude. "Thanks," he finally said. "Most of the time it feels like somebody tossed me over one of those Christmas boats into the deepest part of the lake and all I'm doing is floundering."

"You just need to trust yourself a little more," she said as they reached his pickup truck and he opened the door for her. "Sounds to me as if your instincts are exactly right."

"I don't want to go home yet," Jazmyn said when they were all in the pickup truck and Cole had turned on the heater, which began defrosting frozen fingers and toes.

"I don't, either," Ty said.

Apparently a little warmth gave them a second wind.

"Can we go look at the lights at the park in Shelter Springs? You said you would take us last week but you didn't." Jazmyn's voice held a faintly accusatory tone.

"We had a bit of a complication with Aunt Tricia having to go to the hospital," he reminded her.

"I still want to see it. My friend Anna at school said they have a Christmas tree that's bigger than the mountains!"

"I think that's probably an exaggeration," he said. "You mean you haven't seen enough lights already?"

She shook her head vigorously, an action that Ty mimicked.

"Fine. I'll take you after we drop Devin off."

"Don't you want to see the giant Christmas tree?" Ty asked, a hopeful note in his voice.

How could she refuse? She didn't necessarily need

to see more holiday decorations but she wasn't quite ready for the evening to end.

"Sure. That sounds fun."

Cole gazed at her, his face in shadows and an unreadable look in his eyes, then he shrugged and started driving.

CHAPTER SIXTEEN

DURING THE DARK MONTHS he spent in prison, Cole used to lie on his bunk and imagine what his perfect day would involve. With plenty of time on his hands, he had run through many scenarios in his head.

A clear spring morning spent planting a vast field of barley, where the air smelled of fresh grass and overturned soil and new life.

A summer day, perhaps, riding up into the mountains above the ranch on a fine horse with the sky a brilliant blue overhead and meadowlark and mountain bluebirds flitting through the trees around him.

A fall afternoon of fly-fishing the Hell's Fury with sunlight gleaming on cold swirls of water around his waders and hungry rainbow trout going after his best mayfly.

This particular scenario he was living right now never would have entered his mind—driving through a December night with his kids asleep in the backseat and a light snowfall whispering against the windshield.

But as he drove away from the Shelter Springs town boundary and back around the big lake toward Haven Point with the soft and lovely Devin Shaw beside him, all those other imaginary moments seemed to pale into insignificance.

This. This was perfect.

He wanted to keep driving and driving, all night long.

"I think they're asleep," Devin murmured.

"They have been for about ten minutes now, since we left the park. They've had a long day."

"I guess Christmastime is exhausting when you're a kid."

He smiled briefly, then felt it slide away, replaced by an overwhelming urge to pull over, reach for her hand and tug her into his arms. Then the day would be truly perfect.

What would she do? Would she push him away or would she kiss him back, as she had the other day? Would she taste of mulled wine or of peppermint cotton candy or an intoxicating combination of both?

The memory of their kiss seemed to hover inside the vehicle with them, as tantalizing as it was out of reach. His enjoyment of the evening dimmed slightly and he frowned, upset at himself for yearning for what he couldn't have.

Get over it, already. She wasn't for him.

The evening spent at the Lights on the Lake Festival had been a glaring example of that. She was obviously a valued member of the community, a well-respected physician doing what she could to help her small hometown. Everyone knew her and seemed to love her, seeking her advice or just the chance to talk to her.

What would she ever want with someone like him?

It was a question he couldn't answer and he decided not to ruin the evening by obsessing about it. She was here, wasn't she? She seemed to be enjoying herself, at least judging by the relaxed set of her features and the way she hummed along to the Christmas songs the kids had insisted he play on the truck stereo.

For the short time they had left together tonight, he decided to simply savor the moment, to enjoy the strange, unexpected peace he found in her company.

The song on the radio shifted to some kind of piano version of "O Little Town of Bethlehem" and he relaxed a little more, enjoying the freedom of driving where he wanted while he caught occasional glimpses of color on the lake as the boats that had been in the parade earlier made the return trip back to the Haven Point marina.

"Why can't you give your father a chance?"

So much for the peaceful moment. The relaxed ease seemed to fly out the window as tension crept back in to squeeze his shoulders hard.

"Let it go, Devin. I told you how he abandoned Tricia and me. As far as I'm concerned, he made his choices when he walked away twenty-three years ago. He doesn't get to waltz back in and pretend like nothing has happened and now we can forgive everything and be one big, happy family."

"Maybe he's changed and regrets what he did. I would think you, of all people, could understand that."

Her words hit him like a rock through the windshield. *You, of all people.* A man who greatly regretted the man he had been and the choices he had made, who was trying to change.

Their situations weren't the same.

He turned off the radio. He didn't need Christmas carols about peace on earth right now.

"You've heard of Steps Eight and Nine in twelve-step programs," he said, his voice low.

"The steps about making amends. Yes. I'm familiar with them."

"Then tell me how a father can ever make amends for the harm he caused when he abandoned his kids."

She was quiet and the only sounds in the truck for a long moment were the children's steady breathing and the wipers slowly beating back the snow.

"It's not my place to defend the choices your father made," she finally said. "I couldn't anyway, because I don't know what was in his head."

"You're right. You don't. If you did, you would see his head is filled only with thoughts of himself." He couldn't seem to help the cold, harsh, ugly tone or words.

"I will just say," she went on stubbornly, "that maybe he didn't see it as abandoning you. If you try to look at things from his perspective, maybe he didn't know what else to do. His job required him to travel and he knew he couldn't drag the two of you along with him."

"He could have got another job."

He hated talking about this. He sounded as if he was still the lost eleven-year-old kid, furious at his mother for dying and his father for leaving and the whole damn world for not turning out the way he wanted it to.

"Was your life so terrible with your grandparents?"

"Of course not," he said. "They were great. My grandparents were decent, loving, hardworking people. That's not the point. We weren't their responsibility until he dumped us here."

"Would your life have been better if you had stayed with your father? If he had just left you to babysitters or nannies or housekeepers while he traveled?"

"We'll never know, will we?"

His grandparents had been wonderful but they had already been in their late sixties when he and Tricia had shown up. His grandfather had tried to be the father Stan wasn't but he was tired most nights from running the ranch. He'd already had one valve replacement and his congestive heart failure left him unable to play ball in the backyard or coach soccer teams or even exercise much control over a willful, wild teenage boy.

Cole had started drinking when he was fourteen. By the time he was sixteen, his drinking was out of control—though that hadn't stopped him from winning high school rodeo competitions and going on to college for a few years before going on to the PRCA.

He sometimes wondered if a stronger male influence might have turned the tide for him—not that he would ever blame his grandfather for his own choices.

"I shouldn't have brought it up," she said. "He just looked so lonely tonight, I thought it was worth trying one more time to see if there's any chance you could soften your stance a little to let him interact with the children a bit more."

"I won't," he said firmly.

"I get it. I'm sorry. Your scars are your own and I have no business poking at them. Forget I mentioned it."

"I will, if you tell me what your scars are."

"My scars? I don't have any."

She was lying and both of them knew it. "Sure you do. You can start by telling me why your sister is so protective of you."

She opened her mouth and he thought for sure she was finally going to tell him but she pointed out the window.

"We'll have to save that for another time. Looks like we're here."

He wanted to keep driving until she talked to him—it was only fair, after she gave him the third degree, right?—but the day had been long and he probably needed to get his kids home to their beds.

Beyond that, he didn't think she would appreciate being quasi-kidnapped.

With a resigned sigh, he pulled into her driveway and left the vehicle running to keep the children warm as he walked around to her side to let her out.

Though the snowfall was still light, the driveway and sidewalk were covered with about half an inch of powdery precipitation.

"Be careful," he said as he opened the door for Devin. "It's slicker than you'd think. Hold on."

He knew he probably shouldn't be so thrilled when

she slipped her hand through the crook of his elbow and grabbed tight. "The last thing I need is a broken arm," she said.

He was fiercely aware of the warmth of her against him as they made their way up the walk, of the soft scent of berries and vanilla teasing his senses and leaving him achy and hard.

She seemed small and slight walking beside him, her head barely reaching the top of his shoulder, but size could be deceptive. Within her small stature, she was fiery and determined, the kind of woman his grandmother would have called a dynamo.

At the house, she unlocked the front door and opened it slightly. Warmth and light spilled out of the open doorway into the winter night but Devin hardly seemed to notice.

"I had a great time," she said. "It was so fun seeing the boat parade through the eyes of your children. Thank you for sharing them with me for the evening."

"No, thank you. Jazmyn and Ty loved having you with us."

"And you?"

Despite the teasing note in her voice, awareness still seemed to bloom between them like crocuses burrowing through the snow toward the light.

"I did, too. Probably too much, truth be told." He muttered the last in a low voice he hoped she didn't hear.

She sent him a startled look beneath her eyelashes. "Sorry?"

"Nothing. Never mind." He forced his features into

a polite smile. "Anyway. Thanks. It was good for the kids to be part of it. We all had a great time, especially the last little while, looking at the lights."

"That's one of my favorite parts of Christmas, seeing how everyone decorates their little corner of the world."

He had never given it much thought before and hadn't really spent much time looking at Christmas decorations but she had made the evening fun.

"Well, if I don't see you again before Christmas, I hope it's a merry one."

"Thank you, but you'll probably see me Monday afternoon. That's the day I'm coming back to the ranch with my yoga class, remember?"

Right. The hot spring. The reminder sent a jumble of conflicting feelings tangling through him. Foremost among them was a burst of joy to know he would be seeing her again in just a few days—followed quickly by a pinch of unease at just how happy that made him.

"Right. We'll plan on it."

He was in serious trouble here, if just the idea that he would see her again made the night seem touched by magic, filled with possibilities as bright as the ornaments he could see on her Christmas tree glowing inside.

Yeah. He had it bad. That must be why the next words slipped out of his mouth before he really had time to think them through.

"If you want, your class can stop at the house afterward for hot chocolate and cookies. Letty and the kids have been baking up a storm and we have more Christmas goodies than we know what to do with. The kids would enjoy having someone to share them."

He immediately regretted the invitation and wanted to snatch it back. She made him do and say the *craziest* things and he had no idea why.

It was too late to rescind the offer. She gazed at him with green eyes drenched with delight. "Oh, Cole. Thank you. Everyone would truly love that."

"It's no big deal. Just cookies and hot chocolate."

"Don't tell me it's not a big deal. You don't even want my friends to be at the ranch, yet you've been so very kind to us."

He couldn't let her look at him as if he was some kind of hero. They both knew better.

"I'm not kind," he growled. "I'm a selfish bastard."

She scoffed lightly. "Right. Because only someone completely selfish would invite a bunch of older people he doesn't even know—and doesn't really *want* to know—over for refreshments at his house, purely as a favor to me. I don't think anyone would consider that selfish. What would you possibly hope to gain?"

He did the only thing he could think of to show her exactly what he wanted from her, the same thing he had ached for since the last time she had been in his arms.

He pulled her into the house, yanked her against him and lowered his mouth to hers.

The kiss came out of nowhere. One moment they were talking about her senior citizen yoga class, the next she was pressed against the console table in her foyer with her arms wrapped around him while he kissed her with a fierce hunger that stole her breath away.

She wasn't about to complain—not when she was exactly where she wanted to be at last. She kissed him back, loving the taste of him, mint and chocolate, and the security she always felt in his arms.

On some level, she recognized they couldn't keep this up. The timing couldn't have been worse, with the children out in the car.

She didn't want to let go, though. She wanted this amazing heat to go on forever, to strip away all these layers between them and tug him down onto the sofa just steps away, where they could be closer...

Through the heat and the hormones, she was aware of something else, something deeper—a terrifying thread of tenderness that seemed to be twisting and curling around her heart. It would be entirely too easy to fall hard for him.

It might already be too late.

She froze for only a moment but it was enough, apparently, for him to come to his senses. He slid his mouth away and gazed down at her, eyes still blazing with desire.

A muscle flexed in his jaw. "You asked about my motives," he said, his voice gruff. "How's that for motive?"

"K-kissing me?" Her voice wobbled just a bit on the words.

"For starters. It's all I can think about when I'm around you. I keep telling myself I need to stay away from you, then I do crazy things like take you to the

Lights on the Lake Festival and invite your yoga class over for hot chocolate and cookies."

He stepped away and shoved his hands into the pockets of his coat. "You make me lose control and I *hate* it. I've come too far, fought too hard to gain mastery over myself, my actions, trying to become someone I can maybe one day respect again. Then I only have to touch you and I completely lose my head. Case in point, I spent all evening telling myself all the reasons why kissing you again is a lousy idea, yet here we are."

She blinked at that. He had been thinking about kissing her all evening while they were watching the boat parade and sharing peppermint cotton candy and walking through the fair? At least she knew she wasn't the only one.

"Why is kissing me such a lousy idea?" she had to ask.

He frowned, looking fiercely dangerous in her foyer. "You know as well as I do this thing between us can't go anywhere except a few stolen kisses. The well-respected town doctor and the surly alcoholic ex-con. You couldn't find a worse mismatch!"

His continued emphasis on their different paths was beginning to annoy her. She refused to face the pain caused by his assertion that anything between them was doomed, at least for now.

"Why do you define yourself wholly by your past? Why don't you call yourself the surly single father horse trainer? That seems more accurate to the man you are today."

A little corner of his mouth twitched, as if he wanted to smile at her description and she pushed her point.

"I also have to take exception that you always seem to bring up only one dimension of my existence. Yes, I'm a physician. Yes, I hope my patients respect and like me. But I'm so much more than that."

She faced him, aware her hands were still trembling. "I'm a woman with foibles and quirks and needs and desires. I'm a good friend and a loving sister. I eat too much ice cream and don't like to do sit-ups and I watch trashy TV sometimes when I'm stressed. I love to read popular fiction and play Spider Solitaire and learn new things."

I'm a cancer survivor.

She didn't say the words, even though they defined her just as much as her occupation did.

"My point is, we are all complicated beasts but you seem to only see yourself through one filter—who you once were and the mistakes you once made. That seems a pretty narrow focus and I don't think it's healthy. And you can trust me on that. Apparently I'm a well-respected doctor."

She couldn't tell if her words resonated with him. He gazed at her for a moment, then sighed. "I'd better go. The kids are alone in the car. I shouldn't have left them this long. Thank you for coming with us tonight. Jaz and Ty had a great time and so did I. I guess I'll probably see you Monday."

"Good night."

She closed the door after him, then moved to the

big picture window in the living room of her parents' house. In the dark solitude of the room, she watched him back out of the driveway, then turn toward Evergreen Springs, his headlights illuminating the light snowflakes drifting down.

She was coming to care for him and his children entirely too much. It would be entirely too easy to fall in love with Cole Barrett. She didn't know if she had ever met anyone who so desperately needed a little tenderness and gentleness in his life. He deserved someone to love him, to help heal the scars of his past.

That someone couldn't be her, Devin reminded herself.

She knew all about fixing battered bodies but she couldn't simply waltz in and fix everything that was broken in Cole Barrett's life.

CHAPTER SEVENTEEN

"OH, MY OLD KNEES can't wait for this," Hazel Brewer declared as the truck bounced on a snowy rut in the road.

"Neither can my bad hip," her sister, Eppie, said. "After last week's soak, I felt better than I have in years. Even Ronald commented that I was skipping around the house all weekend like a spring chicken, didn't you, Ronald?"

"Yep."

Ronald Brewer was a man of few words, which made Devin adore him even more.

Devin drove her old pickup truck carefully up the plowed drive toward the Evergreen Springs ranch house, apprehension fluttering inside her.

She wasn't sure she was ready to see Cole again after that sizzling kiss and these tender feelings that seemed to be growing inside her.

"I've been looking forward to this all weekend," Barbara Serrano declared. "Besides the festival craziness on Saturday, we've had Christmas parties booked at the restaurant every night for three weeks. I just want to find a quiet corner somewhere, close my eyes and tune the world out."

Devin could relate to that. She had a couple of emergencies with patients in her practice and had been back and forth to the hospital all day Sunday, and then it seemed half her patients decided to catch various colds and flus over the weekend. She hadn't had a moment to breathe all day long.

"I'm so disappointed this will be our only other time to soak in the hot spring," Eppie said. "Are you sure we can't make this a regular thing, Devin?"

"Yes," Hazel agreed. "Surely you could work your womanly wiles on that handsome hunk of rancher and get him to change his mind."

Devin made a noncommittal sound. She wasn't sure she'd ever had womanly wiles and if she did, they weren't very much in evidence these days. She wasn't sure she could persuade him of anything.

"I'm sorry, ladies. Cole has made it clear he doesn't want big crowds and craziness at the hot spring. He allowed us to come a few times only as a special favor to me. As I mentioned, he has been very gracious to invite us to the house afterward for cookies and hot cocoa. I'm afraid we will have to be content with that."

Under other circumstances, she might have tried to convince him to let them use the hot spring on a regular basis but that didn't seem the best idea right now, given how awkwardly they had left things between them after the festival.

Her truck passed the house and she tried not to be too obvious, looking around to see if she could catch a glimpse of Cole like some kind of girl in junior high school riding her bicycle past the house of the cutest boy in school.

The snowman and his little friend stood sentinel out front, still with the pinecone eyes and stick arms. They had now been joined by a snow blob on four distinct legs. It took her a moment to figure out by the rope around it and another one dangling from one of the snowman's hands that the blob was supposed to be a dog of some sort, with a collar and a leash.

No doubt that was Ty's work, with perhaps a little help from his sister.

Her truck climbed the hill, engine growling in four-wheel drive, with Archie Peralta following closely in his big Chevy Suburban containing several more people from their yoga class.

Finally the road plateaued and a moment later the little hut beside the hot spring came into view, smoke curling out of the chimney again.

Cole had obviously come up earlier. With everything else he had to do at the ranch, he still made sure the road was plowed and a fire set in the warming hut.

What a dear, kindhearted, impossibly stubborn man. How was she supposed to protect her heart from him?

Cole's pickup truck was parked in front of the warming hut and the heart in question seemed to give a sharp little kick—until she saw a woman behind the wheel and recognized Letty.

Of course. When she had spoken with the housekeeper earlier in the day during her five-minute lunch break, Letty had told her she would be driving up with the children and would meet them at the warming hut. She must have taken Cole's big pickup truck that had better traction and four-wheel drive, rather than her own smaller and lighter SUV.

"Here we are," Devin said brightly, doing her best to ignore the disappointment seeping through her like water trickling toward the Hell's Fury.

She pulled up behind the truck and started helping her patients out of the pickup and SUV, since well-seasoned joints sometimes had a tough time with the greater heights of bigger vehicles. While she was helping Eppie out of the backseat of her king cab, Ty bounded over to her.

"Hi, Dr. Devin. Hi! We get to go soak in the water with you."

"Hi, kiddo. I'm so glad! Hi, Jazmyn."

His sister looked as if she wasn't in a very good mood. She didn't respond, just gave a heavy, put-upon sigh.

"Everything okay?"

"I wanted to wear my pink bikini swimsuit but Letty made me wear the blue one-piece. She said it might be a little warmer but I don't care. I don't like it. I'd rather wear the pink one."

"You'll probably be glad once you take off your sweats." Devin smiled, trying to distract her. "Are you ready to soak?"

"I am!" Ty exclaimed. "I remember that we can't get water in our mouths or put our heads under the water."

"Absolutely right. This isn't like a swimming pool

or a bathtub and you don't want to swallow the water. Sometimes there are bad bugs that can make you sick. Just stick close to me or Letty and we'll watch out for you."

She was helping Eppie ease into the warm, healing waters when yet another vehicle pulled up behind Archie's, this one a smaller SUV. A moment later, she gave a mental groan as she watched a familiar figure walk toward them wearing swim trunks and carrying a towel.

"Who's that?" Eppie asked.

"You know who that is," her sister said. "That's Stanford Barrett. Iris's son."

"He's our grandpa. Only, we're not supposed to talk to him," Ty announced. "He has a supercute dog named Buster."

"Hey, Stan," Archie said with a smile. "Good to see you."

"Mind if I crash the party?" Stan asked. "Archie told me the other day you were coming and a soak sounded like just the thing on a December Monday afternoon.

What was she supposed to do here? She glanced at the children and then back at him. "You know I don't mind," Devin answered. "But then, it's not my opinion that matters, is it?"

"No. But I reckon I own a quarter share of the hot spring, so you can't really keep me out of it, right?" he answered.

He took any decision out of her hands by stringing his towel in the lower branches of a cottonwood hanging over the water and slipping into the warm, steamy waters.

"Ahhh. Now, this is heaven."

"Grandpa. Hi." Ty beamed at him. So much for not talking to the man.

Stan gave him a perfunctory wave, though she sensed he would like to do more. Devin was relieved when he moved to the far side of the thirty-foot-wide pool and struck up a conversation with Paul.

He remained distanced from the larger group there the entire time they soaked and seemed to be trying his best to stay away from the children, as their father had asked. She could only be grateful that he hadn't put her in an even more difficult position.

While they soaked, Ty jabbered about Santa coming that week and how he had only two more days of school and about the project he was making for his father. Jazmyn seemed to share his excitement at the approaching holidays but she also seemed to be trying hard not to show it.

Mindful of safety, they let the children soak for only thirty minutes or so before Letty ushered them into the changing hut.

She was talking to Barbara, Eppie and Hazel about their upcoming plans for Christmas when she spotted a horse trotting up the hill toward them. Cole sat loose and comfortable in the saddle, wearing a shearling coat and a black cowboy hat.

She wanted to sink down into the water and disappear, or at least find a convenient snowbank to hide her suddenly flaming face, as he dismounted with fluid grace.

"How's the water today?" he asked.

"Perfect," Eppie answered, her lined face glowing and her eyes bright. "Are you sure we can't talk you into letting us move up here permanently so we can soak the winter away?"

He gave one of his rare, genuine smiles. "I'm glad you're enjoying it."

"Devin here tells us this is our last time to soak. We may have to do some serious negotiating to see if we can convince you to change your mind and let us come up here again," Barbara Serrano said. "Maybe we could work out a trade in free meals from the diner."

"Devin just needs to try harder to persuade you. Surely she can come up with *something* you might want," Hazel said with a suggestive little sideways look that Devin seriously hoped Cole didn't notice.

"Now, ladies, we talked about this," Devin said, her face hot with mortification as she tried to ignore the sudden remembered heat of being in his arms that made the 108-degree water seem tepid. "Cole generously allowed us use of his hot spring, even when it has traditionally been closed to the public. We can't be greedy and push him for more than he wants to offer."

Before the women could wind up for the argument she could see brewing on their wrinkled expressions, the children came out of the changing hut with Letty drying their hair.

"Hi, Dad," Ty chirped, skipping over to him and petting the horse's mane. "We soaked in the water and it was super fun and we didn't put our faces in at all, because it's gross."

"Is that right?"

"Yep. And even though Grandpa is here, we didn't talk to him at all," Ty assured him.

Cole jerked his head up from his son, craned his neck around and found his father through the curling steam coming off the water on the far side of the natural soaking pool. The polite friendliness on his features melted away into the familiar frustrated anger at the sight of him.

His father waved away steam. "Hey, son."

In an effort to defuse the situation, Devin tried for distraction. "Now that the kids are out, let's take turns changing in the hut Cole has been kind enough to warm for us. Ladies first."

The women grumbled a bit but started making their way toward the rock steps. Devin moved forward to help Eppie with her bad hip but Cole beat her to it. He offered a strong hand to her and gave her support while she maneuvered the steps.

"Why, thank you," Eppie said with a girlish giggle that made Devin smile. The two elderly sisters were notorious flirts.

"You're welcome."

"Are we still having hot cocoa at your place?" Hazel asked. "Devin mentioned it earlier."

"I guess that's the plan."

"Oh, good. We brought our famous almond short-cake bars to share."

"Sounds delicious," he answered. "Here, watch your step. Take my arm and I'll help you get to the hut so you don't slip."

"Your nice coat will get all wet, though," Hazel said.

"I don't mind. I'd rather have a wet coat than see one of you lovely ladies get hurt."

Why did he have to be so sweet? It made it so very difficult for her to resist him, even though she knew she had no choice.

Hazel and Eppie seemed to be dragging out the short walk to the warming hut, the rascals, so they could continue holding on to a big, strong man. By the time they made it to the door, she and Barbara were nearly there.

"I was going to see if you needed help but it looks like you made it," he said. His gaze shifted down her body then back up so quickly it would have been funny, if her nipples weren't swollen and hard from the contrast of warm water to mercilessly cold air.

"We're good," she mumbled, certain her face must be fiery red by now. "Come on, ladies. Let's hurry so the men can change."

Oh, he had it bad.

Cole couldn't seem to stop staring at Devin, all warm and pink and delicious. She wore a green one-piece swimming suit that molded to her lithe form and made the spit dry up in his mouth.

Had everybody noticed him staring? He wasn't sure but the older women seemed to give him knowing looks before they slipped into the hut, and Devin seemed unusually flustered.

Inside the hut, he could hear her helping the others change. She was such a nurturer, always taking care of everyone around her.

Did she see him as just another wounded bird, one more broken creature for her to tend?

"You ever need cash, you could really rake it in by developing this place a little more," Archie Peralta said from inside the soaking pool. "You'd just have to put in a couple more changing huts and maybe some better steps, for us old turkeys."

"And maybe a concession stand selling hot cocoa," Ronald Brewer chimed in.

He couldn't imagine anything he would hate more. He had come to the ranch for solace, wide-open space to rebuild his life. The last thing he needed was for the place to be overrun with people.

"I appreciate the suggestions. Right now, I'm not really interested in going into the hot springs business."

"It's not a bad idea."

Cole's jaw set at his father's contribution to the conversation. He didn't want to engage Stan but he had to disagree.

"It's a terrible idea. I don't want a bunch of strangers traipsing around the ranch. Present company excluded, of course."

"This kind of natural mineral spring is rare and special," Stan said. "You could certainly capitalize on the exclusivity of it, allowing only a few people a day to use it for a commensurate fee."

He frowned. "Evergreen Springs is a cattle ranch and it's becoming a horse training operation of some renown. As long as I own the majority share, that's how it's going to stay."

Stan looked as if he wanted to argue but he closed his mouth. Smart of him. As far as Cole was concerned, his father had lost the right to make decisions for the ranch when he walked away from it as a young man without looking back. He couldn't expect to show up now and start pushing his weight around, changing things and inserting himself into a family that didn't want him.

Devin and one of the Brewer sisters—Eppie, he thought—came out of the changing hut a moment later. Devin had changed into a tracksuit and parka and her hair hung in wavy curls around her face.

"The others are almost done, if you gentlemen want to start making your way out of the pool."

Stan was the first one out. "Think I'll just head back to my place to change," Stan said. He dried off with a big beach towel and wrapped it around him, apparently not at all bothered by the brisk December air.

"Better hurry or all of Hazel's almond shortcake will be gone," Eppie said with a bright smile. "Don't worry, though. We'll try to save you some hot cocoa."

Cole tensed. It was one thing for his father to be here at the hot spring. He didn't know how to prevent that. But Stan wasn't welcome at the house.

Stan dropped the smaller towel he was briskly rubbing around his still-thick hair and gave Cole a quick look, then turned to Eppie. "I appreciate that, but I'll have to take a rain check, though I do love almond shortcake. I'm afraid I have to get back. I have a puppy who causes havoc if I'm away too long."

"His name is Buster and he's *so cute*," Jazmyn gushed.

Stan smiled down at her with clear affection that made Cole grind his teeth. What a pitiful ploy, to use a puppy to get to his children. The obvious manipulation pissed him off maybe even worse than Stan showing up at the ranch out of the blue.

"It's sure nice to see you again, Stanford," Eppie said. "You've been away far too long. Your mother would have been happy to know you've finally come home."

Ever the charmer except to his own children, Stan kissed her cheek and then, with a quick look at his son, he did the same to Devin before he climbed into his silver SUV and headed down the mountainside.

"I wish we could see Buster again," Ty said, his voice soft and dreamy, maybe even a little sleepy from soaking in the relaxing mineral waters.

The boy leaned his damp head against Cole's arm, a spontaneous, heartwarming gesture of trust and affection from this boy he loved so much.

"He's the cutest dog ever," Jazmyn said in the same sort of wistful tone.

Cole watched his father go, his chest thick with a jumble of emotion.

His life had seemed so much easier when he had just been trying to make a go of a small Idaho ranch on his own and driving as often as he could manage to wherever Sharla had taken the kids this time.

Easier wasn't the same thing as better, though. He wouldn't change anything, even with his father's presence on the ranch like a constant burr beneath his saddle.

AFTER EVERYONE CHANGED and the caravan wended its way back to the ranch house, Cole made sure his guests were set up with refreshments under Letty's expert care before he grabbed a piece of Hazel's famous almond shortcake on a plate and retreated to his office.

He was deep in the midst of going over the quarterly financial statement from his accountant when a soft knock interrupted him.

"Yeah. Come in."

Somehow he wasn't surprised to find Devin there with a plate full of a few more cookies and a mug of hot cocoa.

He didn't care about the snacks. She was the one who looked good enough to eat.

"I snagged a few more cookies for you before everybody left."

"Is the party over, then?"

She laughed softly. "If that was a party, it was a very low-key one. Everybody is all loose and relaxed after soaking in your mineral spring. I think Paul actually might have fallen asleep over his cocoa for a minute."

He managed a smile, even as she came closer to set the plate on the edge of his desk, stirring the air currents with the flowers-and-strawberries scent of her.

"I just stopped by before leaving to thank you once more for allowing us to use the spring this week. I guess it was fairly obvious that everybody enjoyed it very much."

"You're welcome."

She didn't move away. If he reached out a hand, he could tug her into his lap...

"Your father skipped the hot cocoa soiree, I noticed."

"He at least had the wisdom to know that while I can't prevent him from moving freely around the ranch, this is my house and he's not welcome here."

She sighed, leaning against the edge of the desk. "I wish you could have seen him while we were in the water. I could tell from his face that he wanted so badly to talk to Ty or Jazmyn, but he forced himself to stay away from them."

"Good."

"Okay, I know this is none of my business. It's your family, your choice. But I just have to say this one more time, and then I'll drop it forever, I swear. Your father is trying to reach out. That's an amazing gift and I don't think you see it. My own father is gone and I would give anything to have the chance to spend a little more time with him while I had him."

"My father is not yours."

"I get that. Believe me. What I don't understand is, given the hard road you have traveled yourself, why can't you accept that someone else might just be trying to climb over rubble left from the choices he's made?"

"You can't step in and heal this one, Devin. Let it go."

"I don't want to heal anything," she protested. "I just see a man who would like to be part of his grand-children's lives and two lost and hurting children who need all the love and support they can find at this painful time in their lives."

"How would it help Ty and Jazmyn to develop a relationship with their grandfather, only to sustain another loss when he gets tired of whatever game he's playing and moves on?"

"But what if it's not a game?" she pressed. "What if your father sincerely wants to make a change in his life? He's come all this way. Why else would he do that?"

He pushed away from the desk and rose, furious with her, with his father, with the whole screwed-up situation—furious mostly at himself, for so desperately wanting something he could never have, because of a lifetime of poor choices.

"The decisions I make for the good of my children are none of your concern."

"I know that, but—"

"But nothing. Stay out of my family's business, Dr. Shaw, unless it relates to the medical care you give my sister."

She paled as if he had just shanked her in the gut. He felt like the world's biggest ass and wanted to tell her he was sorry, that he didn't mean any of it, but maybe it was for the best. If he was harsh enough to her, she might finally take her soft compassion and her sweet kisses and stay the hell away from him. Maybe then, he could go back to trying to figure out how he was going to get along without her.

"So I'm back to being *Dr. Shaw* now?" she asked quietly.

"Yes. That's the way we should have kept things."

He didn't want to hurt her but he didn't know how else he could regain a little control over the situation. He should never have let things go so far, let her slip into their lives and their hearts.

"I appreciate all your help these last few weeks with the kids but as far as I'm concerned, this is the end of things. I agreed to let you and your friends use the hot spring twice and you have. That's it. I fulfilled my side of things and now we're done."

Her face paled a shade further, leaving her eyes a stark, wounded green.

Was he destined to hurt every single person who ever had the misfortune to come into his world?

He wanted, more than he had ever wanted any-thing—even his freedom during those hellish months in prison—that things could be different for them.

That *he* could be different.

"We're done. Just like that." Her voice wavered just a little before she seemed to find control.

Though his heart felt as if it was cracking apart, he

forced a casual shrug and put on his best *playa* smile, the one he used to use on all the hot little things who couldn't wait to get him out of his Wranglers.

"If my circumstances were different, I might be tempted to stretch things out a little longer. I've been a long time without sex and you're a beautiful, enthusiastic woman. We obviously have chemistry together and it would be fun to see where things go."

"Fun." Now her voice didn't wobble at all. It was flat, hard, emotionless.

"Sure. I think the two of us would really rip up the sheets together, don't you? But I've got two kids to consider—kids who just lost the only constant in their life, no matter how unstable their mother might have been. They need my full attention right now. I don't have time for the distraction of a fling with you, no matter how tempted I might be by what you've been offering since the day we met."

She stared at him, eyes huge in her face.

"Besides that," he forced himself to go on, "I've got Sharla's mother breathing down my neck, trying her best to take custody of the kids. I can't give Trixie any more grounds to appeal. I'm sure you can understand that. For both our sakes—all our sakes, really—it would be best if you stayed away from Evergreen Springs, now that I've fulfilled my side of the bargain."

"Well. That's certainly clear enough." Her hands were shaking a little but she shoved them into her pockets. His chest felt achy and tight, as if he'd just run to the top of the Redemptions and back.

Had he pissed her off enough? He couldn't tell. There was still a shadow of doubt in her eyes, as if she suspected he was deliberately trying to push her away. She was too insightful, damn it.

He decided he had no choice but to ramp things up. He had always been particularly talented at taking a bad situation and making it worse. Why stop now?

"Consider yourself fortunate," he drawled. "We never got around to screwing, so at least you don't have that complication to add to the mix. I don't like breaking hearts if I don't have to."

She stared at him for a long moment, until he felt small and stupid and worthless. Any doubt or confusion in her eyes had been completely eradicated. Now she just looked at him with all the disgust he thought should have been there all along.

"Oh, certainly. You can be sure I'll be thanking my lucky stars from now until next Christmas for that."

She rose from the chair and walked out without another word.

As soon as she left, he wanted to call her back. He wanted to race after her, wrap his arms around her, bury his face in her neck and beg her to forgive him. He wanted to tell her he didn't mean a word he said, that he needed her, that he would try to make a little peace with his father if she thought that was for the best.

He did none of those things, of course. He sat at his desk, wishing—as he had never wanted a damn thing in his life—that he could be the sort of man she deserved.

DEVIN WALKED OUT of the ranch office with her head high and her spine straight while her emotions seemed as fragile and frayed as antique lace.

I don't have time for the distraction of a fling with you, no matter how tempted I might be by what you've been offering since the day we met.

The words seemed to race around her head and she wanted to die of humiliation. He had seen what she refused to face, that she had been attracted to him, that she had wanted him, from the very beginning.

Of course he wouldn't want her in return. Why would he? Sure, he had kissed her and pretended to be attracted to her but only because she was warm and willing and *there*. She didn't have anything that would keep a man interested for long.

Her hands were trembling. *All* of her was trembling and she was suddenly ice-cold, as if she had walked out of the warm, soothing waters of Evergreen Springs into a raging blizzard.

She walked down the hallway to the great room, where she spotted the beautiful Christmas tree he had cut down. The time decorating it with his darling children would always be precious to her.

So many memories of the past few weeks poured through her. Listening to him sing Christmas carols in the afternoon hush of a quiet barn, enjoying the boat parade through the eyes of his children, driving through Shelter Springs to look at Christmas lights.

Heated kisses and tender moments.

Had she imagined the feelings growing between them? Had they been entirely lopsided? If so, he was an amazing actor, much better than she would ever have guessed. Maybe his time in prison had taught him how to conceal his true emotions.

She stopped dead. Prison. Of course.

That scene in his office had been the act. That wasn't the man she knew, the one she'd fallen in love with. He had been trying to push Devin from their lives.

The surly ex-con washed-up rodeo star and the well-respected town doctor. Isn't that what he had said the other night?

She had just been played. He had wanted her to see him as the womanizing player he used to be as a reminder of all that he had done.

She wanted to march back into the office and throw his words back at him, to see if she was right.

She couldn't, she realized as a fresh wave of pain washed over her. Whatever was the truth, even if he had feelings for her, he had made it plain he didn't want her in their lives. That, at least, was no act.

Oh, it would hurt to walk away from him and from the children she had come to cherish.

The worst thing was knowing it was her own fault. She had pushed herself into their world, knocking over barriers and objections from him, certain she could help them.

McKenzie had told her more than once that she suffered from some kind of Messiah Complex, the fierce need to try repairing everything broken within her sphere.

She couldn't deny it. To some degree, everyone

who entered the medical profession suffered from it a little. She loved to fix people.

Her own recovery—which plenty of her doctors and nurses weren't shy about calling nothing short of miraculous—played a big part in that. *She* had been healed thanks to advances in modern medicine and perhaps the natural healing effects of Lake Haven, thus she felt a great obligation to extend the same gift to others.

Of course, that Messiah Complex was quickly beaten out of most first-year medical students by the reality of life and the frailties and idiosyncrasies of the human body. She had learned early that she couldn't heal everyone.

In Cole's situation, she had only wanted to help. She had fallen for his kids—prickly, bossy, adorable Jazmyn and sweet, sweet Ty—and had wanted to ease their pain a little. Now she was afraid she would only cause them more pain when she extricated herself from their world.

What choice did she have? Cole had made it plain she was no longer welcome at Evergreen Springs.

She wasn't sure how long she stood in the entryway, trying to summon the strength to walk out those doors for the last time. She was close to it when Letty walked out of the kitchen and found her there.

"You're leaving?" Letty asked.

Yes. Forever. Devin forced a smile, even though her heart ached.

"I have to go. I…should run to the hospital to check on a few of my patients."

"You work too hard, my dear."

Work was all she had. The rest of her life stretched ahead of her, empty and barren. She loved Cole and his children and the idea of walking away from them devastated her.

"If the people of Haven Point would just stop getting sick, I wouldn't have to," she managed. "Where are the kids?"

"They're finishing their homework."

"I'd…like to say goodbye," she said.

She walked in and found them both squabbling over one last cookie on a plate. Ty finally broke it in half and gave the larger piece to his sister, a sweet gesture that broke her heart all over again.

"Hey, kids," she said in a falsely cheerful tone. "I have to go."

"Oh!" Ty gave a disappointed look. "I wanted you to stay for dinner. We're having chicken strips and baked fries. Letty makes the *best* fries."

"Why are they still called fries when they're baked, not fried?" Jazmyn asked.

"I'm not sure. Whatever the reason, your dinner sounds delicious. I'm sorry to miss it but I have to leave. Can I have a hug?"

Ty jumped up, wrapping his arms around her waist tightly. She clung to him for a long moment and finally kissed the top of his head, which smelled of shampoo and little-boy sweat.

"Goodbye, my dear."

Jazmyn stood more slowly, her gaze narrowed as

if she suspected something wrong but couldn't figure out what it might be.

She gave her a hug, then stepped away, still looking at her with suspicion in her eyes that looked so much like her father's. "Bye, Devin."

"I hope you have a wonderful Christmas," she said. To her dismay, her voice wobbled a bit on the last word and she quickly ordered her features into smooth lines.

"Christmas isn't for four more days. Won't we see you before then?" Jaz asked.

"I doubt it. I'm going to be very busy working through the holidays. People still get sick at Christmas, I'm afraid. But merry Christmas. I'm sure it will be magical. Christmas always is. Goodbye, my dears."

She walked out before the sharp-eyed little girl could see the tears brimming in her eyes.

Out in the hall, she paused only long enough to grab a tissue off a handy box on the console table there. To her dismay, Letty followed her, concern on her features.

"Is everything okay, Devin?"

"Yes. Fine. I think my sinuses must have been affected by the minerals in the water today. Listen, thanks for the cookies and hot chocolate. Everybody loved the little post-soak party."

"It was Cole's idea but I was happy to help."

"Thanks, especially for being here for Cole and the kids."

"It's been my pleasure," Letty assured her, still

looking at her with concern. "I feel lucky to have the chance."

"Take care of them," Devin said. Somehow she mustered a smile from somewhere deep inside, then walked out into the cold and the gathering darkness.

CHAPTER EIGHTEEN

A HOSPITAL CAFETERIA was a lousy place to celebrate Christmas Eve—even when you were one of the medical professionals and not a patient or member of a patient's family.

The staff had done their best to make the cafeteria as cheerful as possible. A Christmas tree glowed in one corner and paper garlands created by the pediatric patients and staff had been looped around the doorways.

Festive decorations aside, it was still a hospital cafeteria. Christmas Eve was for home and hearth, for gathering around the fireplace and telling stories, singing songs, playing games, enjoying time with family. Not for being in the clinical setting of a medical facility.

Devin tried not to feel too sorry for herself. Okay, her brown-bag turkey sandwich wasn't her ideal late lunch on Christmas Eve but she had known what she was giving up when she volunteered to fill in during the holidays for the regular emergency department physicians. They all had families at home. Since she had only a couple of cats who barely deigned to notice she was there most of the time, she had been willing to make the sacrifice.

She refused to let herself dwell in self-pity. She was so tired of herself after the past few mopey days.

How were the children? she wondered. Were they excited about Santa coming that night? Had Cole found the last few items on their wish lists?

She hoped Ty received the LEGO set he had his eye on and that Jazmyn got the American Girl doll she had mentioned only about a dozen times.

Devin sank into a booth in the mostly deserted cafeteria, wishing she had at least asked one of the nurses working that day to have lunch with her.

She wouldn't feel lonely. That was a choice, a voluntary one that she refused to make. She would sit here and eat her turkey sandwich and leaf through the favorite collection of inspiring Christmas short stories that she reread every year.

Her holiday wouldn't be all bad. Though her mother was on an extended cruise with a friend, Devin and McKenzie were planning to get together the day after Christmas.

Meanwhile, she was doing something worthwhile with her holidays. She was here offering her help to people who needed it. She would be dealing with the food poisonings from bad potato salad, the overexertion from snow shoveling, the box cutter injuries from impatient people trying to open ridiculous packaging.

And she would continue to do it with joy, she decided as she sat there in the cheerless cafeteria. No matter how down she might feel inside, she would bring her very best self to help people who weren't at the hospital by choice.

She was just indulging in a snickerdoodle she'd brought in from a plate one of her neighbors had delivered the night before when she spied a familiar handsome older gentlemen walk into the cafeteria.

Cole's father.

She couldn't seem to escape Cole, wherever she was.

Stanford's shoulders seemed more stooped than usual as he looked at the choices available for Christmas Eve lunch. The food service would be available only for dinner that day, so the options now mostly included premade sandwiches in the cooler, fruit and snacks.

He grabbed an apple and a bag of potato chips, paid for them and then started to sit down when he spotted her in the corner and switched directions.

"Hey, Doc."

She couldn't help a pang of sympathy for the man. He looked more alone than she was.

"I'm afraid the selection is limited for now but they're serving a turkey dinner later, if you're still around."

He held up the apple and chips. "This will do me. I just needed a little something to tide me over."

"I'm guessing you've been to see Tricia. I haven't had a chance to see her yet today. I was planning to stop in briefly after I eat. How is she?"

Worry creased his still-handsome features. "Tired of being here and ready to pop those babies, I guess.

I don't really know. She didn't say much. She did seem more uncomfortable than usual today, though."

How did Tricia feel about her father visiting her? Devin had the impression by some of the things she had said that Tricia was a little more willing to let her father work his way into her life than Cole. She had been younger when the two of them came to live with their grandparents. That might be why she didn't hold fast to the same bitter anger he did.

Stanford's features looked suddenly bleak and he gazed down at his apple as if he didn't recognize what it was. "I had to visit her today. After the next few days, I don't think I'll be very welcome."

She didn't like the sound of that. "Why? Has something happened?"

He gripped the apple more tightly, giving her a small smile that looked falsely hearty. "Oh, nothing. Never mind. You know, I've changed my mind. I think I'll eat my snack on the way home. Buster will be ready to go out soon. Merry Christmas to you, Dr. Shaw."

"Merry Christmas," she answered automatically.

Still troubled by the cryptic conversation, she finished her sandwich quickly and then hurried out of the cafeteria toward Tricia's room to ask her about it.

As she made her way through the hospital, it occurred to her, belatedly, that Cole might very likely be there with the children, visiting his sister.

She should have thought of that. She hadn't seen him since the evening he had basically told her to keep away from him and his children, closing the door on her as effectively as he shut down his father.

Her throat felt tight with the familiar aching sadness she hadn't been able to shake since that day. She missed them all terribly and felt as if any joy she might have found in this wonderful season of hope and light had seeped out of her as she drove away from Evergreen Springs.

She paused outside Tricia's room. What would she do if Cole and the children were inside? She sighed. She would be professional and detached and as polite as she could manage. What other choice did she have?

When she walked inside, however, she found Tricia alone in the room she had decorated to make it feel more like home. Her still-bandaged ankle rested on a pillow and she had a magazine propped on her huge-with-twins belly but seemed to be staring into space, not reading.

"Hi." Devin pinned on her brightest smile. Sometimes that confident, calming smile was the best gift she could give her patients. "How is everyone today?"

Tricia shifted on the bed. "Achy. I can't seem to get comfortable, no matter what I do. My back is killing me."

Devin looked at her more closely, taking in the tightness of her features, the flush in her cheeks. "Any contractions?"

Tricia shrugged listlessly. "More Braxton Hicks."

"When was the last time Dr. Randall gave you an exam?"

"Tuesday, before he left town."

He had gone to Utah for a ski vacation with his family. Devin had talked to him before he left about the possibility that Tricia might go into labor and they had agreed that she and his colleague Dr. Strong would deliver in that case.

"When was the last time the nurses hooked you up to the monitors?"

"This morning. Everything was fine then."

A great deal could change in a few hours. "I'd like to take a look at things, if you don't mind, and perhaps have the nurse hook you back up to the monitor."

A few moments later, she pulled off her gloves. The exam confirmed what she had seen on the printout from the monitors. She gave Tricia that comforting smile again and reached for her friend's hand. "Guess what? Those aren't Braxton Hicks."

Tricia sucked in a breath. "Are you serious?"

"Full-fledged labor, my friend. You're dilated to a four already. Merry Christmas, Tricia. Looks like you're going to have two more presents than you were expecting."

"Now? Today?"

"Apparently." She paused, feeling her face heat in a way that was completely unprofessional. "Do you need to call your brother?"

"He's on his way, actually, and should be here in a few minutes. He and the kids are having their Christmas Eve dinner here with me—a spinach lasagna you and your friends brought over for them. Jaz picked it for their dinner because it was red and green, Christmas colors."

"Clever. But you're going to want to hold off on

lasagna—and anything else—for now. Don't eat anything. I'll call Dr. Strong and let him know."

"Will they be all right?" Tricia asked, her voice thin-edged with fear. "Are they big enough?"

"They're thirty-seven weeks today, which is officially considered full-term. They'll probably be on the small side, which they would have been anyway, being twins, but I have a feeling they'll be fine."

Tricia leaned back against the pillow, her eyes dazed. "They're really coming today. I can't believe it. My babies."

Devin smiled, folding Tricia's fingers in hers. This was one of her favorite parts of being a family physician, helping to bring new life into the world.

It was also one of the hardest, emotionally. While doing her residency and internship and since she had opened her practice, she had been involved in dozens of deliveries. Each was an amazing experience, life-affirming and joy-filled, even on the rare occasions when things didn't go as expected.

They were also emotionally draining and clawed at the scabs around her heart.

"Since this is your first pregnancy, it might take a while," she said calmly to Tricia. "It's nearly two-thirty now. There's a good chance they might not be here until Christmas Day. On the other hand, your body has been getting ready to deliver since your accident, so things might progress faster than expected. I'm going to call the nurses in and get you moved up to the labor and delivery floor and call Dr. Strong and

Dr. Randall on his vacation to let them both know what's going on and see how they want to proceed."

She regretted the necessity, but she would also have to call in someone to cover for her in the emergency department. Her partner—and Ben Kilpatrick's father, Russell Warrick—was the logical choice as he didn't have young children. He had grandchildren but she knew he was going to visit them Christmas evening.

Tricia was her friend and she was alone. Devin wasn't going to miss this delivery.

While she was going over what she had to do, she suddenly realized Tricia had gone quiet, her features pale.

"What's wrong?"

She gripped Devin's hand. "I'm not ready. How can I do this by myself?"

"You won't be by yourself. I'll be there the whole time, along with Dr. Strong and an excellent team of nurses and techs on the labor and delivery floor."

"I don't mean the delivery itself, though I'm scared to death of that. I mean afterward. I don't know if I can handle twins by myself. What if I'm a terrible mother?"

Devin shoved aside her to-do list and her own emotional scars that had no place here. "Listen to me. You're going to be a fantastic mother, Tricia. I've seen you with Ty and Jazmyn and you're great with them. And you won't be by yourself. You'll have Cole to help you and Letty, who can't wait to take care of you and those babies of yours. Your father, too, if

you let him." She smiled. "And don't forget Jazmyn.
Knowing her, she'll insist on being your number one
helper, whether you want her to be or not."

Tricia gave a small laugh, the color returning to her
features. "Yes. Yes, of course. You're right."

Her features suddenly tightened and she pressed
a hand to her abdomen. "I can't believe this is it. The
real thing."

"Yes. And what a wonderful Christmas it will be
for all of you."

She smiled, gave her patient's hand another squeeze
and then hurried out of the room to start the wheels in
motion for everything she needed to do to help Tricia's twins arrive safely.

FIVE HOURS LATER, as darkness descended and Christmas lights popped around the lake that gleamed a
shiny black outside the window, it became obvious
Devin's prediction would come true.

Labor had progressed quickly and it appeared as if
Tricia would indeed have a Christmas Eve delivery.

"You're doing great," she told her friend. "A few
more hard contractions like that and we'll be in transition and ready to rock and roll."

"What's this *we* business?" Tricia muttered, though
she gave a tired smile as she said it.

Devin checked the monitors on the babies. Both
had healthy, regular heartbeats, and all seemed to be
proceeding normally. The babies were both in good
position.

Because everything was normal and routine, even

with the multiple birth component, Dr. Strong hadn't been eager to abandon his family's Christmas Eve party if he wasn't needed here. He had stopped in a few hours earlier and seemed content that Devin had things under control.

"I wouldn't do a single thing differently. Nothing," he had told her in consultation out in the hall. "She's obviously more comfortable with you than me, since I've only met her once. I'm fine with letting you take point on this one, if you're okay with it."

"I am," she'd said. She appreciated his confidence in her and this wasn't her first time delivering twins, but she was still anxious for Tricia's sake.

"I'm only five minutes away if there are any complications at all or if you think we might be heading toward needing a C-section at any point. I'll lay off the eggnog at the party, just in case I'm needed here."

"Thanks, Kent. I'll keep you posted."

She was grateful to know he was close if Tricia ran into any difficulties, but so far everything was going smoothly.

"Thank you for everything, Devin," Tricia said after the next contraction. "I'm so glad you're here, even though I know this wasn't the way you planned to spend your Christmas Eve."

"No. I planned to be in the emergency department, dealing with all the domestic fights and the food poisonings and the stitches from people not knowing how to work their new electric knives."

Tricia's weak smile fell away at the sudden noise of commotion out in the hallway.

"What's going on?" she asked, craning her neck to hear better. "That sounds like Cole."

Devin's shoulders went taut. Over the past five hours, Cole and the children had been in and out of the room. Things had been predictably awkward and they had hardly exchanged two words, both focused on Tricia and trying to ignore the tension between them.

The loud male voices in the hall continued and Devin could see it was distressing her patient.

Sylvie Taylor, the maternity nurse helping Tricia, looked at the door. "Do you want me to check it out?"

"No. Stay here. I'm sure it's nothing but I'll go take a look."

She headed for the door, just as they distinctly heard the words *my wife*, which elicited a gasp of shock from Tricia.

"That's...impossible!" Tricia exclaimed.

"What is?" Devin asked, just as the door burst open and a tall, wiry, handsome man burst through with Cole close behind and lurched toward the bed.

"Patricia."

"I'm sorry, sis. I tried to stop him." Cole followed the man, looking big and tough and dangerously angry.

"You're in labor," the man exclaimed. Devin hadn't expected the British accent from Tricia's husband— or that Sean Hollister would look haggard, unshaven and wan.

"You've been in hospital for two weeks and you never bothered to say a word to me. You blocked my calls, you didn't respond to my messages or my emails. I get one lousy text message saying you're staying with your brother and I'm not to contact you. You didn't seem to care that I was going crazy for worry. I told myself you're pregnant and hormonal and not yourself, thinking you'll come to your senses and be home any day. But then the days turned into weeks and you still wouldn't answer my calls."

"You knew where she was," Cole growled, looking ready to drag the man behind his horse for a few hundred miles. "You could have come out here to Idaho anytime to see her in person."

"I wanted to. God knows, I wanted to. I started to a dozen times, but I was afraid of making things worse, pushing you further away, and then this morning I had finally decided, to hell with it, I was driving here anyway to have things out with you once and for all. Just as I'm on my way out with my bag packed, I get a phone call from Stanford, who tells me in no uncertain terms, with a great deal of unflattering terms, what a son of a bitch I've been."

Tricia frowned. "My…father called you?"

"Yes. Earlier this morning. He told me I deserve to rot in hell for leaving you here alone with a sprained ankle and two babies you've been trying for two weeks to keep from coming too early. Why didn't you tell me, Tricia?"

"What difference would it have made?" she snapped.

"I would have been here, from the very beginning! I could have helped you through this, damn it. Instead, you shut me out, like you've been doing from the moment you found out you were pregnant."

"I shut you out?" Tricia flushed and Devin saw her heart rate rise on the monitor. "I did everything I could to involve you in the pregnancy. You wouldn't even come to the last ultrasound!"

He raked a hand through shaggy hair. "Because you told me very clearly that I didn't have to come. In fact, you made it sound like you didn't want me there. You deliberately scheduled the ultrasound for a time you knew I had an upcoming trip and would be away, just like every other prenatal appointment. You scheduled them all when I was traveling or had meetings I couldn't miss, even though I was careful to give you my calendar."

In response, Tricia only moaned in pain as another contraction rolled over her. Her hands clenched the side rails of the bed and her abdomen visibly tightened under the sheet.

Sylvie, eyes wide as she watched the ongoing drama, froze for a moment, so Devin stepped in. "That's it. That's the way, my dear," she said calmly to her patient.

When it was over, Tricia sagged against the pillows with her eyes closed. "Do we have to discuss this now?" she said to her husband, her voice sounding weak, muffled. "I'm only a few contractions away from having these babies. I don't need this right now. I would like you to leave."

Cole moved closer, all wide shoulders and dangerous, menacing muscles. "You heard her. You need to leave."

Hollister gaped at his brother-in-law and then at his wife. "I'm the father! Don't I have the right to be here?"

"You didn't want these babies and you didn't want me. As far as I'm concerned, you have the right to go to hell."

The last word came out on a sob. As fervent declarations went, it was a little on the cheesy side but Devin decided she would give Tricia some allowances for being in labor and in pain.

"I never said I didn't want you. I love you!"

"But not the babies."

He raked a hand through his hair again. "Neither of us wanted children. We said it to each other a thousand times. And then you get pregnant. With twins!"

"Not by myself, if you recall," Tricia said heatedly, just as another contraction washed over her, stronger this time. They were definitely heading into transition. The contractions were coming faster and stronger.

When the wave of pain was over, Sean Hollister looked even more pale than Tricia.

"Please…go," she whispered, looking devastated. Her heart rate climbed another notch on the monitor and Devin decided she needed to step in.

"I'm afraid I have to ask you to leave the room," she said. "I can't kick you out of the hospital unless you're deemed a security risk but the mother gets final say about who can remain in the delivery room."

"Even when they're my babies?"

"Yes. I'm sorry."

Cole crossed his arms over his chest like a bouncer in a nightclub, ready to throw his brother-in-law out on his ass, Devin was sure.

The man looked even more devastated, his eyes hollow and filled with so much pain that Devin couldn't help feeling a little sorry for him.

"I need to say one more thing. You told me to go to hell. Where do you think I've been this last month? I haven't slept more than an hour or two at a time since you left. I keep waking up and hoping this is some kind of nightmare and you'll be there. I'm bollocks at work and can't focus on a thing and I've lost a stone in the last month."

He gripped her hand, a desperate look in his eyes. "Whatever else you think of me, I love you, my darling. I never stopped. I love you and…and I love our son and daughter. Here. I brought something for them."

Out of the pocket of his suede jacket, he pulled two tiny onesies out. One was pink and said Daddy's Sweetheart and the other was blue and said Daddy's Little Man.

"Oh," Tricia whispered.

Out of the corner of her gaze, Devin saw the nurse press a hand to her mouth, eyes watching the unfolding drama as if it was more exciting than the tele-novelas all the staff watched on their breaks.

"I bought these the day you told me you were having twins," Hollister said, his voice shaking with suppressed emotion. "I'd forgotten about them, stuffed them in a drawer in my bureau and only just found them when I was throwing things in a bag to come here. I'm sure they're too big but…maybe they'll fit in a month or two."

Tricia said nothing, only gazed between the little onesies and her husband.

At her continued silence, he drew in a shaky, defeated breath and stepped away. "I… May I stay here at the hospital until they're born, just to see them and make sure you're all…safe?"

At that word, Tricia hitched in a wobbly breath.

The man sank to his knees beside the bed and grabbed her hand. "Please, Patricia. Please don't make me leave. I'm begging you. I want to be here for you and for the babies. I'll stay in the corner and won't say a word, but please. Let me stay."

"Oh, Sean." She grabbed the onesies with her other hand and clutched them to her breast, then burst into noisy sobs.

"Don't cry. Don't cry. I'll go. I'm sorry."

After a moment and another contraction, her sobs subsided. She shook her drenched head on the pillow and then curved her hand up and pushed a lock of hair out of his face. "You need a haircut and a shave. You look as lousy as I do," she said.

"I've never seen you more beautiful," he said fervently, eyes blazing with emotion.

Beside Devin, Sylvie gave a small, breathy sigh of delight.

Devin didn't know what to think. She thought of the heartbreak Tricia had shared with her, the fear that her husband would never be able to love their children. It had been a great enough fear that she had left him over it.

This man looked like someone completely enamored of his wife. He also looked nervous about becoming a father, but that didn't necessarily mean he wouldn't be a good one. Perhaps he was one of those men who had a tough time showing their deeper emotions—the natural anxiety a man would have facing impending fatherhood of twins—and perhaps Tricia had interpreted that as him not wanting the babies.

Devin thought it just as likely that Tricia's own background had colored her perception. While she wasn't as bitter as Cole and had begun to reestablish a relationship with Stanford, her father had walked out at an impressionable age and certainly must have left scars and insecurities.

Perhaps this had been a preemptive strike. Maybe Tricia had been subconsciously looking for things that proved her husband wanted to abandon her and the babies, just as Stanford had abandoned her and Cole, and had fled the situation to protect herself and her children from future hurt.

Not that the reasons mattered now, not when Tricia's body was tensing with another hard contraction. This time, her husband was there to wipe her face and murmur encouragement.

"So that's it?" Cole demanded when the contraction had passed. "After a month of ignoring you and the babies, he just gets to walk back in like nothing has happened?"

Tricia turned from her husband to her brother. "These babies are going to be here within the hour. I don't have time to figure out if I'm making the right decision. I only know I love him. He's my husband and the father of my children and if he wants to be here, I want him here. That's the only thing that matters right now."

Cole looked baffled by the whole situation. "Your choice, I guess. Since you don't need me now, I'll go back into the waiting room with the kids. Just know that if you change your mind, I'm just out there. I'll be more than happy to come in and toss him out into the snow for you."

"Thank you, Cole."

She gave him a ragged smile. After a moment, Cole walked to the bedside. "For the record, I love you, too. You're one of the strongest women I know. You got this."

He kissed the top of her head in a tender gesture that made Devin's heart ache and then turned away. As he did, his gaze met Devin's. She thought she saw something flash there, raw and emotional, then he nodded curtly to her and walked out of the room.

THIS WAS NO new revelation to him, but Cole did *not* understand women.

All these weeks of misery, of Tricia being completely convinced the man didn't love her and their children, and now his sister was willing to let her husband back, just like that. It made no sense to him—but then, it wasn't his decision, either. If Tricia wanted

Sean here now while she went through the pain of labor and delivery—if she was willing to work through their issues, despite the past rough few weeks—Cole had to support her. Even if he didn't understand what had just happened in there.

His mind kept straying to Devin. She wore green scrubs, with her luscious hair pulled back into a tight braid. She had looked brisk and efficient and in control—except that moment when her eyes had met his just as he walked out, when deeper, unfathomable emotion had stirred there.

He couldn't tell if she was angry with him or if he had glimpsed something else.

He wanted to march back in and ask her but he supposed she was a little busy right now, delivering his sister's twins and all.

With a sigh, he pushed the memory away and walked out to the waiting room, where he found the kids still watching one of their favorite Christmas movies.

They were snuggled together on one of the sofas under a blanket one of the kind labor and delivery nurses must have brought them, like two little puppies. As he watched, Ty covered a yawn.

Poor things. This wasn't the way they all intended to spend Christmas Eve. It was now nearly 8:00 p.m., about the time they should be settling down in their beds to dream about Santa and what he might bring the next day. Instead, they were stuck in a hospital waiting room.

They'd been wonderfully patient through the

whole thing and as he stood in the doorway, he was consumed with love for these two little creatures doing their best to adapt to the circumstances life had handed them.

Jazmyn spotted him in the doorway first. Her eyes brightened. "Did Aunt Tricia have her babies?" she asked.

He walked inside. "Not yet. Soon, though."

"She's really gonna have them *tonight*? On Christmas Eve?" Ty asked in an awestruck voice.

"Looks like it."

"Are we going to stay the whole time, until she does?" Jazmyn asked.

What else could he do? He should probably take the kids home but he didn't feel good about leaving Tricia, even though her husband was there now. "I'm pretty sure it's close now. Do you mind waiting a bit longer."

"No. I want to see them. Can we hold them?"

"Probably not tonight but maybe tomorrow. Thanks for keeping an eye on Ty for me."

"You're welcome."

She looked at the television set, then back at him. "Who was that man you were mad at before?"

"I didn't like when you yelled," Ty added.

He could only imagine how frightening that must have been for his kids when Sean had walked in, bold as brass, and Cole had lost his temper.

He was careful to keep control around the children. They had probably never seen him truly angry.

"That's her husband. Your uncle Sean." He still

thought it was sad that the children had never met Tricia's husband, since Sharla had despised his sister and would never have made the effort to connect, even when she was in California.

"Why were you so mad at him?" Ty asked, still giving him wary looks.

He sighed. "It's a long story. He made Aunt Tricia sad and I didn't want him to do it again."

"Is he in there now, with Aunt Tricia?" Jazmyn asked.

"Yes. He's going to stay until the babies come."

"Will Aunt Tricia go back to California now?" she asked.

"Maybe. I don't know what will happen."

She seemed to accept this with equanimity. Ty yawned and snuggled down into the sofa.

He thought again they should be home in their own beds but he would get them there eventually. If nothing else, this would be an unforgettable Christmas, the year they waited for new cousins along with Santa Claus.

They watched for a few more moments, until the closing credits, then Jazmyn turned to him. "Will you read us a Christmas story?" she asked. "While we were waiting for you, we went through all the books on the bookshelf until we found some. You said we could read stories tonight."

She pointed to a stack of five or six Christmas stories. What a funny kid she was. Before he knew Tricia was in labor, he had told the kids they could watch a Christmas movie and read some books that evening to celebrate the holiday. The venue and the circumstances might have changed but Jazmyn would hold him to what he had said, no matter what.

"Sure. Sounds perfect. Let's see what we have here."

He picked up the pile and leafed through it until he found a story that looked appealing.

"Scoot over. You need to sit in the middle so we can both see the pictures," Jazmyn directed.

Someday she was going to make an excellent four-star general. Or maybe a prison warden.

He almost laughed at the irony of that as he complied and moved to the middle of the sofa. Once the children were settled with their blankets around them, Cole started reading.

This wasn't at all the way he intended to spend Christmas Eve, he thought after the third book—this one about mischievous Christmas trolls—but it wasn't bad, either. Jazmyn had her chin resting on his biceps so she could see the pictures and on his other side, Ty was quiet and still.

He turned to the next page just as he sensed the presence of someone else. He looked up and his mouth tightened at the sight of his father standing in the doorway, his features strained and his parka covered in snowflakes.

That same helpless frustration as always washed over him. He opened his mouth to ask his father what the hell he thought he was doing there but then just as quickly closed it. He figured he had done his share of yelling for the night.

"Has she had the babies yet?" Stan asked urgently.

"Not as far as I know. How did you know she was in labor?"

Stan moved into the room. "Hollister texted me that he was here and that he was staying through the delivery. I suppose you think I shouldn't have told him she was in the hospital. One more thing for you to hate me over."

Cole couldn't seem to dredge up any anger, as much as he wanted to. How many times had he hounded Tricia to call her husband over the past month? He had almost called the man himself a few times but had always backed down at the last minute, figuring his sister had the right to manage her own life.

Maybe if he *had* called Sean, they could have avoided this last-minute drama.

"He's here now. Don't know what either one of us can do about it at this point."

"I hope I did the right thing."

He wasn't about to give his father absolution. "Tricia wants him to stay, so I guess that's the end of it."

"I suppose you're right." Stanford sank into the sofa across from them. "I interrupted. I'm sorry. Go back to your story."

He was going to wait here with them? Cole swallowed down his irritation. He couldn't ask the man to leave. It was a public space and he didn't have that right. He supposed he would have to tolerate it, for Tricia's sake.

Feeling itchy and uncomfortable, he returned to

the story. When he finished, Jazmyn gave a happy sigh. "That's a great story."

"I like it, too," Ty said sleepily. He was three-quarters of the way asleep. A little push in the right direction would send him over the edge.

"Why don't you two close your eyes and stretch out on that other sofa."

"I'm not sleepy," Ty said, smothering a huge yawn.

"You don't have to sleep, just rest for a minute. I'll let you know when Aunt Tricia has her babies." Cole picked up his son and carried him across the space to the other sofa. "Jazmyn, there's room on this other end for you. You can come down here and read to yourself for a minute."

"I guess I could."

"Do you want me to carry you?"

"I'm not a baby," she said, picking up her blanket and carrying it to the other sofa. He helped her get settled and handed her a book, but he could tell even as he returned to his own spot that she would soon be asleep like her brother.

Sure enough, ten minutes later, both children were dozing on the sofa. He glanced at his watch. It was after nine. Tricia had officially been in labor nearly seven hours, and probably longer than that, unofficially. How much longer?

He leaned his head back on the sofa and closed his eyes, wishing he'd brought some paperwork with him to pass the time. The moment he closed his eyes, he pictured Devin again, cool and competent in the delivery room.

It was another snapshot for the collection he was saving in his mind. He added to the one of her vibrant and alive out in the pine forest. Sweetly solicitous to her elderly friends at the hot spring. Bright with excitement during the light parade on the lake. Warm and deliciously responsive as she kissed him...

His father's voice interrupted the internal slide show just at the best part.

"You're a good father, son."

He tensed, then deliberately forced his shoulders to relax.

"Doesn't feel like it, most of the time," he admitted. He loved his kids but he wasn't sure he was doing any of this right. He had a hard time staying consistent with rules. He yelled at them sometimes when he was at the end of his rope. He didn't know how to ease their heartache over their mother, especially when he had come to despise her in recent years.

"Take it from someone who wasn't. A good father, I mean. You've got the stuff." Stan gave a smile that was tinged with emotion. "Not many men are strong enough to step up and do what it takes in your circumstances. I know I wasn't."

At his father's low words, Cole gazed at him. This was the closest Stan had ever come to admitting he might have been wrong to walk away from his kids.

"Those two are lucky to have you," Stan went on, his voice gruff.

He was the lucky one. His children gave his life meaning and purpose.

"We have each other," he said.

"As it should be," Stan said with a nod. He was quiet for a long while. When he finally spoke, his voice was subdued. "I wanted to tell you, I'm leaving Evergreen Springs."

Cole gazed at his father. He'd been expecting that announcement for some time. Instead of the relief he might have expected, he was startled to realize he mostly felt sad.

"I'll probably wait a few days to see how things shake out with Tricia and Sean and the babies," Stan went on, "then I'll get out of your hair. I guess I'll go back to Denver. I've still got my house there sitting empty. I'm sure you'll be glad to see the last of me."

"I can't say I'm surprised. That's what you do, isn't it? You leave."

Stan sighed. "I guess I deserve that. I don't want to leave this time. I've got nothing in Denver anymore. I never did, really. But I don't want to stay here when my presence is making you so unhappy, son."

Now the anger started to simmer. "Don't make this about me. It's about you. It's always about you."

He saw his father's hands tighten on his thighs. Stanford gazed at the sleeping children, then back at him. "When I found out about Sharla's accident, I thought maybe this was my chance to help you. To finally be there for you like I should have been when you and Tricia were young. I suppose I hoped we could find some kind of peace after all these years, but I can see now I'm only making things harder for you. That's not what I wanted at all. I'm sorry. For everything."

The low, emotional apology seemed to yank his feet right out from under him. Cole felt as if he'd just been dropped hard off a bronc.

If he didn't know better, he would swear his father was genuinely contrite.

Was he? Or was this only another manipulation?

Given the hard road you have traveled yourself, why can't you accept that someone else might just be trying to climb over rubble left from the choices he's made?

He heard Devin's voice in his head. Was she right? Was Stan really just trying to find some way to atone for the choices he had made, trying to build some connection now in an effort to help Cole and his children?

As if he had conjured her, she suddenly appeared in the doorway of the waiting room. She had lines of fatigue around her mouth and her eyes drooped with exhaustion. Still, her soft loveliness took his breath away.

"Oh. You're both here." She mustered a smile.

He rose anxiously and saw his father do the same.

"How is she?" he asked.

"And the twins. How are they?" Stan added his voice.

"Everyone is doing wonderfully. The babies are on the small side, as we expected. Five pounds eight ounces for the girl and five pounds six for her brother, but other than that, they're perfect in every way."

His father whispered a heartfelt prayer of thanks and Cole had to agree.

"Can we see her?" Cole asked. He included his father in the plural pronoun, a big step for him.

"For a few moments tonight. You can come back tomorrow and stay all you'd like but she's very tired and needs to rest. Oh, and I would ask you to go in one at a time."

He wanted to kiss her—not romantically, though he wanted that, too, but out of gratitude for her care of his sister. He had treated her poorly when she didn't deserve it. Of all the things he regretted in his life, that was near the top.

"I can stay with the children, if you'd like."

"Thanks." The word seemed wholly inadequate but he didn't trust himself now to say more.

When he headed for his sister's room, he found the door open. Inside Tricia was holding one baby and Sean in the chair next to her bed was holding the other. They wore identical expressions, both looking stunned and overwhelmed and completely besotted at becoming parents of twins.

Tricia beamed at him and stroked a finger down the baby's cheek. "Look what I did. Isn't it amazing?"

He laughed a little and stepped forward to the bedside to kiss her cheek.

"Amazing," he agreed. The word came out raspy from his raw throat and he had to clear it a couple of times. "They're beautiful. Just beautiful."

Right now they looked like a couple of little squashed eggplants, but they were hers, which made them beautiful.

"This is Jack and this one is Emma."

Emma had been their mother's name. He had wanted to name Jazmyn that but Sharla had refused, calling it too old-fashioned. It all worked out, as those things tended to do. Right now, he couldn't picture his daughter as anything but Jaz, but Emma seemed perfect for this little dear.

"You did good, kid."

"I know." She beamed. Right now in the exhausted euphoria following birth, she seemed completely different from the anxious woman she had appeared even yesterday. "Thanks. But I had help. Devin was amazing, wasn't she, Sean?"

Hollister nodded. "We were both nervous wrecks. Completely mental, but she was so calm throughout the entire thing. She's a darling."

She was. Absolutely. He nodded as his throat felt raw all over again. Emotions washed over him, sweetly tender. He stared at the couple and their children as the truth seemed to kick him right in the gut, harder than a feisty mule.

Devin *was* a darling. She was *his* darling.

He loved her.

He closed his eyes, wondering how in the world this whole thing had spun so completely out of his control. He was in love with Dr. Devin Shaw. He loved her courage and her kindness, her intelligence and her compassion.

Everything.

Instead of treating her with the tenderness that seemed to be washing into every corner of his heart, he had been crude and harsh to her, had done everything he could to push her away.

"Are you okay?" Tricia asked him.

"Yeah," he lied. He wasn't okay by a long shot. "I'm just so proud of you. You're going to be a terrific mom, Trish."

The little boy in her arms yawned hugely and she traced his cheek again with her finger. "You know, I think I am."

Still reeling from the shock, he nodded to both of them. "I'll get out of your way. Devin said you need your rest."

"Thank you for staying to the end."

"It's not the end. It's the beginning. Anyway, we're family. That's what we do." He leaned in and kissed her again. When he rose, he gave Sean a hard stare. To his credit, the man returned his look with a steady one of his own.

Cole wasn't sure he was ready to forgive him for whatever he had done to hurt Tricia but since she apparently had put it behind them, he could do nothing less. Jack and Emma needed their father, plain and simple. If Sean was willing to step up and do the job, as Stan had talked about, Cole figured he owed it to his sister to ease the man's way.

"If you need a place to crash while you're in town, we can probably find room at the ranch," he said to his brother-in-law.

Surprise flickered in the man's gaze briefly, then was gone. "Thanks, mate. I don't want to leave Patricia or the babies tonight, so I'll probably try to sleep a bit here, but perhaps I could bunk for a few hours at your place tomorrow."

"Sure."

"Dr. Shaw said we can probably leave the hospital day after tomorrow," he went on, "but I doubt any of us will be up to the flight for a few more days after that. I'm sure I can persuade Aidan to fly us home to California with him and Eliza and Maddie after New Year's. Would it be all right if we stayed with you until then?"

"You know you can."

It was Christmas Eve, he suddenly remembered. What a perfect time for new life and new beginnings— other than in a few years when the twins would probably hate that their birthday might always get a little lost in the holiday craziness.

He still needed to go home, get the kids to bed and do the whole Santa thing, something Tricia and Sean would be dealing with all too soon.

"I need to go but I'm afraid Jazmyn and Ty will never forgive me if I don't let them see the babies before we go. If it's all right, I'll just bring the kids to the doorway and they can say good-night and merry Christmas."

"Absolutely." Tricia smiled.

"Oh, and Dad's out in the waiting room. I guess I should have warned you. He wants to come in."

She blinked in surprise. "He's been waiting the whole time?"

"The last hour or so. Want me to send him back or are you too tired for a visitor?"

"You can send him back for a few minutes, I suppose."

"I'll do that." He paused. "Merry Christmas, sis."

She gave him a wobbly, joy-filled smile. "The best Christmas ever."

He was glad she thought so. Right now he was having a tough time feeling in the holiday mood when it seemed as if his life has just been shaken like a snow globe.

Both kids were awake when he returned to the waiting room. To his dismay, Devin was still there. At the sight of her, his heart seemed to expand like the Grinch's and he wondered how the hell he hadn't figured out his feelings before now.

When he was with her, he felt different. *Better.*

"They're beautiful, aren't they?" she said. The words were light but for some reason, her features were closed and she didn't meet his gaze.

"Absolutely," he said. "You did great, Doc."

Her mouth twisted into what might have passed for a smile to someone else but he knew it wasn't.

Something was wrong and somehow he sensed it was more than her completely justifiable anger at him for his paltry effort to push her away the other day. This was something else. She seemed jittery and anxious, very unlike herself.

Keeping half his attention on her, he spoke to his father. "Tricia said you can go back if you want."

"I'll do that." He rose and went to Devin. "Thank you, my dear, for helping her through this. We'll never forget what you've done."

"You're w-welcome." She mustered another fake-looking smile as Stanford gave her a quick hug but Cole didn't miss the way she was quick to extricate herself.

"I need to…" Her voice trailed off and she gestured blindly toward the hall. "I've got to go. Merry Christmas. All of you."

"Try to get to sleep or Santa won't c-come," she said to the children, then she smiled at everyone except him and hurried from the room.

"What's wrong with her? What did you say to her?" he demanded of Stan.

"Nothing!" Stan frowned after her. "Everything was fine until just a minute ago. Ty gave her a big hug and told her merry Christmas and he loved her. After that, she just sort of shut down."

"Did I do something bad?" Ty asked, distress on his little features.

Cole kissed the top of his son's head. "Not at all, son."

I did.

Despite the mistakes he had made, he sensed this was about more than him being an ass to her.

"Dad. I need to go talk to her. I hate to ask but can you… Do you mind hanging out with the kids for a few more moments?"

Stanford stared at him, eyes shocked. Like Cole, he must have realized the significance of Cole's request. He was trusting him with his children without anyone else there for a buffer. Somehow it felt as if they had both turned a corner.

"Of course," Stan said quickly. "Of course. Take your time. We'll be fine. Talk to Dr. Shaw."

It truly *was* a night for new beginnings and second chances.

Some part of him would always struggle to understand the choice his father had made after their mother died. It wasn't the one *he* would have made, but holding on to that old pain wasn't the answer. He couldn't rob his children of the chance to have one more person in their lives to love them.

He wasn't sure which way Devin had gone but was lucky enough to run into the labor and delivery nurse who had been helping Tricia.

"I'm looking for Dr. Shaw. Have you seen her?"

"Oh. You just missed her," Sylvie said. "There's a rooftop patio garden and we all go there sometimes to hang out or decompress. She said she needed some fresh air, so I think that's where she was heading."

"Do I need a code or a key card or anything?"

"No. It should be open."

"Thanks."

He took the elevator up a level and followed her instructions toward the patio, hoping she was right and Devin had truly come this way.

What would he say to her? He had no idea. He just couldn't bear the thought of her in pain, especially if he had caused it.

As he came off the elevator, he spotted a figure clad in green scrubs slipping through a door, just where the nurse had told him she was going.

He followed her and discovered she was in an

outdoor courtyard of sorts, protected on three sides by the building and open on the other to the lake and the Redemption Mountains. With heavy wrought-iron chairs and tables, it looked as if it had been created as a place of contemplation and reflection, a quiet corner with a beautiful view.

Though it was cold, it wasn't bitterly so, probably because it was protected from a crosswind. It also looked as if some sort of heating system of the hospital vented here, which warmed the air somewhat.

Still, Devin only wore thin scrubs. He moved closer to her and saw she was trembling.

"Are you crazy? It's Christmas Eve, it's snowing and you don't have a coat."

She turned at his voice. Her features were a pale blur in the moonlight, her eyes huge and stark. In her eyes, he saw shock and dismay at the sight of him, before she quickly averted her face.

"Go away," she ordered roughly.

He ignored her. What else could he do?

He was wearing a sweater, which he quickly pulled off. "Here. Wear this. It's not much but at least it's better than what you have on."

"I don't want your sweater." She didn't take it from him, stubborn woman, so he moved closer and wrapped it around her shoulders. They were trembling, he realized.

"What's wrong?"

"Don't be nice to me now," she said, her voice hushed and small. She still wouldn't look at him.

"I'm sorry. You're right. Give it back."

His dry tone elicited a tiny, strangled laugh. She turned slightly, just enough for him to see the tears trickling down her cheeks.

At the sight, his chest ached and his throat felt raw and tight. "Devin," he murmured.

He couldn't stand it. He had no choice. He opened his arms and wrapped them around her. She stood rigid for just a moment before she sagged against him and let out a little sob. She didn't put her arms around him, but she didn't pull away, either.

Her slim frame trembled but he didn't think it was from the cold. "What is it? I can't help unless you tell me what's wrong."

"Please. I'm okay. Sometimes it just hits me, that's all. I just…need a minute."

"What hits you?"

She was quiet, her cheek pressed to his chest, and he thought she wasn't going to answer for a long moment. When she did speak, her voice sounded tattered and tired.

"I was fine through the delivery. I was great even afterward, after things were cleaned up and the pediatrician brought the babies back all weighed and bundled up like little burritos. I was even fine when Tricia had me hold both of the babies so Sean could take a picture of me with them. I held it together, just like I always do. Then, when Ty hugged me a few minutes ago and told me he loved me, I just…lost it."

She wept silently and Cole could do nothing but hold her, baffled. A few stray snowflakes drifted down and under other circumstances, this would have been beautiful, with the moonlight on the water and the snow-covered mountains in the background. He barely noticed, unable to bear her distress.

"I don't understand," he finally said. "Why would you be upset about Ty hugging you?"

"I'll never have that. The baby, the delivery, the doting father like Sean was. Even worse, I'll never have the sweet little boy throwing his arms around me and telling me he loves me."

He frowned. "Why would you say that? You've got plenty of time."

"I have time. I just lack the necessary equipment to get the job done."

He stared down at her and she must have felt his gaze. At his continued silence, she pulled away, wrapping the sweater around her.

"What do you mean?" he finally had to ask.

"It's nothing. I shouldn't have said anything."

"Devin. Tell me."

She looked down at the water for a moment, then back at him. "When I was sixteen, I was diagnosed with cancer."

The word, ugly and dark, seemed to roar to life between them. Cancer. Oh, how he hated that word. Devin had cancer, when she was only a teenage girl. The reality of it overwhelmed him.

So many things made sense now. Her sister's over-protectiveness. Devin's words to him that everyone on earth faced trials and loss. *Nobody gets to walk through this world on a trail littered with rose pet-*

als, she had said. *Thorny bushes, deep ravines, jagged glass. Everybody faces something.*

This must have been what she meant.

What an amazing woman, he suddenly realized, falling hard for her all over again. What incredible strength and courage it must have taken for her to go into medicine in order to help others as she, perhaps, had been helped.

"Is everything okay now?" he had to ask.

"I've been in remission for more than ten years. Everything's fine. I had a scare last summer but it turned out to be nothing, so yes, I'm okay."

"I'm so sorry you had to go through that," he murmured.

She blinked a little at his solicitude. "It sucked," she said simply. "When I was a girl, I wanted two things out of life, to be a doctor and to become a mother. I've always loved kids and I wanted a half dozen of them. Because of the cancer, I had to have a...a hysterectomy when I was seventeen."

"Oh. That must have been heartbreaking."

The compassion in his voice somehow slid past the cold and the snowflakes, a warm little candle burning in the storm of her emotions.

"It's still the hardest part of the whole cancer gig. I was okay with the radiation when my hair fell out. Kenzie shaved hers, too, and we had a great time picking out wigs. I dealt with the chemotherapy that made me sick all the time. We made it through the fear and uncertainty to the other side. All that is in the past and seems like a distant memory but I still hate that I can never have children."

She had never told another soul this deep pain in her heart, not even her sister, though she suspected McKenzie must have guessed how hard the hysterectomy had been on her, emotionally.

Why she shared this intimate part of her cancer journey with Cole Barrett, of all people, she had no idea.

"Just because you can't give birth doesn't mean you can't be a mother. If you want kids that badly, you can adopt them. What's the big deal? There are tons of kids out there who need love."

Despite the raw jumble of emotions tangling through her, she almost laughed at his matter-of-fact tone. "Just like that."

"Why not? Problem solved. You can call the adoption agency tomorrow. The day after, anyway. Tomorrow's Christmas."

Now she did laugh. She never would have expected it, given her tangled emotions, and it sounded small and strangled but it was still a laugh.

"Adoption is not a new concept, believe me. If I ever do have a child, that will naturally be the route I'll have to take. It will be wonderful, I'm sure, and I won't care where the baby came from once it's in my arms. But some part of me is still a little melancholy that I'll never have the chance to go through what your sister did today."

"The pain and the stretch marks and being laid up for weeks in the hospital?"

"Not that part, obviously. The rest of it. Feeling a baby kick inside me, knowing she is growing healthy and strong because of me. Being able to nourish her at my breast. It's an amazing, miraculous thing that I can never fully understand, no matter how many years of education and training I might have."

She had been emotional enough from delivering a healthy set of twins for Tricia and Sean. Then, when she had spent a few moments with Jazmyn and Ty, she had felt such a rush of love for them, quickly followed by despair at the realization that she could never have a role in their lives.

It had all been too much for her poor battered heart and she had retreated here, to this quiet spot on top of the bustling hospital.

"The act of giving birth is only one tiny part of being a mother. You get that, right? Just like being a father is much more than simply an honorary title given to somebody with fast enough little swimmers in the right place at the right time?"

"I know." She pulled a tissue from her pocket and dried her eyes, touched more than she wanted to admit that he would try so hard to comfort her. "Most of the time it doesn't bother me. It just is and I can't change it now. But once in a while when my defenses are down, I indulge in a little pity party."

"Why were your defenses down?"

She thought about making some kind of excuse about her busy holiday schedule and the extra work she was doing to cover for the emergency physicians. Something about the quiet night and the stars glittering above them and the inherent magnitude of Christmas Eve prompted her to be honest.

"It's been a rough week for me," she admitted softly.

"Has it?" He gave her a searching look, filled with concern and regret and something more, something she couldn't identify in the cold moonlight.

She should stop now. The smart course would be to hand him back his sweater, wish him Merry Christmas again and part ways, but she couldn't do it. He had come looking for her, had held her when she cried, had looked at her with blue eyes that blazed with emotion.

She had told him something she hadn't shared with anyone else. She might as well make a complete fool of herself and tell him the rest of it.

"It's not every week a woman falls in love and has her heart broken at the same time."

She heard his intake of breath, sensed the sudden tension of his muscles.

He said nothing, just stared at her, and she was grateful for the cold night air against her suddenly heated face.

"Forget I said that, please. Apparently delivering twins is really good at removing all my internal filters. I'm sorry. I didn't mean to make things even more awkward between us. You made it plain you don't want me. I get it."

He made a rough, strangled sound low in his throat. "Don't want you? Is that what you think?"

"What else? You basically told me to stay away

from you and your children. You couldn't have been more clear."

"You don't get it, do you?" His voice was low, intense. "I only tried to push you away to keep myself from grabbing on tight and never letting go."

She caught her breath at his words, trying to make out his features in the moonlight. All the sounds of the night seemed magnified suddenly. The ever-present lake wind in the trees, an owl somewhere far below, a distant dog barking. Her pulse seemed to thunder in her ears.

Despite the snowflakes fluttering down, a warm glow seemed to begin at some point in her chest and spread throughout her limbs. A wary sort of hope.

"That sounds perfect," she finally whispered.

"Perfect, yes, but also completely impossible. Can't you see that?"

"No," she breathed. "Why is it impossible?"

He stepped closer and his gaze met hers, raw and anguished. "I'm in love with you, Devin. You're the most amazing woman I've ever met. I wish I could live my life over again to change the situation, to change what I've done and where I've been. I'm the worst possible man for you and we both know it."

"I'm beginning to think you're the *only* man for me."

He closed his eyes and sucked in a breath as if she had sliced through skin with a forged scalpel.

"I'm an ex-con, Devin. Don't you get it? I beat a man badly enough to put him in a hospital like this one for weeks. I don't know why, whether I was defending

myself or just pissed off, because I was too drunk and
don't even remember it. I'm an alcoholic burned-out
rodeo cowboy with a prison record."

The pain in his voice broke her heart. Why couldn't
he see himself the way everyone else saw him? After
just one night with him at the Lights on the Lake Festival, McKenzie raved about what a great guy he was.
All the nurses were half in love with him from his frequent visits to see his sister while she had been hospi-
talized. Letty wanted to adopt the man, for heaven's
sake.

His perception of himself was completely skewed
and she didn't know how to make him see that.

"That's not the man I fell in love with. The man I
love is devoted to his children, he is sweet to his sister, he is kind to senior citizens and horses and dogs.
He makes me feel things I never expected."

He looked as if he wanted to drink in her words
like McKenzie's dog Rika at the lake after a hard
run. But after a moment, his features turned stony
and cold. "You say that as if you're talking about two
different men. Before and after. I'm one man. I'm the
one who wasted so much time in my life with hard
living. I own my mistakes and I know I'll have to live
with them for the rest of my life."

She didn't know how to get through to him and she
was suddenly afraid she wouldn't be able to. *I'm in
love with you, Devin.* She clung tightly to the words,
folded them deep inside her heart.

They had a chance for happiness here and she
couldn't let him throw that away. In a last, desperate

effort, she grabbed his big, calloused hands in hers. These hands that had once been used as weapons but that could also hold a sick child and train a horse and touch a woman with sweet tenderness.

"In a few hours, it will be Christmas, Cole. The time for peace on earth and goodwill toward men. It's a wonderful time for forgiveness—and that includes forgiving yourself. Don't you think it's time you gave yourself a break? You paid for your crimes and you made full restitution. More important, you're trying to live an honorable, decent life now. That matters far more to me than the mistakes you made once."

He gazed at her for a long moment and she saw something tentative stir in his eyes, something warm and bright that began to push away the bleakness there. He touched her cheek with his thumb, wiping away a stray tear that hadn't frozen yet. His fingers were trembling, she realized, and she was humbled and overwhelmed that she could have that sort of effect on this hard, tough man.

"I don't deserve a woman like you," he said gruffly. For an instant, she felt the beginnings of a dark, awful despair that none of her words resonated with him, but then—before that had time to take root—he gave the lopsided smile she loved so much.

"But I sure as hell would like to do my best to try."

He lowered his mouth to hers and she gave a half sob, half laugh and threw her arms around his neck. The cold night air, the exhaustion from her long, difficult day, the pain and loneliness of the preceding week—none of it mattered. The only important thing was the heat of his mouth on hers, his arms holding her tight against hard muscles.

She didn't know how long they kissed while the snowflakes swirled around them and the stars glittered overhead but finally he pulled away. "We're crazy. Both of us. It's below freezing out here and snowing."

"That's funny. I'm not cold at all."

He pressed his forehead to hers. "I don't want to say it but I need to go back downstairs. I...left the kids with my father."

She stared. "You did? This *is* a night for miracles."

He gave a rough-sounding laugh, then paused and gazed up at the snowflakes spiraling down. "I guess if I'm going to start learning how to forgive myself, I should probably make a stab at forgiving him, too."

Just when she thought her happiness had peaked, he added another layer to it. She almost burst into tears all over again. Instead, she hugged him close and kissed him again.

"I really do have to go," he said reluctantly a few minutes later.

"Yes. Of course. The children need to be home in bed."

She led the way back inside the building to the elevator and was touched that he held on to her hand, even when he pushed the button.

"Are you done working for the night?" he asked when they were in the elevator car.

"Yes. I'm working in the emergency department again tomorrow night, though."

"I want to ask you something and I don't quite have the right words."

"What is it?"

He shook his head, looking embarrassed. "Never mind. I think you've done enough today, between delivering twins and knocking a certain stubborn cowboy on his ass when he needed it."

"All in a day's work." She smiled.

"Like I said. The most amazing woman I've ever known." He shifted. "Here's the thing. You've done so much to help me with Christmas this year. The tree, the decorations, the food. Finding Letty, who's been a godsend. But I need help with one more thing."

She knew how difficult he found it to ask for anything and was touched all over again that he would do it, anyway.

"I still have to take care of the Santa thing for my kids after they're asleep and I have no idea what I'm doing. I told you I've never done Christmas before, except when Jazmyn was really little. Would you consider coming to the ranch tonight and helping me?"

She caught her breath. Of all the things he might have asked her, that never would have occurred to her, but at this moment, she couldn't envision anything she wanted more.

"You could even stay the night in one of the guest rooms if you want, so you can be there when they open their presents in the morning. I might need help corralling the crazy, especially when I give Jazmyn the border collie puppy I picked up last week at the auction." He gave a rueful smile. "I know. What was I thinking?"

"You're thinking you have a daughter who's been through a traumatic life change and needs the steady, unconditional love a pet can provide."

"It sounds good when you say it that way," he said drily. "I have a feeling I was just bending to the relentless pressure."

"She'll be thrilled, either way," she assured him.

"I only know that if you help me, I'll even fix you breakfast. I make a pretty mean Western omelet and I'm particularly good at cinnamon toast."

How was it possible that her Christmas Eve had gone from seeming so lonely to this wild surge of joy?

She hugged him, more in love than she could ever have imagined, as the joy bubbled through her, finding all the places that had been so cold for so long. She loved this man, despite his past—or maybe *because* of it, because of the good and decent man who had emerged from the rubble.

"Why, Cole Barrett," she said softly, "that is absolutely the best Christmas gift you could ever give me."

Hours later, after the clock struck midnight and Christmas officially arrived, Devin lay on the couch with her head on Cole's chest. A fire burned in the fireplace, warm and comforting, and the colorful Christmas tree with the crystal angel on top provided the only light in the room.

All the stockings were filled and wrapped gifts were clustered underneath the tree, waiting for the children to wake in a few hours, and his old dog Coco lay on a rug in front of the fire, snoring softly.

The house looked so different from the first time she had seen it. The garlands and ribbons and lights were part of it, of course. They made it a warm, appealing place filled with holiday cheer.

It was more than that, though. The house was filled with love now.

Coco snuffled in her sleep and Devin lifted her tired head to look at the dog. "Where's the puppy?" she suddenly remembered.

Cole gave a rueful smile. She had a feeling she would never get tired of seeing it.

Like his house, he looked so different from the gruff, taciturn, humorless man she had thought him the first time she had met him at the hospital. This man laughed and teased and stole kisses the whole time they had been filling the stockings and wrapping a few last-minute gifts.

"My hired man's been taking care of him since we picked him up at the auction. I'm meeting Joe down at the barn at five-thirty for the handoff."

"That's less than four hours from now. You need some sleep."

"How can I sleep when I have the woman of my dreams in my arms?" Cole murmured. He pulled her down for another kiss and she realized *this* was what she would never get tired of. This heat and wonder and tenderness.

After another long moment, he pulled her up. "You're right, though. We do need to sleep. You've had a long day, saving lives and delivering babies. It's too bad it's so late and we can't leave the kids alone or I'd sneak you up to the hot spring. You deserve it after today and I can't imagine anything better than Christmas Eve under the stars with you. Maybe next year."

After the past difficult week, she could hardly believe they might *have* a next year—or the year after that and the year after that.

A string of magical Christmases looped together like Ty's paper chains stretched out ahead of them and she could hardly contain the joy inside her.

"You know I only want you for your hot spring, right?" she teased.

He laughed gruffly and nipped her bottom lip. "Yeah, that's kind of what I figured. What other reason would a woman like you be here with a guy like me?"

With a happy sigh, she kissed him tenderly. "Love," she finally answered, her voice low in the quiet house. "The very best reason of all. Merry Christmas, Cole."

His smile against her mouth was all the answer she needed.

* * * * *

She started reading and, as usual, it only took a few pages before a hush fell over the room. The children were completely enthralled—not by her, she was only the vehicle, but by the power of story.

She became lost, too, savoring every word. When she neared the climax, she looked up for dramatic effect and found the children all watching her with eager expressions, ready for more. Her gaze lifted to the parents and she spotted someone she hadn't seen before, a man sitting with the back row of parents, a young girl beside him.

He had brown hair shot through with lighter streaks, a firm jaw and green eyes the color of new leaves.

This had to be the hot dad Frankie meant.

Her heart began to pound fiercely; so loud in her ears she wondered if the children could hear it over the microphone clipped to her collar.

She knew this man, though she hadn't seen him for years.

Flynn Delaney.

She would recognize him *anywhere*. After all, he had been the subject of her daydreams all through her adolescence.

She hadn't heard he was back in Pine Gulch. Why

was he here? Was he staying at his grandmother's house, just down the road from the Star N? It made sense. His grandmother Charlotte had died three months ago and her house had been empty ever since.

She suddenly remembered everything else that had happened to this man in the past few months and her gaze shifted to the young girl beside him, blonde and ethereal like a Christmas angel.

Celeste's heart seemed to melt.

This must be her. His daughter. Oh, the poor, poor dear.

The girl was gazing back at Celeste with her eyes wide and her hands clasped together at her chest as if she couldn't wait another instant to hear the rest of the story.

Everyone was gazing at her with expectation and Celeste realized she had stopped in the middle of the story to stare at Flynn and his daughter.

She felt heat soak her cheeks, appalled at herself. She cleared her throat and forced her attention back to the story, reading the last few pages with rather more heartiness than she had started with.

This was her job, she reminded herself as she closed the book, helping children discover all the delights to be found in good stories.

She wasn't here to ogle Flynn Delaney, for heaven's sake, even when there was plenty about him any woman would consider ogle-worthy.

Flynn didn't think he had ever felt quite so conspicuously out of place—and that included the times he had walked the red carpet with Elise at some Hollywood premiere or other, when he had always invariably wanted to fade into the background.

They all seemed to know each other and he felt like the odd man out. Was everybody staring? He didn't want to think so but he seemed to feel each curious sidelong glance as the residents of Pine Gulch, Idaho, tried to figure out who he was.

At least one person knew. He was pretty sure he hadn't imagined that flicker of recognition in Celeste Nichols's eyes when she'd spotted him. It had surprised him, he had to admit. They had only met a few times, all those years ago.

He only remembered her because she had crashed her bike in front of his grandmother's house during one of his visits. Charlotte hadn't been home so Flynn had been left to tend to her scrapes and bruises and help her get back up the road to the Star N.

Things like that stuck in a guy's memory bank. Otherwise, he probably would never have made the connection between the author of his daughter's favorite book, *Sparkle and the Magic Snowball*, and the shy girl with long hair and glasses he had once known in another lifetime.

He wouldn't be here at the library if not for Celeste, actually. He had so much work to do clearing out his grandmother's house and really didn't have time to listen to Dr. Seuss, as great as the story might be, but what other choice did he have? For the past four months, Olivia had been a pale, frightened shadow of the girl she used to be. Once she had faced the world head-on, daring and curious and funny. Now she was afraid of so many things. Loud noises. Strangers. Crowds.

From the moment she'd found out that Celeste, the author of her favorite book, lived here in Pine Gulch, where they were staying for a few weeks—and was the town's children's librarian who also hosted a bi-monthly story hour—Olivia had been obsessed with coming. She had written the date of the next event on the calendar and had talked of nothing else.

She was finally going to meet the Sparkle lady and she couldn't have been more excited about it if Celeste Nichols were Mrs. Santa Claus in the flesh.

For the first time in weeks, she had shown enthusiasm for something and he had jumped at the chance to nurture that.

He glanced down at his daughter. She hadn't shifted her gaze away from Celeste, watching the librarian with clear hero worship on her features. She seemed utterly enchanted by the librarian.

The woman was lovely, he would give her that much, though in a quiet, understated way. She had big green eyes behind her glasses and glossy dark hair that fell in waves around a heart-shaped face.

She was probably about four years younger than his own thirty-two. That didn't seem like much now but when he was a teenager, the time she'd crashed her bike, she had seemed like just a little kid, thirteen or so to his seventeen.

As he listened to her read now, he remembered that time, wondering why it seemed so clear to him, especially with everything that had happened to him since.

He'd been out mowing the lawn when it had happened and had seen her go down out of the corner of his gaze. Flynn had hurried to help her and found her valiantly trying not to cry even though she'd had a wide gash in her knee that would definitely need stitches, and pebbles imbedded in her palm.

He had helped her into his grandmother's house and called her aunt Mary. While they waited for help, he had found first-aid supplies for her—bandages, ointment, cleansing wipes—and told her lousy jokes to distract her from the pain.

After Mary took her to the ER for stitches in her knee and he finished mowing for his grandmother, he had gone to work fixing her banged-up bike with skills his father had insisted he develop.

Later that day, he had dropped it off at the Star N and she had been almost speechless with gratitude. Or maybe she'd just been shy with older guys, he didn't know.

He had stayed with his grandmother for just a few more weeks that summer, but the few times he had seen Celeste in town at the grocery store or the library, she had always blushed fiercely and offered him a shy but sweet smile.

Now he found himself watching her intently, hoping for a sight of that same sweet smile, but she seemed to be focusing with laser-like intensity on the books in front of her.

She read several more holiday stories to the children,

then led them to one side of the large room where tables had been set up.

"I need all the children to take a seat. We're going to make snowman ornaments for you to hang on your tree. When you're finished, they'll look like this."

She held up a stuffed white sock with buttons glued onto it for eyes and a mouth and a piece of felt tied around the neck for a scarf.

"Oh," Olivia breathed. "That's so cute! Can I make one, Dad?"

Again, how could he refuse? "Sure, if there are enough to go around."

She found a seat and he propped up the wall along with a few other parents so the children could each have a spot at a table. Celeste and another woman with a library name badge passed out supplies and began issuing instructions.

Olivia looked a little helpless at first and then set to work. She seemed to forget for the moment that she rarely used her left hand. Right now she was holding the sock with that hand while she shoved in pillow fluff stuffing with the other.

While the children went to work, Celeste made her way around the tables, talking softly to each one of them.

Finally she came to them.

"Nice job," she said to his daughter. Ah, there it was. She gave Olivia that sweet, unguarded smile that seemed to bloom across her face like the first violets of springtime.

That smile turned her from an average-looking

woman into a breathtaking creature with luminous skin and vivid green eyes.

He couldn't seem to stop staring at her, though he told himself he was being ridiculous.

"You're the Sparkle lady, aren't you?" Olivia breathed.

Color rose instantly in her cheeks and she gave a surprised laugh. "I suppose that's one way to put it."

"I love that story. It's my favorite book *ever*."

"I'm so happy to hear that." She smiled again, though he thought she looked a little uncomfortable. "Sparkle is pretty close to my heart, too."

"My dad bought a brand-new copy for me when I was in the hospital, even though I had one at home."

She said the words in a matter-of-fact tone as if the stay was nothing more than a minor inconvenience. He knew better. She had spent two weeks clinging to life in Intensive Care after an infection ravaged her system, where he had measured his life by each breath the machines took for her.

Most of the time he did a pretty good job of containing his impotent fury at the senseless violence that had touched his baby girl, but every once in a while, the rage swept over him like a brush fire on dry tinder. He let out a breath as he felt a muscle flex in his jaw.

"That's lovely," Celeste said with a quick look at him.

"It's my very favorite book," Olivia said again, just in case Celeste didn't hear. "Whenever I had to do something I didn't want to, like have my blood tested or go to physical therapy, I would look at the picture of Sparkle on the last page with all his friends and it would make me feel better."

At Olivia's words, Celeste's big eyes filled with tears and she rocked back on her heels a little. "Oh. That's...lovely. Thank you so much for letting me know. I can't tell you how much that means to me."

"You're welcome," Olivia said with a solemn smile. "My favorite part is when Sparkle helps the animals with their Christmas celebration. The hedgehog is my favorite."

"He's cute, isn't he?"

The two of them gazed at each other in perfect charity for a moment longer before a boy with blond hair and a prominent widow's peak tried to draw Celeste's attention.

"Ms. Nichols. Hey, Ms. Nichols. How do we glue on the hat?"

"I'll show you. Just a minute." She turned back to Olivia. "It was very nice to meet you. You're doing a great job with your snowman. Thanks for letting me know you enjoy the book."

"You're welcome."

When she left, Olivia turned back to her project with renewed effort. She was busy gluing on the button eyes when the woman beside Flynn finally spoke to him.

"You're new in town. I don't think we've met." She was blonde and pretty in a classic sort of way, with a baby on her hip. "I'm Caroline Dalton. This is my daughter Lindy. Over there is my son Cole."

He knew the Daltons. They owned much of the upper portion of Cold Creek Canyon. Which brother was she married to?

"Hello. I'm Flynn Delaney and this is my daughter, Olivia. We're not really new in town. That is, we're not staying, anyway. We're here just for a few weeks and then we're going back to California."

"I hope you feel welcome here. This is a lovely place to spend the holidays."

"I'm sure it is, but we're not really tourists, either. I'm cleaning out my grandmother's home so I can put it up for sale."

He could have hired someone to come and clean out the house. There were companies who handled exactly that sort of thing, but as he and Olivia were her only surviving descendants, he felt obligated to go through the house himself.

"Delaney. Oh, Charlotte! She must have been your grandmother."

"That's right."

Her features turned soft and a little sad. "Oh, everyone adored your grandmother. What a firecracker she was! Pine Gulch just doesn't feel the same without her."

His *life* didn't feel the same, either. He hadn't seen her often the past few years, just a few quick semiannual visits, but she had been a steady source of affection and warmth in his chaotic life.

He had barely had the chance to grieve her passing. He hadn't even been able to attend the memorial service held by members of her church congregation for her here. He had been too busy in the ICU, praying for his daughter's life.

"I miss her, too," he said quietly.

Her eyes looked at him with kindness and warmth. "I'm sure you do. She was an amazing person and I feel blessed to have known her. If you need help sorting through things, please let me know. I'm sure we could find people to give you a hand."

With only a little more than a week to go before Christmas? He doubted that. People were probably too busy to help.

He didn't bother to express his cynicism to Caroline Dalton. "Thanks," he said instead.

"Despite your difficult task, I hope you enjoy the holidays here."

Yeah, he wasn't a huge Christmas fan for a whole slew of reasons but he saw no reason to share that with a woman he just met.

"Daddy, I can't tie the scarf. Can you help me?" Olivia asked.

She *could* use her left arm and hand. He'd seen her do it at therapy or when she lost herself in an activity, but most of the time she let it hang down uselessly. He didn't know how to force her into using it.

"Try again," he tried.

"I can't. It's too hard," she answered plaintively. He sighed, not wanting to push her unnecessarily and ruin her tentative enjoyment of the afternoon.

He leaned down to help her tie the felt scarf around, just as Celeste made her way back around the table to them.

"I love that snowman!" she exclaimed with a smile. "He looks very friendly."

Olivia's answering smile seemed spontaneous and genuine. Right then, Flynn wanted to hug Celeste Nichols on the spot, even though he hadn't talked to her for nearly two decades.

His little girl hadn't had much to smile about over the past few months. He had to hope this was a turning point, a real chance for her to once more return to his sweet and happy daughter.

At this point, he was willing to bring Olivia to the library every single day if Celeste could help his daughter begin to heal her battered heart.

Chapter Two

She was late.

By the time she helped the last little boy finish his snowman, ushered them all out of the meeting room and then cleaned up the mess of leftover pillow stuffing and fleece remnants, she was forty minutes past the time she had told her sisters to expect her.

They would understand, she was sure. Hope might tease her a little but Faith probably wouldn't say anything. Their oldest sister saved her energy for the important things, like running the cattle ranch and taking care of her children.

She stopped first at the little foreman's cottage, just down the driveway from the main house. It felt strange to be living on her own again after the past year of being back in her own bedroom at the main house.

She had moved back after Travis died the previous summer so she could help Faith—and Aunt Mary, of course—with the children and the housekeeping.

Hope had lived briefly in the foreman's house until she and Rafe married this fall. After she moved into the house she and Rafe purchased together, Faith and Mary had taken Celeste aside and informed her firmly that she needed her own space to create. She was a bestselling author now and while Faith loved and appreciated her dearly, she didn't want Celeste to think she had to live at the ranch house the rest of her life.

Rather reluctantly, she had moved to the foreman's cottage, a nice compromise. She did like her own space and the quiet she found necessary to write, but she was close enough to pop into the ranch house several times a day.

As she walked inside, her little Yorkie, Linus, did little spirals of glee at the sight of her.

She had to smile, despite her exhaustion from a long day, the lingering stress from the phone call with Joan and the complete shock of seeing Flynn Delaney once more.

"How was your day?" she asked the little dog, taking just a moment to sink onto the sofa to give him a little love. "Mine was *crazy*. Thanks for asking. The weirdest I've had in a long time—and that's saying something, since the entire last year has been surreal."

She felt her tension trickle away as she sat with her dog in her quiet living room while the Christmas tree lights that came on automatically gleamed in the gathering darkness. Why couldn't she stay here all evening? There were worse ways to spend a December night.

Linus yipped a little, something he didn't do often, but it reminded her of why she had stopped at the house.

"I know. I'm late. I just have to grab Aunt Mary's present. Give me a second."

She found the gift in her bedroom closet, the door firmly shut to keep Lucy, her cat, from pulling apart the tissue paper inside the gift bag.

"Okay. I'm ready. Let's go."

Linus's tail wagged with excitement but Lucy curled up on the sofa, making abundantly clear her intent to stay put and not venture out into the cold night.

Celeste made her way through lightly falling snow to the ranch house, a sprawling log structure with a steep roof and three gables along the front.

She went in the back door into the kitchen with Linus scampering ahead of her. Delicious scents of home greeted her—roast beef, potatoes and what smelled very much like cinnamon apple pie.

As she expected, her entire family was there; all the people she loved best in the world. Aunt Mary, the guest of honor, was busy at the stove, stirring something in the pot that smelled like her heavenly brown gravy, while Faith, her oldest sister, was pulling a pan of rolls out of the oven as Hope helped the children set the table, where her husband, Rafe, sat talking with their neighbor Chase Brannon, who was just like one of the family.

The children spotted Linus first. They all adored each other—in fact, the children helped her by letting him out when they got home from school and playing with him for a little bit.

"There you are," Faith exclaimed. "I was beginning to worry."

"Sorry. I sent you a text."

Faith made a face. "My phone ran out of juice sometime this afternoon but I didn't realize it until just now. Is everything okay?"

Not really, though she wasn't sure what bothered her more—the movie decision she would have to make in the next few days or the reappearance of Flynn Delaney in her world. Somehow, she couldn't seem to shake the weird feeling that her safe, comfortable world was about to change.

"Fine," she said evasively. "I hope you didn't hold dinner for me."

"Not really. I was tied up going over some ranch accounts with Chase this afternoon and we lost track of time."

"Fine. Blame me. I can take it," Chase said, overhearing.

"We always do," Hope said with a teasing grin.

Chase had been invaluable to their family since Faith's husband died and Celeste was deeply grateful to him for all his help in the subsequent dark and difficult months.

"I'm happy to blame you, as long as that means I wasn't the cause of any delay in Aunt Mary's birthday celebration," Celeste said with a smile as she headed for her great-aunt.

She kissed the woman's lined cheek as the familiar scent of Mary's favorite White Shoulders perfume washed over her. "Happy birthday, my dear. You are still just as stunning as ever."

Mary's grin lit up her nut-brown eyes. "Ha. Double sevens. That's got to be lucky, right?"

"Absolutely."

"I don't need luck. I've got my family around me, don't I?"

She smiled at them all and Celeste hugged her, deeply grateful for her great-aunt and her great-uncle Claude, who had opened their hearts to three grieving, traumatized girls and given them a warm haven and all the love they could need.

"We're the lucky ones, my dear," she murmured with another hug, before she stepped away.

For all intents and purposes, Mary had been her mother since Celeste turned eleven. She had been a wonderful one. Celeste was all too aware that things could have been much different after their parents died, if not for Mary and Claude. She and her sisters probably would have been thrown into the foster care system, likely separated, certainly not nurtured and cared for with such love.

She had a sudden, unexpected wish that their mother could be there, just for a moment, to see how her daughters had turned out—to meet her grandchildren, to see Hope so happily settled with Rafe, to see the completely unexpected success of their Sparkle book.

December always left her a little maudlin. She supposed that wasn't unexpected, considering that had been the month that had changed everything, when she and her sisters and parents had been hostages of a rebel group in Colombia. Her father had been killed in the rescue effort by a team of US Navy SEALs that included Rafe Santiago, who was now her brother-in-law.

She wouldn't think about that now. This was a time of celebration, a time to focus on the joy of being with her family, not on the past.

She grabbed an olive out of a bowl on the counter and popped it in her mouth as she carried the bowl to the table.

"I talked to Joan this afternoon," she told Hope.

"I know. She called me, too. I reminded her that any decision about making a movie had to be made jointly between us and each of us had veto power. Don't worry, CeCe. I told her firmly that I wouldn't pressure you. You created the Sparkle character. He belongs to you."

That wasn't completely true and both of them knew it. She might have written the words but it was Hope's illustrations that had brought him to life.

"I don't know what to do," she admitted as Faith and Mary joined them at the table carrying bowls and trays of food.

"Your problem has always been that you overthink everything," Mary pointed out. "You know someone is going to make a Sparkle movie at some point. It's as inevitable as Christmas coming every year. People love the story and the characters too much. If you like this production company and think they'll do a good job with it based on their reputation, I don't know why you're dragging your feet."

Mary was right, she realized. She was overthinking,

probably because she was so concerned with making the right decision.

She hated being afraid all the time. She knew it was a by-product of the trauma she and her sisters had endured at a young age, but neither Hope nor Faith seemed as impacted as she had been.

Hope seemed absolutely fearless, spending years wandering around underdeveloped countries with the Peace Corps and then on her own, teaching English. Faith had plowed all her energy and attention into her family—her marriage, her children, the ranch.

Celeste's life had become her job at the library and the stories she created.

In some ways, she supposed she was still a hostage of Juan Pablo and his crazy group of militants, afraid to take a move and embrace her life.

"Everything's ready and I'm starving," Mary said cheerfully. "What are we waiting for? Let's eat."

The children quickly slid into their usual seats. Celeste sat between Joey and Chase.

Dinner was noisy and chaotic, with several different conversations going at once.

"How did story time go?" Faith asked when there was a lull in the conversation.

She instantly remembered the shock of looking up from Dr. Seuss to see Flynn and his daughter.

"Good." She paused. "Charlotte Delaney's grandson, Flynn, and his daughter were there. I guess he's in town to clean out Charlotte's house."

"Flynn Delaney." Hope made a low sound in her throat. "I used to love it whenever he came to stay with Charlotte. All those times he used to mow the lawn with his shirt off."

Celeste dropped her fork with a loud clatter, earning her a curious look from Hope.

"Really?" Rafe said, eyebrow raised. "So all this time I should have been taking my shirt off to mow the lawn?"

Hope grinned at him. "You don't *need* to take your shirt off. You're gorgeous enough even when you're wearing a parka. Anyway, I was a teenage girl. Now that I'm older and wiser, I prefer to use my imagination."

He shook his head with an amused look but Celeste was certain his ears turned a little red.

"You said Flynn came into the library with his daughter," Faith said, her voice filled with compassion. "That poor girl. How is she?"

Considering Flynn's connection to Charlotte, whom they all had loved, everyone in Pine Gulch had followed the news reports. Celeste thought of Olivia's big, haunted eyes, the sad, nervous air about her.

"Hard to say. She didn't use her left arm while we were doing the craft project but other than that she seemed okay. She's a big Sparkle fan, apparently."

Hope smiled at this. Her husband, on the other hand, merely looked curious. "Who is Flynn Delaney and what happened to his daughter?" Rafe asked.

"It was all over the news three or four months ago," Chase said. "Not long after Charlotte Delaney died, actually."

"You remember," Hope insisted. "We talked about it. He was married to Elise Chandler."

Understanding spread over Rafe's handsome features. "Elise Chandler. The actress." He paused. "That poor kid."

"Right?" Hope frowned. "What a tragedy. I saw on some tabloid in the supermarket that Flynn never left her side through the whole recovery."

Somehow that didn't seem so surprising, especially considering his devotion to his daughter during story time.

"What happened to her?" Louisa asked. At eleven, she was intensely interested in the world around her.

Her mother was the one who answered. "Elise Chandler was a famous actress," Faith said. "She was in that superhero movie you loved so much and a bunch of other films. Anyway, she was dating someone who turned out to be a pretty messed-up guy. He shot Elise and her daughter before shooting and killing himself. Even though she was injured, Olivia managed to crawl to her mother's phone and call 911."

Celeste had heard that 911 call, which had been made public shortly after the shooting, and the sound of that weak little panic-stricken voice calling for help had broken her heart.

"She seems to be doing well now. She told me she loves the Sparkle books and that her dad used to read them to her over and over again in the hospital."

"Oh, how lovely," Hope exclaimed. "You should take her one of the original Sparkle toys I sewed. I've still got a few somewhere over at the ranch."

"That's a lovely idea," Mary exclaimed. "We should do something for that poor, poor girl. It would have broken Charlotte's heart if she'd still been alive to see Flynn's little girl have to go through such a thing."

"You *have* to take it over there," Hope insisted. "And how about a signed copy of the book and the new one that hasn't come out yet?"

Her heart pounded just at the *idea* of seeing the man again. She couldn't imagine knocking on his door out of the blue. "Why don't *you* take it over? You're the illustrator! And you made the stuffed Sparkle, too."

"I don't even know him or his daughter."

"Like that's ever stopped you before," she muttered.

"It would be a really nice thing to do," Faith said. "I baked an extra pie. Why don't you take that, too?"

All day long, people had been pushing her to do things she didn't want to. She thought longingly of jumping in her SUV again and taking off somewhere, maybe Southern California, where she could find a little sunshine, but she couldn't just leave her family. She loved them, even when they pressured her.

She wanted to tell them all no but then she thought of Olivia and her sad eyes. This was a small expenditure of effort on her part and would probably leave the girl thrilled.

"That's a very good idea," she said. "I'll go after dinner. Linus can probably use the walk."

"Perfect." Hope beamed at her as if she had just won the Newbery Medal for children's literature. "I'll look for the stuffed Sparkle. I think there's a handful of them left in a box in my room."

What would Flynn think when she showed up at his house with a stuffed animal and an armful of books? she wondered as she chewed potatoes that suddenly tasted like chalk.

It didn't matter, she told herself. She was doing this for his daughter, a girl who had been through a terrible ordeal—and who reminded her entirely too much of herself.

Don't miss
A COLD CREEK CHRISTMAS STORY
by RaeAnne Thayne.
Available December 2015 wherever
Harlequin Special Edition books
and ebooks are sold.
www.Harlequin.com

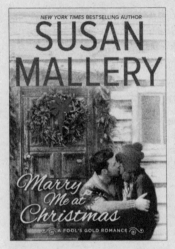

HARLEQUIN®

SPECIAL EDITION

Life, Love and Family

Celeste Nicholas prefers to keep to herself in her hometown of Pine Gulch, Idaho... That is, until one of her children's stories becomes a major success.

Millionaire Flynn Delaney has moved back home to help his little girl heal from losing her mother. Celeste holds some indefinable magic for them both. Can Flynn find a family, and true love, in the one who got away?

SAVE $1.00

on the purchase of A COLD CREEK CHRISTMAS STORY by RaeAnne Thayne {available Nov. 17, 2015} or any other Harlequin® Special Edition book.

Redeemable at participating outlets in the U.S. and Canada only. Not redeemable at Barnes & Noble stores. Limit one coupon per customer.

52613076

Canadian Retailers: Harlequin Enterprises Limited will pay the face value of this coupon plus 10.25¢ if submitted by customer for this product only. Any other use constitutes fraud. Coupon is nonassignable. Void if taxed, prohibited or restricted by law. Consumer must pay any government taxes. Void if copied. Inmar Promotional Services ("IPS") customers submit coupons and proof of sales to Harlequin Enterprises Limited, P.O. Box 3000, Saint John, NB E2L 4L3, Canada. Non-IPS retailer—for reimbursement submit coupons and proof of sales directly to Harlequin Enterprises Limited, Retail Marketing Department, 225 Duncan Mill Rd., Don Mills, Ontario M3B 3K9, Canada.

U.S. Retailers: Harlequin Enterprises Limited will pay the face value of this coupon plus 8¢ if submitted by customer for this product only. Any other use constitutes fraud. Coupon is nonassignable. Void if taxed, prohibited or restricted by law. Consumer must pay any government taxes. Void if copied. For reimbursement submit coupons and proof of sales directly to Harlequin Enterprises Limited, P.O. Box 880478, El Paso, TX 88588-0478, U.S.A. Cash value 1/100 cents.

5 65373 00076 2 (8100)0 12098

COUPON EXPIRES JAN. 29 2016

Available wherever books are sold, including most bookstores, supermarkets, drugstores and discount stores.

www.Harlequin.com

® and ™ are trademarks owned and used by the trademark owner and/or its licensee.
© 2015 Harlequin Enterprises Limited

HSECOUP1015

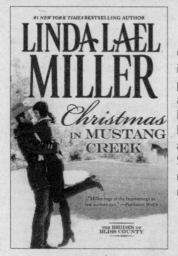